Matters of the Heart

By Heather M. Green

For Julie who inspired me.

For Fran and Kaidence who are fighters.

And for Courtney who gave me the courage in the first place.

Acknowledgements

A special thanks to Breanna Chandler for letting me interrupt her busy schedule to get medical info. And to Eric for schooling me on Texas lingo.

More special thanks to the doctors and nurses who work to provide our loved ones with a greater quality of life. You do it with a smile on your face even after twelve plus hours on the clock. One doctor, in particular, inspired a portion of James' story. Elder Russell M. Nelson, a talented heart surgeon and pioneer in operations on the aortic valve, told of his failures and subsequent intense study and education to save lives. Your story touched and inspired me deeply. Thank you for not giving up.

A gigantic thank you to my proofreaders- Hadlee Green, Courtney Green, Breanna Chandler, Paula Maddock, Amy Church, and Shanda Richey. I could not have done it without you. Last the best of all the game is my husband, Gil. Your patience is endless. Especially when the glare of my computer screen is your unnecessary night light into the wee hours of the morning. Your helpfulness is constant. Especially during my freakouts with missing computer files. This book wouldn't exist without you. I love you.

Chapter 1

Sophie

"I give up," I sighed morosely, slowly pushing the front door closed with both hands, and dramatically flinging myself down on our second hand sofa. I pulled my shirt away from my chest a couple of times to encourage some air flow. It seemed I'd traded the uncomfortable San Antonio night for our sweltering three bedroom apartment.

"What happened this time?" my roommate and best friend, Adri, asked from the kitchen." Air conditioning is out again, by the way."

"So you decided to help out by turning on the oven? Thanks," I said wryly. "You don't even want to know about the date. You wouldn't believe it if I told you," I called in to her.

Adri appeared in the doorway, a bowl of cookie dough in one arm. "Come drown your sorrows in cookies. They're fresh from the oven I turned on to help us appreciate the very limited times our air conditioner actually works. Ha."

I jumped up, my ridiculous excuse for a date and the miserable heat wave forgotten, and made a beeline for the kitchen counter where warm chocolate chip cookies awaited. I grabbed a bowl from the cupboard, a cookie, and the praline ice cream from the freezer and layered a sundae calorie bomb topped with caramel syrup and sliced almonds.

"Mmm," I moaned around the first therapeutic bite and took a seat at the table. "This is what was missing tonight. You know me better than I know myself."

"No. I know your dating record and wanted to be prepared with comfort food that we can spend hours working off tomorrow," she told me, sliding another tray of cookie dough into the oven.

"I knew I loved you," I told her, my eyes closed to better concentrate on the mingling flavors. "What I would like to know is, where are all the normal guys? What about me is so offensive to the dating gods that I am continually subjected to these abstract-type people of the male species?" I took another bite of my sundae and chewed slowly, letting the comfort flavors of warm cookie and cold vanilla and caramel ice cream meld and reduce my spiked post-date blood pressure. "It's my fault really," I acknowledged. "I should have had enough sense to lock the door when Flavius the Gladiator arrived to pick me up."

"His name is Flavius?" Adri asked dubiously, a giggle working its way past her grinning lips. "I knew I should have skipped that last work meeting." She eagerly joined me at the table for the retelling.

"Count your blessings," I told her, swallowing another bite of ice cream. "But his nicely defined quads would have made you proud." Adri choked on her cookie and I pounded her on the back as I muttered, "I averted my eyes during the entire car ride." Who knew a tunic could make you blush. I gave up on the pounding when her choking started to sound suspiciously like laughter.

"Flavius is his gaming name," I explained over her amusement. "It went well with the apparent theme of the night as evidenced by the other costumed couples we challenged. I stuck out like a sore thumb."

"More like an achilles heel," Adri laughed at her own joke. "It was really rude of you to miss the costume memo." She giggled again. "Next time maybe you will listen to me and avoid those who would ruin your life by setting you up on blind dates."

I groaned. "A friend of a friend of my parents. With you and this ice cream sundae as my witnesses," I crossed my heart with my spoon, "I will never go on another blind date."

Adri raised her own partially eaten cookie in silent support and took another huge bite. "How did the rest of the night go?"

"He graciously apologized to the others on my behalf for my lack of proper gaming attire. For a minute I thought they'd chain me to something like Jaba did to Princess Leia, only I was a little more fully clothed. They were willing to overlook it this time, but could not overlook the fact that I didn't have an avatar. When Flavius suggested we set one up for me so I could join in the gaming, I thought, okay, it's worth a trial run. So we did. I hate to be the party pooper, but two and a half *hours* later --he and the two other couples were in character the whole time, mind you-- I got his attention long enough to ask if he had something else planned for the evening. Guess what he told me?"

The buzzer on the stove brought Adri to her feet. "I have no idea." She glanced up from transferring cookies to a cooling rack, fascination evident on her face.

"He said he could go all night. He didn't even acknowledge my cry of shock because suddenly Brutus and men had forced their way past the blockade and the war was turning. And not in Flavius' favor. Apparently, he has these parties that do go all night. They dress up in costumes-"

"Of course..."

"-and like fourteen hours later-- no sleep, very minimal food, and even more minimal bathroom usage-- he sleeps for a couple hours and is at it again.

"On the upside, he told me he'd let me know when the next game night was so I could come in costume. I'm really considering that Princess Leia bikini thing…"

Adri snorted.

"He just quit his third job this month because the company wouldn't work around his gaming schedule," I continued. "I don't know... Maybe I'm a snob, but what happens when his electricity gets shut off due to nonpayment? He'd probably only notice because his game would be interrupted."

Adri pointed the spatula at me. "He'd probably go to someone else's house and play there."

"Well, he's not coming here. How do people live like that? Life isn't real to them anymore-- the game world is. It's nuts," I said shaking my head.

"They wrapped things up pretty early for you," Adri commented.

"No. I'm sure they're still at it," I told her with a sigh.

"How'd you get home?"

"I called an Uber. Flave probably doesn't even know I'm gone. But I'm seriously thinking about getting a toga."

Adri's head jerked up from the cookie dough to stare at me in disbelief. My lips twitched and we both burst out laughing.

"They seem pretty lightweight and cool, as opposed to our suffocating apartment," I reasoned between laughs.

When our laughter subsided a few moments later, I said, "On a more serious note, I'm checking out that building I saw the other day over in the strip mall near the Riverwalk. Hopefully this time next week, you will be looking at the proud owner of some office space." I high-fived her happily. "Where is everyone?" I asked as I headed out of the kitchen and down the hall to the bathroom to brush my teeth.

"Hope is on a date. Ideally having more success than you had-"

"Amen," I called back to her.

"-And Kortney is still at work. As soon as these cookies are finished, I'm going to bed. It's been a long day."

"Do you want me to finish them?" I asked her around a mouthful of toothpaste. "An wha tie do oo wanna run to'orrow?"

"Go spit. That's gross," she whined. "You're dripping on the floor!" She pushed me toward the bathroom, muttering under her breath. I laughed all the way. She knew me, but I knew her better.

"Good night," I sang out as I shut my bedroom door.

James

"Hey, Kaley bug. What's up?" I answered around my water bottle after the third ring.

"So, that friend of mine has been asking about you again. Can you come for dinner this weekend and meet her?" my sister, Kaley, asked.

"Can pigs fly yet? 'Cause you know that was the stipulation," I responded, wiping my sweaty face with my shirt and motioning for Andy to go ahead without me.

"Come on, James. She is pretty and nice and successful. You'd love her. I promise."

"How pretty? How successful?" I asked warily.

"Oh, sheesh. You want a frumpy hermit? One of those ladies who has like fifteen cats and- " she asked in exasperation.

"No…" I interrupted. "Who said I want anyone? I just…I'm not ready." I reminded her, shouldering my gym bag and pushing against the door with my body before heading out of the gym and into the dark Portland night. "You'll be the first to know when I am."

"It's been like seven years, James. When will you be ready? You are too young to spend the rest of your life alone. You aren't getting any younger."

"Am I too young or not young enough, Kaley? Which is it?" She huffed in response. "I'm thirty-two and I'm not alone. I have all my patients at the hospital. And I have Andy," I teased. The sooner I could get her upset, the sooner she'd end this conversation.

"Now I know you've lost it," she muttered, irritation seeping through the phone. *Perfect.* "Our cousin, Andy? Is that who you are referring to? He's as much company as a Chia Pet."

I laughed in amusement at her Chia Pet comment. It's funny how we come to view those closest to us. Andy was anything but inorganic. Cocky? Yes. Overbearing? At times. But stone-faced and still? Never. I laughed at the very idea. Absurd. My mind conjured the image of Andy perched on the counter, expressionless, awaiting my return from work each day. Ha!

Kaley continued undeterred. "It's time to let go of the past and move on."

All thoughts of laughter gone, I sighed and pushed a hand through my sweaty hair. It needed a trim a couple weeks ago. "No, Kaley. No."

"Fine. I'm just trying to help because I love you and want you to be happy," she said, playing the martyr.

"You're just *trying* my patience. And I'm telling Andy you called him a Chia Pet."

"You do that. He'll think it's a compliment." She hung up.

I sighed again. I knew I infuriated her, but for crying out loud... I was happy. I was. Having a woman on my arm wouldn't make me any happier. Unfortunately, I knew that from experience. I unlocked my apartment door and headed for the shower. Another twelve-plus hour day at the hospital with no one to come home to other than the "Chia Pet."

I was happy.

Chapter 2

Sophie

"I found it," I sang to my brother through the phone. "It's beautiful and I'm finally going to go for it!" I went on without a pause. "I may be pushing thirty and not married-- well, okay, technically I'm only twenty-nine-- but I'm only pushing thirty and ready to set up my own business. Finally," I sighed with relief. I would have gone on. I was just getting started, really. But the distinct silence on the other end of the line when there should have been exaggerated gushing-- if brothers ever gush-- made me pause mid start.

"Trev, aren't you excited for me?" I asked, a little wounded by his lack of enthusiasm. After all, he was the one who had been pushing me for at least a year now to quit playing second string and strike out on my own in the world of sports therapy. Now that I had finally dug deep and found the courage, he was silent.

"I'm sorry, Soph, but we just got back from the ultrasound and it looks like there might be something wrong with the baby." I could hear the anguish in Trevor's voice and was instantly contrite. And worried.

"Wrong? What do you mean wrong?" I questioned. "What did the OB see? What makes her think something is wrong? And why are they only finding it now?" I tend to ramble on without much room for breathing when I am nervous or excited. It's a habit that drives my brother-- and only sibling-- up the wall most of the time. This time, especially, was no exception.

"I don't have all the answers yet, but we are meeting with a pediatric cardiologist next week and will go from there. If there is a problem, I may need some help out here. I hate to ask, especially with the news about your sports therapy office, *finally*, but we have to go C-section, so Stacy will be down for the first six weeks or so anyway. That's when we'd need the most help. Then there is the possibility of an extended stay for the baby in the NICU to think about. Visits, feedings, I don't know what all else. And then Jeran..." He blew out a loud breath.

Trevor was referring to my spitfire two year old nephew, Jeran. If he weren't so cute, I think Trevor and Stacy would have sold him to the gypsy's long ago. But how can you resist those blond curls and cherub cheeks? Beneath those angel cheeks and curls, I hate to say, brewed the heart of a little devil. What a stinker! But I digress and I hadn't heard anything Trevor had been saying.

"...some friends from church, but they obviously can't be here full time. I really hate to ask with the recent major announcement of your therapy business-"

"You said that already," I interrupted. "Sorry. Go on."

"-*But* would it be possible for you to put your career on hold for a few months to come out here when the baby is born?" He pushed on without a pause, reminiscent of my prattling tendencies. Must be hereditary. "I know how that sounds, believe me, but we'd pay you, of course, kind of like a nanny. With Mom and Dad out of the country on a humanitarian mission and Stacy's mom's health on the decline, we don't know what else to do. I'm really worried." A pause then, "Sophie, what are we going to do?" I felt tears well in my eyes as my strong big brother's voice broke.

"Trev, of course I'll come," I reassured, gulping back tears. "Since I found the perfect spot for the new office, I was going to quit at the clinic soon anyway. I was only going to start out by leasing the new space until I get established. Let me find out what that entails and then I'm there," I told him, mentally going over all that I needed to do before I could make a two thousand plus mile road trip from Texas to Portland, Oregon to live as a nanny for an undetermined amount of time. My room in the shared apartment, my Sunday school class, my volunteer reading tutor position at the elementary school…

"Stacy's due in six weeks, right?" I asked. "If I get everything squared away here, I could be there in a little over two weeks with drive time. That would give me time to get settled in before the next little devil joins the family." I smiled in relief when I heard Trevor chuckle.

"Soph, I don't know how to thank you." A little of the tension and worry dissipated from his voice. "I know it's a huge sacrifice to put your life on hold like this, but we'll love you forever. And who knows, you may find the perfect guy in your spare time. You know, different sea, different fish."

"Yeah, well, you'd better love me forever anyway, buddy. And what spare time? I've met my nephew, remember?" I responded. "Just take care of that wife and baby and I'll see you soon. Love you, Trev," I told him, then pushed end on my phone.

"I can't believe you are driving all the way to Oregon by yourself instead of flying!" Adri said over lunch at the Riverwalk the next day. "If you knew how long you'd be staying, I'd go with you. Wouldn't it be fun to do a road trip?"

"I love a good road trip," I said, laughing. "Remember that time back in college you had this crazy idea at midnight to go for a road trip. We drove for hours trying to find that beach and finally gave up. We had to split a hotel room to get some sleep so we didn't get in a car accident."

"I totally remember because you wanted to just pull into a Walmart parking lot, sleep for a few hours, and then drive back home to make it to our classes." Adri was working up a belly laugh.

"You were so afraid we'd get arrested if we stayed in the parking lot." I grinned, pointing at her.

"We probably would have, but that's not the best part," she said, barely containing her laughter. "We drove all that way and gave up, but when we woke up the next day, we realized," she clapped her hands and we practically shouted in unison, "we were only a mile from the beach!" We burst into uncontrollable laughter and I had to cover my mouth to muffle the sound so we didn't get ourselves kicked out of the restaurant.

When our laughter finally died down, I wiped my eyes and said, "I can't believe I'm really doing this. It's going to be so strange to live with my brother again. Strange and a little horrible." I shuddered. "You sure you can find someone to take my spot at the apartment? I'll be there for two months at least. I worry that you won't find anyone and then be stuck with my portion of the rent every month." I charged on, not waiting for her response. "If you find I left anything you think I'll need, ship it and I'll send you reimbursement. You know, I don't have a memory in the last five years that doesn't have you in it..." I mused, feeling the melancholy set in.

"You're doing that sentence vomit thing again. But it does feel kind of final." Adri agreed, absently stirring her drink with her straw.

"Yeah. It does," I sighed. "Thanks, Adri, for everything. I don't know how I would have made it through the last couple of years' dating fiascos without your calming influence." I reached over and squeezed her hand. "You are a good friend."

"The best," she agreed smugly. "I'm letting you get the bill."

Chapter 3

Sophie

The next two weeks passed in a frenzied blur. Now I found myself rolling down the window of my cramped Honda, turning up the radio, and holding my drooping right eye open with my thumb and index finger. *Maybe it's time for a break*, I thought as I looked for the next freeway exit.

I pulled into a parking space on the outskirts of a Walmart parking lot and turned off the car. I thought about calling Adri and making her guess where I was, but instead laughed at the beach memory, silenced Google Maps on my phone, and made sure the doors were locked. I reclined my seat back and closed my tired eyes. Just about halfway through this little journey, I smiled as I drifted off.

Water surrounds me and I know instinctively that I'm swimming in the Pacific looking for a certain species of fish. I'm plucking fish from the water one by one and shaking my head then flinging them back. Jeran is sitting upright in the water next to me, repeatedly beating me over the head with a toy hammer and yelling, "Lady. Hey lady, wake up!"

What? I tried to push his hand away and started when my hand touched something cold. My eyes flew open and swung from left to right in a panic as I tried to make my dream mesh with reality. I stifled a scream and put my hand to my rapidly beating heart when a knock sounded on the car window next to my ear. I tugged on the lever to return my seat to the upright position and fumbled for the keys in the ignition and then the button to roll down my window. A hard hat, orange reflective vest wearing construction guy was peering down at me through my now open window, a scowl on his face.

"Sorry to wake you," he told me, not sounding very sorry at all. "We are closing off this section of the parking lot for repaving. I need you to move your car to that section over there," he informed me, pointing toward the store behind me.

"Oh, okay. Sorry," I apologized around a yawn as I watched him walk away shaking his head. I sat for a minute zoning, staring at nothing out the windshield. I shook my head to clear the remaining fuzziness and talked to myself as I started my car. "The Pacific, fish, and hammers to the head, huh?" I muttered. "That better not have been a vision of things to come."

As the scenery changed from sagebrush and partially planted, spring green open fields and farms to lush green trees, waterfalls flowing from rocky outcroppings, and thick vegetation, I knew I had crossed into Oregon. Excitement bubbled in me at seeing my brother and his family, kissing Jeran's chubby little cheeks, and making a trip to the ocean. Lighthouses perched on rocky outcroppings, stretching for the sky and tide pools full of sea anemones, crabs, and sea stars were just waiting to be discovered. My favorite place on earth. This was going to be a refreshing adventure.

The view driving into Portland was breathtaking. Bridges spanned the Willamette River that housed watercraft from fishing boats to luxury houseboats and sternwheelers to massive barges. This looked like a place where things got done.

I pushed the 'get directions' button on my phone. "Speak to me Google," I instructed as I wound around streets and up and down hills to get a feel for the city. I pulled into Trevor and Stacy's driveway around dinner time, exhausted and filled with nervous anticipation. How would my life change in the next few months?

I had called ahead to let them know my expected time of arrival, so I wasn't surprised when the front door flew open and Trevor came bouncing down the steps with Jeran toddling behind as fast as his little legs would let him go.

Trevor held out his arms for a hug as I hurried up the walk. "It's so good to see you. Glad you finally made it."

"I hope dinner's on the table 'cause I'm starving," I teased, hugging him back. "And you," I turned to Jeran and smiled down at him, "are such a big boy now. When I saw you last, you were a teeny baby." I held my hands up in front of myself about a foot apart from each other to show him how small.

"Your house is really nice, Trev." I admired his cute Victorian home with a tree and flowers in the landscaped front yard. I noticed the house sat high enough to view the Willamette River in the distance. "I bet you couldn't believe all the green when you moved here. For a Texas girl like me, this is the Garden of Eden." Trevor laughed as he lifted one of my suitcases from the back seat of my car. I grabbed the other suitcase and Jeran's hand.

Jeran started talking a mile a minute about showing me his toys. I couldn't believe how well he spoke, and to a stranger. If we could communicate, we could get along. I wouldn't get too excited yet, however. This was the angel side I was seeing right now. Trevor assured me there is a devil in there somewhere.

Stacy called to us from the living room as soon as the door opened. Trevor set the suitcases down in the hall and led me into the living room. "I'll give you the grand tour later. Come see my glowingly pregnant wife."

I rushed past Trevor and bent over the couch to give Stacy a one armed hug. "Look at you!" I gushed. "If I ever have kids, I want to look like you. You make such a cute pregnant lady. How are you feeling? What do you hear about the baby?"

Stacy laughed at my rapid fire comments and questions. "I'm sorry." I apologized. "I've been talking to myself for the past few days. You know how I am. I'm not very good company for myself, I've realized."

"You and Jeran should get along well if you don't care that you will talk over each other and never get any answers with so much to say." Trevor grinned.

I scowled at him. "Rude," I said. To which he laughed.

I took a seat next to Stacy on the couch and pushed her forward a little to rub her back. She let out a bliss-filled sigh and closed her eyes. "Where have you been the past seven plus months?" She murmured. "This was a good decision, getting you up here. I could get used to this."

"So tell me what you know about the baby's condition," I cued while continuing the massage.

"Well, first of all let me say that we feel we were led to Portland when we were looking to settle in Oregon," Trevor said and reached for Stacy's hand. "The OHSU Hospital has an excellent pediatric cardiologist named Dr. David Harmon. While the hospital doesn't rank as high as hospitals in Boston or Texas, we feel good about this hospital. We've spoken with Dr. Harmon a few times already and he's confident and competent in what he does."

"We liked him from the first visit and know he will be a blessing to the baby. He's had many successes and we are grateful to have him in our corner." Stacy finished with a hesitant smile. A trusted doctor was one less thing to worry about, but I could tell they weren't completely at peace with the whole situation yet. I couldn't blame them. The unknown is a scary place to be.

"Dr. Harmon did more tests and says the baby has a ventricular septal defect. It's a common congenital defect where there is a hole in the wall separating the two lower chambers in the heart."

"What does that do?" I asked.

"The hole allows blood to travel across the hole from the left pumping chamber to the right pumping chamber and out into the lung arteries. The good, oxygenated blood mixes with the oxygen-poor blood. That means the heart and lungs have to work harder and the lungs can become congested. It's difficult to diagnose in utero and sometimes isn't even diagnosed until adulthood because if the hole is small, it will usually close on its own."

"How did they even diagnose it then?" I wanted to know.

"The hole in our baby's heart appears to be so large-- that's how it was caught on the ultrasound-- that it may get smaller on its own, but it will never fully close. If he can't gain enough weight or shows other signs of heart failure, he will have to have it repaired soon after he is born."

"What does that involve?"

"There are three types of repairs and we are still deciding which one to go with. He will stay in the hospital for about a week for monitoring and testing, and if surgery is necessary, he will be in the hospital for *at least* a week more. If there is inflammation around the heart or infection, the stay will be longer. After he is born, it's a waiting game for a while, unfortunately."

"So, it's a C-section for sure then?" I asked.

"Yes. The doctor is worried that the stress of labor will be too much for the baby," Trevor explained.

"And they want him out quickly to monitor his condition," Stacy added. "Just one more month and I'll be able to touch my feet again, she sighed in relief, rubbing her distended stomach.

"Say 'four weeks,'" Trevor told her. "That sounds like less time to wait than one month. Then he sighed like he carried the heavy burden instead of his wife. "And I'll be able to sleep again."

Stacy smacked his arm. "Nice, Trev. When have you missed a night's sleep in the last eight months?" She raised her brows at him, challenging him to come up with an answer. "That's what I thought," she grinned.

"I was only trying to be a part of this important conversation."

Stacy and I rolled our eyes. *Please...*

"How are you feeling today?" I asked Stacy as we strolled through their neighborhood a week later. Jeran was talking excitedly from his stroller about the toys he would play on at the park and the stray dog we had just steered around. The day was going to be another partly cloudy yet beautiful one. I could get used to these milder Oregon temps. I'd already have the AC cranked up high if I was still in Texas and it was only nine-thirty in the morning.

"I'm okay. A little crampy today," Stacy sighed, rubbing her giant belly. "Only three weeks to go. I'm to the point where I'm so uncomfortable that I'm ready for this to be over, but then I'm afraid of the heart stuff, so I'd like to keep him in indefinitely."

I laughed at the image my mind conjured of her still pregnant years from now. "Just be glad you aren't an elephant. They are pregnant for almost two years. Imagine trying to get the baby out after that amount of time…"

"I feel like an elephant," she complained.

"Mommy's a elphant. Mommy's a elphant," Jeran chanted.

"Good one," I whispered to Stacy, smothering a chuckle. "Nothing like the constant reminder you are going to get now. That ought to make you feel real good."

In an attempt to turn the conversation from Stacy's size, I spoke to Jeran over the stroller visor, "Jeran, when shall we go to the zoo and see the mommy elephant?" That's all it took to hijack his current thought process and he was off telling stories of giraffes, lions, and monkeys.

"How do you want to work a schedule while I'm here?" I asked as we turned up another street. I still couldn't believe how alive and fresh everything was here. I looked around at the yards in wonder. Roses the size of my palm bloomed everywhere leaving a delicious floral scent hanging in the air. I breathed in deeply and smiled. "I was thinking I could go to the hospital early in the mornings and then again in the evening when Trevor gets home from work for the first six weeks or until you feel up to going yourself. I'll get most of the meals and Jeran and I will entertain each other during the day while you rest."

"Maybe Trevor could go in the mornings before work when the doctors make their rounds so he can discuss any issues and so you'd only have to go once a day," Stacy suggested. "I don't want to wear you out. I'm hoping he can be bottle fed breast milk and not need a feeding tube. It's just so hard to plan when we don't know exactly what we are planning for. There are so many variables. I would like to read some stories with Jeran every day at naptime. That way, he will have his mommy time," she said as she ruffled his hair. He squealed and struggled to get away. Luckily he was belted in.

"The schedule will change after my six week ban, I'm sure. And then again when the baby comes home from the hospital. Thank you for doing this, Sophie." She put her hand on my arm and gave it a light squeeze. I smiled at her and announced to Jeran that the park was up ahead. His excited laughter and bouncing in the stroller broadened my smile. There was nowhere else I'd rather be.

James

"Hey, bro," Kaley said into the phone. "You coming to church with us again this week?"

"Of course."

"Good. You can stay for dinner afterward."

I pushed an aggravated sigh through the phone. Would she ever quit? "I smell you from a mile away. Who is she this time? And have you been talking to Mom and Dad again?"

"Please. That's not the only reason I ever call you."

"Oh yeah? Name one time in the last three months that you have called just to shoot the breeze." A pause. "I didn't think so. Come on, spill."

"Fine. Mom was giving me a hard time about not coming to visit, about how it's time for another baby, about any other thing you can think of that isn't going according to her timeline. If you would just hurry up and do something with your life, it would really take the pressure off," she whined.

I rolled my eyes. "Right, Kaley. Let me get right on that."

"Seriously, though. Bring Andy this time so you won't feel trapped or backed into a corner or however you feel when you see someone of the opposite sex and simply meet this girl. You don't have to marry her. Just meet her. That's all I ask. That way I can report to Mom that you met someone and she will leave me alone for a few days."

I glanced at Andy who was holding up the basketball and motioning impatiently to his watch and rolled my eyes in a silent apology. "You make me sound like I have a phobia of women. I *was* married once, remember? I do still like women. I'm just too busy to get involved right now."

"That's the point-"

"Oh, Kaley," I interrupted, urgency in my voice. "That's my pager. Sorry. I've got to go."

"You are a liar. I heard the basketball. Tell Andy to get a life and I'll see you two this weekend."

"Phew," I breathed out as I hung up. "Sorry about that," I told Andy, tossing my phone onto my gym bag. "She invited you to dinner this time, too."

"Awww, man," Andy whined.

"She invited someone she wants you to meet," I told him and laughed inwardly as he perked up. "I'm just there to help the conversation flow."

"Food and women- two of my favorite things. Okay. Enough talk." Andy inbounded the ball. "Prepare to get smoked."

"Maybe," I shrugged smugly. Who cares if I won the game or not? I just won a major battle off the court.

Chapter 4

Sophie

We moved around the house the morning of Stacy's C-section like we were performing a slightly nerve wracking dance. Stacy hummed softly while packing a bag and wrapping a gift she got for Jeran to welcome his new brother. Trevor paced and switched on the television. Then, restless, he'd switch it off and pace again. Occasionally, he'd ask Stacy if she needed anything.

Finally, when I thought I'd go crazy with anticipation, Stacy sat down on the couch and pulled Jeran on her lap as far as he could fit with her basketball shaped stomach between them.

"Daddy and I need to go to the hospital so the doctor can get your brother out of my belly. I'll be gone for a few days, but Aunt Sophie will be with you. You be a good boy for her, okay?"

Jeran patted her tummy. "Yup," he said.

Stacy kissed the side of his head. "I love you, buddy."

He lay his head on her belly. "Love you, Mommy." Then he scooted off her lap and took my hand. "Mommy is going to get my baby," he said matter-of-factly. "Let's go to the pahk."

I choked on a laugh. "Tell your daddy goodbye."

He briefly raised his hand, not even looking in Trevor's direction. "Bye, Daddy."

"Hey," Trevor laughed at Jeran's disinterest and picked him up. "You give me loves." Trevor covered Jeran's small face with kisses and tickled his stomach.

Jeran struggled and squirmed in his arms. "Okay. Okay," he cried, putting a hand on Trevor's face to pull it down to his lips. When his lips and Trevor's cheek met, Jeran blew a zerbert on Trevor;s cheek and burst into giggles.

Trevor cried out in mock outrage and lowered Jeran to the floor. Jeran ran from his father, still giggling. "You get back here, you little stinker," Trevor called. He grinned at Stacy and took her hand, helping her up from the couch.

"Thanks again, Sophie," Stacy said as they made their way to the door.

"Don't worry about us. Go have a baby. We'll be praying for you." I slung an arm around Trevor's waist and gave it a light squeeze. "Call or text to let us know."

I closed the door softly behind them and turned. "Little stinker," I called, "come out, come out wherever you are." I heard a faint giggle, grinned, and moved stealthily toward the happy sound.

"Jeran, guess what?" I asked excitedly, pushing end on my phone and pointing to an empty space on a wooden puzzle board.

"What?" he answered distracted, attempting to shove the puzzle piece into the spot I indicated.

"Daddy called and your new brother is at the hospital. We need to get you super clean so we can go see him."

"I don't wanna get clean," he protested and held up his hands and inspected them then turned them over and showed them to me. "I clean awedy."

"Wait. I see a dirty spot," I said as I kissed his chubby cheek. "And there's one here." I kissed the other cheek. "And I think there's another one here." I moved to nibble at his very ticklish neck and he shrieked and wriggled to get away. "How about we use bubbles?"

"Yay fo bubbles!" he yelled racing ahead of me to the bathroom.

Yay for bubbles, I thought as I quickly retrieved the dish soap from the kitchen and followed him into the bathroom. I leaned over and started the water filling the tub. "What do you want to name your brother?" I asked as he held up his arms for me to lift his shirt over his head.

"I think…" he paused to think with a small pointer finger on his lips. "I think Gampa would be good."

I smiled. "What would we call Grandpa then? What about zebra?" I reached out and tickled his naked belly.

He shrieked and pushed my hand away and climbed into the warm water. "Umm, that's not a vewy good name," he told me as he raised skeptical eyes to mine.

"Ok. How about puppy?" I tried again with a smile.

"Yeah. Puppy's good."

"Or what about Wilbur or Daffy or Scooby?" I suggested facetiously.

"No. I don't like those names. I think puppy is good. O apple juice." He picked up a handful of bubbles and dropped them on top of his head. I scooped some up and applied them to his chin and grabbed the hand mirror to show him. I laughed at his delighted grin.

"I look like Santa," he giggled. "Maybe we should call my butha Santa."

"What about Oscar the Grouch or Daniel Tiger?" I tried again. "Or Thomas Train?"

He paused with a handful of bubbles in the air. "Maybe…" He shrugged his shoulders, uncommitted.

"Let's ask Daddy when we get to the hospital- " My phone ringing cut me off.

"Hey, Adri. What's up?" I answered, shoving the phone between my ear and shoulder and grabbing a towel for Jeran.

"I wanted to tell you that I've been looking at ticket prices and I'm thinking of coming up to visit."

"That would be awesome," I squealed. "When are you thinking and I will check on tickets too?"

"Well, not for at least a month. I need to arrange time off from work. So what's happening with you, supernanny? Are you all settled?"

"Yeah. And Trevor just called and the baby is here. I'm just getting Jeran out of the tub so we can go to the hospital." I looked around me. "Speaking of Jeran…Where is he?"

I hung the towel on the back of the door and headed down the hall. "Jeran?" I called through the house. "Hey, Adri, I hate to cut this short, but Jeran is running naked somewhere in the house and the last time that happened it was like a puppy all over the floor."

"Good luck. Don't rub his nose in it," she laughed and hung up.

"Jeran! You get back here, you little monster."

I heard the ding of the elevator and bounced on the balls of my feet as I watched the doors slowly open to the twelfth floor of the Kohler Pavilion. Didn't they know we were in a hurry? It took all the persuasion skills I was blessed with to drag Jeran through the parking garage and into the elevator. When we finally made it to the elevator, it took more skills, some of which I didn't know I possessed, to get him off. Big metal boxes with buttons are fascinating to a two year old. We could have ridden in the elevator all day and Jeran would have been entertained. Trevor and Stacy were waiting for us, but Jeran wanted to see his new brother first, and this elevator was trying my patience. When there was just enough room for me to slip through, I readjusted my grip on Jeran's little hand and made my way down the long hall searching for the Neonatal Intensive Care Unit.

I pushed the call button on the wall and waited until I heard, "Can I help you?"

"My name is Sophie Mitchell and I have a big brother with me who's pretty excited to see the Mitchell baby," I told the nurse over the intercom.

"Did you check in at the front desk before you came up?" came the reply.

"Yes, ma'am."

"What was your name again?"

"Sophie Mitchell."

Instead of buzzing me in, I looked up to see a petite nurse in lavender scrubs covered in tiny, multicolored stethoscopes exit the doors to meet me. She checked her clipboard for my name and said, "Because we limit the number of visitors in the NICU, you are only admitted if your name is on the list of approved visitors the parents fill out. I'm sorry, but I don't see your name on the list. You'll have to get his parents to add your name. But wait just a second." She put a finger in the air. "I have an idea."

She smiled at me and pushed the button on the wall as she turned to go back between the doors. I watched as she walked across the room to a small curtained off section. The nurse pushed the curtain aside to reveal a little room with a wooden rocking chair, medical equipment, and an incubator decorated with a colorful homemade name tag and a three by five card with the baby's stats on it. The nurse unplugged some tubes and pushed

Dylan's incubator across the room and up closer to the doors so I could peek at him through the little square window on the door.

My heart melted and I cooed as if he could hear me. I felt tears prick my eyes as I looked at all the tubes hooked up to his little body. How could there even be enough room on his little body for all those tubes? I sent a prayer heavenward that this beautiful baby boy could be strong and fight to stay alive until he could get the help he needed.

I held Jeran up so he could see through the window. "There's your brother," I told him around the hitch in my throat. "Isn't he so cute?"

"My butha," Jeran said in awe. "Cute." I laughed softly and we watched the baby for a few minutes, soaking in his fresh-from-heaven glow. Jeran struggled to get down so I said, "Wave bye-bye to your brother and let's go find Momma and Daddy." I mouthed thank you to the nurse as Jeran waved. We smiled at each other as I wiped my eyes and turned to go.

I admired the soothing nature artwork on the walls as Jeran and I walked briskly down the hall hoping to find Stacy's room quickly. As I turned a corner, glancing at the numbered plaques on the wall beside each door, I saw Trevor. I smiled as I picked up the pace and called his name. The look on his face when he turned and opened his arms to me caused my smile to slip. I ran into his arms as the tears began streaming down his cheeks.

"Oh, Trev, he's beautiful," I cried, squeezing him tight. "You can't even tell he's struggling. From the outside, he looks like a healthy little boy."

I heard Trevor heave a shuddering sigh and felt his tears mingle with mine on my cheek. "There is a huge success rate with this kind of defect, but it's still scary. Stacy is so upset. Post labor hormones…geez." He ran a hand through his already messy hair. "She's not able to get up and around yet. She hasn't even really been able to see him except for a glimpse as they whisked him away." He clung tighter to me and cried softly, his body shaking. "We're both so scared. I love him so much already, you know? I'm so glad you are here." He stepped out of my arms and reached down to pick Jeran up. "Jeran needs you." He hugged him close. "We all need you. Thank you for coming." I squeezed him with one arm around his waist and then stepped back to smack him on the shoulder.

"What's the big idea not putting my name on the approved visitor list?" I demanded. "The favorite aunt...there should be no question," I scolded. He laughed as I hoped he would as he swiped at his eyes.

"I know," he told me apologetically. "Things were so crazy and happening so fast, I didn't have time. Stacy is sleeping now and I don't want to wake her. Let's go get your name on that list and see if you still have the magic aunt touch." He slung his arm around my shoulders.

"My butha sleeps in a box," Jeran informed Trevor. "He have elphant nose." I grinned at Trevor's look of confusion as we headed back to the NICU.

"How was your day, little man?" Trevor asked Jeran over dinner the next night.

"We went to the pahk," Jeran told him around a mouthful of green beans. "I didn't like that gehl. She wouldn't let me slide." Trevor looked at me questioningly.

"There was a little girl who wanted him to play with her, but he didn't want to right then, so she blocked the slide in an effort to force his attention on her," I explained. "This casserole is pretty good. Maybe we could get the recipe."

"Yeah," Trevor snorted around a mouthful, "and every other casserole that will be coming in for the next week and a half."

"Don't look a gift horse…" I reminded him in a sing song voice. "It could be a casserole made by yours truly that we were suffering through tonight."

"Good point. Have I told you yet how delicious this…" Trevor's phone rang interrupting our banter. He checked the caller ID and apologized in advance for breaking the 'no phone at the table' rule.

"I need to get this." He put the phone on speaker. "So you can help me remember everything to tell Stacy later," he whispered.

"Mr. Mitchell, this is Dr. Harmon. I regret that I have to tell you this for more reasons than one, and over the telephone, but I have been in a biking accident and will be out for a few weeks at best." I watched Trevor put a hand to his forehead and close his eyes.

"I have asked a Dr. James Anderson to take over the care of little Dylan. Dr. Anderson is newly out of medical school, but he completed his residency in Boston at one of the best pediatric cardiology hospitals in the country. His training may exceed mine in some instances because I'm finding that I'm getting old. Don't ever get old, Mr. Mitchell," the doctor said with a somewhat pained chuckle. "I have full confidence that Dr. Anderson is the right doctor for your family. He will meet up with you on his rounds at the hospital. I have given him all the information he needs. I wish you good luck and many happy years with your new baby."

"We are sorry to hear about your accident," Trevor said. "We wish you a speedy recovery. Thank you for making us aware of the situation personally. We appreciate the time you have taken with us and Dylan. You are a good doctor and a good man. Thank you. Goodbye."

Trevor pressed end on his phone with a long, weary sigh. "Well, it's back to square one, so to speak. Sure hope this new guy is as good as Dr. Harmon seems to think."

James

"You outta here, nurse Zeke?"I asked, passing him on my way into the NICU.

"You know it," he told me, covering a yawn.

"You need to lay off the partying. Then you could make it through a shift without falling asleep."

"You need to party more," came his joking reply. He nodded down the hall. "You met the Mitchell's yet?" I turned in the direction Zeke indicated in time to see a man lift a toddler and toss him into the air, catching him easily. The toddler and the woman with them had their backs to me so I couldn't make out their expressions, but I watched joy replace the worry on the man's face as he interacted with who I assumed was his son. The little boy squealed in delight when his father tossed him into the air a second time and chanted, "Again, again, Daddy." The man shook his head and lowered the toddler to the floor. With one arm around the woman's shoulders and the little boys hand in his, the family turned and disappeared down the hall. I could hear them talking softly as they went. In the time I had worked in the NICU, it didn't get any easier seeing the pain and constant worry of the unknown that the families endured.

"That lady is pret-ty fine." He raised his eyebrows and grinned.

"Have some respect," I said in disgust.

Zeke shrugged. "It's the truth, Doc."

"I need to get in there," I told him, cutting the conversation short. "Go get some sleep."

"Ms. Gina, who is singing?" I asked, looking up from the computer screen on the desk at the nurses station. I was finishing up my reports on my afternoon rounds before calling it a long day when I heard the peaceful melody filter down the hall like Oregon mist reaching and encompassing everything around it. I thought I was hearing things at first, but when the melody changed dynamics, I concluded it was live, not coming from a phone or radio somewhere.

I walked part way down the hall and peeked around the corner. My breath caught in my chest as I watched a beautiful woman sing softly to the Mitchell baby and I felt physical pain. I couldn't swallow around the lump forming in my throat. Whether it was from her beauty or the tender scene before me, I didn't know. Her long dark hair fell over her shoulder as she lovingly looked down at the baby nestled in her arms. It was as if a bubble of peace surrounded them and I didn't want to disturb it. I'd never seen her and she was someone I'm sure I wouldn't have missed if she'd been in before. I could suddenly empathize with the Grinch when his heart grew ten sizes except that mine was attempting to break through what felt like ten feet of ice surrounding it. I was surprised by the overwhelming desire I had to be where she was, in her circle of peace. I had to meet her.

"That's Ms. Mitchell, Doctor." Ms. Gina told me, standing half way and peeking over the counter for a glimpse of Mrs. Mitchell.

I was suddenly transported back to the hallway this morning watching a little family take advantage of a happy moment on an otherwise emotional rollercoaster. *Or not meet her*, I thought.

"She's a pretty little thing, ain't she?" Ms. Gina continued.

I nodded my head absentmindedly. She was getting around remarkably well for just having had a baby. I did my best to not notice, but she was in great shape. Phenomenal, really. You'd never know she'd had a baby only a few days ago. I squeezed my eyes shut to block out the image of her trim body.

Ms. Gina continued talking, unaware of my internal struggle. "She sings to that baby all the time. She's only been coming for a few days now, but she has a way with the babies. Goes around to each one that belongs to the state and talks or sings to them. You can almost see the babies respond to the singing. We could use a lot more like her." She looked at me thoughtfully. "You should go meet her."

Suddenly, I was terrified to look at Mrs. Mitchell let alone speak to her. The draw I felt to her was not okay since she was a married woman. I'd talked with Mr. Mitchell about Dylan during morning rounds since he had been transferred to my care. One more day without meeting her wasn't going to hurt anything.

"I've got somewhere I've got to be," I lied, grabbing my keys and satchel. I needed to be at my apartment for a shower, so it wasn't really a lie, I justified. "I'll catch up with her another day. Have a good night."

"You as well, Dr. Anderson."

Sophie

Where you from again, Ms. Sophie?" Ms. Gina asked over my quiet singing two evenings later. "I'm detecting a slight twang," she teased.

Mrs. Regina Black, known throughout the hospital and probably most of Portland as Ms. Gina, fit her name in more ways than one. She was from the deep South and her drawl was still thick as molasses after all these years. She liked to tease me about my wimpy Texas twang. Said, "it was barely worth the effort if folks could still understand ya." She was quickly becoming one of my favorites here at the hospital. She was fluffy and gentle and all kinds of motherly goodness. No wonder the babies thrived under her care.

"Yes, ma'am. Texas proud. I'm getting pretty good at keeping the y'alls under wraps, but I can't quite get a handle on the twang." I told the matronly nurse with a smile.

Ms. Gina chuckled and shook her head as she stuck her hand through another incubator window and took the miniature hand of a sick little infant. I gazed at the tender scene in wonder. How did she come here everyday and not feel exhaustion seeping through every pore? She seemed as giving and full of love at the beginning of her shift as at the end.

"I don't know how you do it, how you've done it all these years, Ms. Gina," I told her as I pushed off the floor with my foot to set the rocker in motion again. "I'm more than exhausted when I leave here each night and I only care for one. Inadequately, I might add. You must have been born for this." Her slight blush at my praise endeared her to me all the more.

"Aw, sugar, it's the good Lord who keeps me going. I just try to give a little of His love to each of these sweet babies like He would if He was here," she crooned in a sing-song voice as if she was talking to the baby she was caring for instead of me. Her voice and the steady beeps of monitors in the background enveloped me in a peaceful cocoon.

I snuggled little Dylan closer and leaned my head back against the smooth wood. Listening to Ms. Gina's loving cadence, combined with the warmth of my nephew and the rocking, was likely to put me to sleep.

"Thank you for all you do for my family," I murmured, my eyes getting heavy. "You are an angel."

"And a saint," she added. "Don't I know it."

40

We laughed together and I forced myself up from the hard chair with a quiet groan. "Ugh, this chair sure doesn't get any softer with each sitting. Is it bath night tonight?"

"Sure is. You wanna get the little guy in his birthday suit and I'll get him smelling like an angel again."

I carefully unsnapped Dylan's onesie and slid it up his chest. I pulled his smooth, skinny arms out of the sleeves and over his head. Then I lifted him and transferred him into Ms. Gina's waiting arms. I followed her to the sink and watched as she adjusted the water temperature and, with a washcloth, washed Dylan's little body. When she had him clean and sparkly, she wrapped him in a warmed blanket and handed him back to me. I walked Dylan over to his bed and lifted the side. I leaned down to smother his little forehead with kisses and breath in his yummy baby scent.

When I had his diaper fastened and his clean onesie on, I whispered, "Good night, miracle boy. I'll see you tomorrow."

Ms. Gina came over to help with all the tubes and gave him a soft pat when he was all settled. I put a hand on her shoulder and said, "Take care of him for us."

She reached her big hand up and patted mine. "Me and the good Lord will be watching over him tonight. Don't you worry none now."

How could I worry with her keeping watch? I waved goodbye to a nurse as I walked past the nurses station and paused to swipe my visitor's ID badge before I walked out the doors, comforted in the knowledge that those babies were in Ms. Gina's and the Lord's capable hands.

I had come a little earlier than usual to visit Dylan today. Stacy was being discharged from the hospital and I offered to pick her up so Trevor wouldn't have to miss work. The 'Welcome Home' banner Jeran and I colored hung in the front window of the house. Jeran was having a play date with a little boy from church so I could get Stacy situated at home without having to worry that Jeran was running naked down the sidewalk like he did following his bath yesterday, or digging up all of Stacy's flowers in the front flowerbeds to bury his Matchbox cars. That kid was quick.

I still had a while before Stacy could be discharged and was suddenly craving a pastry. Breakfast had been digested hours ago chasing my nephew. I massaged Dylan for a few minutes more, then closed up his incubator and went in search of Ms. Gina.

"Ms. Gina, I'm headed to the Starbucks over in the Children's Hospital wing. Do you want anything?" I rested both arms on the counter and she looked up from the computer.

"Will you remember my order?" She laughed, knowing I didn't drink coffee and the double mocha latte chai whatever was almost like a foreign language to me.

"Write down all your mumbo jumbo and I'll be good." I waved a hand at a pad of sticky notes.

"How you survive without all that *mumbo jumbo* is beside me, girl. You gotta have some pleasures in this life."

"I can't even say it, how could I drink it? I'll be back." I waved to her and smiled at her laughter as I swiped my badge and walked out the NICU doors.

"Hey, Mrs. Mitchell, right?" I looked up and almost choked on my cranberry orange scone. I quickly racked my brain trying to recall ever meeting this handsome man. I didn't know many people in Portland yet, and definitely no one who looked like this, so I'm sure I'd remember if we'd met. My eyes flicked to his ID badge. "Yes. I'm sorry. Who are you?"

"Oh, I'm sorry. I'm Dr. James Anderson, Dylan's doctor. I took over for Dr. Harmon. I'm glad I caught you. Ms. Gina said you headed this way. I've talked with Mr. Mitchell a couple times, and was anxious to meet you before you went home today as well."

This couldn't be Dr. Anderson. He was way too young to be a doctor. Forget his age. He was way too hot to be my nephew's doctor. If I had to see him multiple days a week, he'd have to check me into the hospital for trouble with my own heart.

"Right." I laughed a little at the formal way he addressed me and Trevor. Was that Ms. Sophie thing going through the whole NICU? I thought only Ms. Gina called me that because of upbringing. And nurse Zeke said it to be annoying. Or was everyone always so formal in this state? "And you are Dr. Anderson," I groaned inwardly at my reiteration of his introduction and of the fact plainly printed on the ID that hung from a lanyard around his neck. I leaned closer and squinted at the ID. *Great picture, by the way.* I gave myself a mental head slap. *Idiot.* "Have a seat." I gestured to the empty chair beside me as I tamped down my embarrassment.

"Thanks. I just finished with a surgery so I can only stay for a minute," he said as he took a seat. "I'll need to get back up there and check on my little patient." Pause. "Speaking of patients, your little guy is a fighter." He smiled.

Sheesh. How could one little smile have such an aerobic effect on my heart?

"I know." I returned the smile. "I can't believe how something so tiny can have so many problems, but such a will to live. He's definitely at least as stubborn as his father." I knew how stubborn Trevor was first hand. Ugh, brothers.

Dr. Anderson chuckled. "He doesn't get any of it from you?"

"Well, it's all in the family, I guess." Why was I blushing? "What made you decide to go into pediatric cardiology?" I asked in an attempt to get the conversation away from myself.

Was that pain that flickered across his face just now before he masked it? He cleared his throat and said, "My youngest sister was born with a congenital heart defect. She died as a toddler. When I saw the pain my parents suffered, I vowed to ease that pain for others, if possible."

I nodded. "I can't tell you how grateful my family is that you are passionate about and dedicated to your profession. How long have you worked at this hospital?"

"Two years now. I'm from Oregon originally. I finished up my residency at a hospital in Boston and then took the opening here to be closer to family."

"Closer to family is good." It had been nice being with Trevor and Stacy again. "Hey, speaking of Boston, did you know that Boston built the first subway system in the United States and the first sewing machine was invented there? There is a house in Massachusetts built entirely of newspaper, and the fig newton was named after Newton, Massachusetts."

Dang it. I'd revealed my nerve induced penchant for spouting useless trivia. Dr. Anderson's eyes widened slightly. He looked like he didn't know whether to laugh or make up an excuse to leave quickly.

"I didn't know all that. Hey, thanks for letting me sit a minute. I don't get a chance to do that very often during my shift." Flee it is. "I'll see you around."

I watched in awe and disgust as he walked away- awe that his scrubs emphasized his broad shoulders, muscular arms and back, and trim waist and disgust that I sentence vomit at the most inopportune times. And he seems like a pretty normal guy. Why can't that kind of guy ever find any interest in me? Sigh.

James

I pushed the up button on the elevator and mentally kicked myself over and over. What was it about that woman that had me sharing like we were old friends and thinking if all women were like she appeared to be, I might be open to relationships again? I closed my eyes against the pain that resurfaced when I recalled the question she had asked me. In truth, my sister had only been one part of the scarring answer. Sure it had been difficult for my family when she passed away, but I had been young and not as affected as I'd made it seem. I'd never tell the other more painful part of the reason I dedicated my life to children's hearts.

When I pictured Mrs. Mitchell's face lit up with her dazzling smile, I couldn't help the smile that spread across my face. And those eyes...were they blue or green? I'd had a hard time looking away. I mentally flogged myself. She's married, for crying out loud. Pretty sure that's one of the Ten Commandments. Maybe that's why I find Mrs. Mitchell so fascinating-she's off limits. That's it. I'm lulled into a false sense of security because I know she's taken; no pressure. I'm safe. Or she is. I shook my head in confusion at my train of thought. But because I know she's off limits, I let my guard down. I needed to be careful. Wary.

Chapter 5

Sophie

It had been a little over a week since Dylan's birth. I was getting pretty used to my routine of entertaining Jeran and keeping up on the laundry and dishes during the day so that Stacy could rest. I drove Stacy to the hospital in the afternoon for feedings. When Trevor got home from work in the evenings, I would leave Jeran and Stacy in his capable hands, pack up the pumped breast milk, and go to the hospital for feedings.

Night time was my favorite time to be in the NICU. The lights seemed softer and the beeps a little less harsh on the ears. I rocked Dylan in the wooden rocker and sang hymns to him softly while he sucked on a bottle. He looked bigger and better to me every day. Hopefully, we'd be able to avoid surgery. Some evenings I would sit and hold him for hours, just to feel his soft sweetness against me. And I pictured him as my baby. Would I ever have the chance to be a mother? Aside from marriage and giving my heart to someone who loved me to the depths of his soul, motherhood was my greatest desire.

I changed Dylan's diaper and made sure he was snug in his bed and told nurse Zeke and Ms. Gina goodnight. I walked out of the NICU doors, leaving Dylan and the NICU for another day. I had just about made it to the stairwell door when I heard, "Ahh, Mrs. Mitchell. Just the person I needed to see."

I hadn't run into Dr. Anderson since last week at Starbucks. I'd seen him leaving the NICU a few nights on his way to wherever he went after work. Except for the unfortunate trivia dump at our first meeting, I thought our conversation had gone well and found myself disappointed that we hadn't had a chance to talk again. Now I spun around to face him, excited for the chance.

I sucked in a breath as I drank him in with my eyes. He looked amazing. And tired. The sleeves of his dress shirt were rolled to mid forearm. His tie hung loosely around his neck. His hair had an adorable disheveled appearance. Probably from running his fingers through it. Although I would have liked to try that out for myself, I kept my hand firmly at my side.

I swallowed and found my voice. "Hey, Dr. Anderson. You're here late."

"Finishing up paperwork. It never ends." The rich timbre of his voice caused my heart to flutter as if a thousand seabirds had just taken flight. What was it about this man? "No running for me tonight," he said with a tired sigh.

"You're a runner?" I grinned in excitement at discovering something we had in common.

"Well, not tonight. I don't want to keep you from getting home to your family, so I'll be brief." I blinked at his abrupt change of topic. "I'm a little concerned with Dylan's lack of weight gain. That's common in infants with his condition, but I don't want him to have to work any harder than necessary with the other things his body is struggling to do." I didn't like his condescending tone suggesting that I was somehow responsible for Dylan's lack of weight gain. "I'd like to start using nutritional supplements in the breast milk at the very least, but I'm leaning more toward a feeding tube," he informed me.

Worry for Dylan niggled at my heart. "I'll talk to Trevor about it. You could discuss your concerns and all the possibilities when you meet with him tomorrow morning." I paused. "But doctor, the nurses haven't seem concerned. Dylan seems fine to me." I hated having to tell Stacy they wanted to switch to a feeding tube. It seemed so invasive on such a small person. Of course, I knew she and Trevor would do whatever was best for Dylan without question.

"I wouldn't be speaking with you if he was fine, Mrs. Mitchell." My eyebrows rose in surprise at his patronizing tone. Was this the same man I spoke with only days ago?

I felt my defenses rise. "If y'all would just be patient, I'm sure y'all will see the results you are looking for," I said through clenched teeth. Why was I arguing with the doctor when he obviously knew more than I did on the subject and anything that would help Dylan was priority?

"As Dylan's doctor and the professional here," he reminded me unnecessarily, "I will have to insist that if he isn't getting enough calories or is getting too tired to finish a bottle, we will have to use a feeding tube. But we will plan on starting supplements with tomorrow's feedings. Don't let your love for him blind you to the issues he's facing and keep him from getting the proper care." With that Dr. Anderson turned and stalked away.

I stood dumbfounded, rooted in my spot. Of all the nerve! It wasn't what he said so much as the superior tone he used that was the problem. *Nice bedside manner, Doc.* I was spitting mad.

James

That woman! Who does she think she is trying to tell me how to do my job? As if she knows anything about anything. How many children has she helped exit the hospital in good health? Zero.

I was still fuming an hour later. But the longer I thought about it, the more I wanted to smile. As I replayed our conversation in my mind, I noticed that her drawl increased in direct proportion to her anger level. It was almost comical and I now found myself wanting to anger her again for whatever perverse reason. I gave myself a mental slap. Married. My smile dimmed. Enough said.

Sophie

"How can you even stand that doctor?" I fumed to Trevor as soon as I walked in the front door. Stacy was resting on the couch, reading Jeran a story, and Trevor sat beside them flipping channels on the television with the remote control. Three sets of eyes turned to me. "He's unprofessional, arrogant, and mean." *And so intense when his brown eyes spark...*I gave myself an angry mental shake.

"What are you talking about? Did something happen today?" Trevor turned off the television and gave me his full attention. "He has been very kind and patient with me," he answered, confusion on his face.

"They are going to add a special nutritional supplement to the breast milk so Dylan gets more calories and gains more weight," I informed them. "You two need to discuss what will happen if they decide to put in a feeding tube." My voice hitched on the words and Stacy looked as if she may start to cry. Trevor reached an arm over and squeezed her shoulder.

"It will be okay, sweetie," Trevor told her. "He is doing well. I'll talk to Dr. Anderson tomorrow morning. They said setbacks are normal."

"I just can't stand to see my baby hooked up to all those tubes and machines." Her tears began to fall. Trevor moved Jeran from between them and pulled Stacy to him, caressing her back.

I knew this would be hard on Stacy. I felt terrible getting so upset about the doctor when it was Dylan I should be worrying about.

"Stacy," I tried, "You've seen how strong he is. He's doing great. Trevor will talk to the doctor tomorrow and then we'll see." I patted her shoulder and lifted Jeran from the couch. "How about a snack, little man?"

"Yay!"

"I'll put Jeran to bed tonight," I called over my shoulder as I carried Jeran into the kitchen.

"We can wead stowies?" he asked.

"After our apple slices," I promised.

"No apples. I want cookies," he pouted.

"It's too late for cookies tonight. But you can have one tomorrow."

"I guess," he sighed dramatically.

I laughed and set him on the counter. "Skin or no skin?" I asked, slicing an apple.

"No skin. It huts my teeth."

"No way. You have piranha teeth."

"What's a pwana?" he asked, his face scrunched adorably in confusion.

"It's a fish with really sharp teeth that eats little boys who love cookies," I told him, tickling his ribs.

He squealed and grabbed at my hands. "We not eat cookies tonight, Aunt Sophie."

"No. But I'm going to eat you." I leaned in and smothered his neck and cheeks with kisses while he screeched and tried unsuccessfully to get away.

"You not a pwana," he declared between laughs.

I looked at him in mock disbelief. "I'm not?" I asked. "You mean to tell me piranha's only live in South America and they don't eat boys who like cookies?"

"Yes," he said importantly. "And you live at home, not South mewica."

"Phew," I blew out. "What a relief. Eat these apples so we can brush our teeth and read stories." I lifted him off of the counter stood him on the floor. With our hands full of apple slices, we made our way to his bedroom for p.j's and stories.

Whe's Mommy and Daddy?" Jeran asked as I took the casserole out of the oven the next night and carried it to the table.

"They are talking in their bedroom about your brother. They should be in a few minutes, though," I told him. "Let me grab the veggies and we'll say a blessing on the food. I can't wait to dig into this casserole."

"What's a cassawole?" Jeran asked.

"It's whatever is left in the fridge all thrown into a nine by thirteen dish and baked til the mold melts in," Trevor told him as he and Stacy entered the kitchen.

"What's mold?" Jeran asked.

"It's green and furry and grows on food," Trevor said in a creepy voice.

"Trevor," Stacy laughed. "Knock it off."

"Seriously, Trev. Look at his face." I gestured to Jeran's horrified expression as he eyed the food I was cutting on his plate.

"We eat gween monstahs?" Jeran whispered. "I not vewy hungwy anymoe."

"No, sweetie," Stacy said as she glared at Trevor. "This is very yummy food that someone made especially for us and we are going to eat it without complaining." She sent Trevor a challenging look.

"It looks delicious," Trevor said with a grimace. "We are so happy to eat another casserole."

I laughed and dug into my food. I didn't mind the casseroles so much when it meant less work in the kitchen for me.

"I'd like to get back to why Aunt Sophie doesn't like the arrogant doctor," Stacy said mischievously. I never should have told her about my Starbucks run-in.

"I wouldn't," I protested. After I got Jeran to sleep last night, I hadn't wanted to interrupt Trevor and Stacy's discussion about a feeding tube. I hadn't had a chance to tell them about my conversation with the evil doctor. I had hoped they had forgotten about it. Apparently not.

"It's not so much what he said as the way he said it," I scowled and turned to Trevor. "Stacy's milk has come in. This morning, she said she felt like she was going to pop. Dylan has fallen asleep a few times while eating, but it's not like he is refusing to eat. Everything should be fine now. And your and my definitions of kind and patient must be very different." I told Trevor, referring to his defense of the doctor during last night's conversation.

Trevor and Stacy shared a look. "Calm down, cowgirl," Trevor grinned. "It's his job to make sure Dylan is gaining weight so we can avoid surgery. Stacy and I were actually going to talk to the doctor about a feeding tube anyway. When we spoke this morning, he was leaning in that direction. He wanted to consult the other NICU doctors, so we'll discuss it more tomorrow morning. It can't hurt, right?" He leaned back in his chair and folded his arms over his chest. "It's just funny to hear the drawl jump out when you get angry. It's always been that way with you. I'm sure everything will be fine the next time you speak with him." Trevor tried to console me.

"If I have to talk to him ever again it will be too soon." I looked down at my plate of food and muttered about know-it-all doctors.

"It won't be too long before Stacy can start going in and you can have a break from all things hospital related," Trevor said.

"Including good looking doctors," Stacy added with a smirk.

I felt my face heat as I snatched my plate from the table. I *never* should have told her about the Starbucks run-in. I rinsed my plate in the sink and stomped from the room. "I hear y'all laughing at me in there!" I yelled back through the house to Trevor.

Chapter 6

Sophie

Stacy was with the baby at the hospital, so I made sure Jeran got to his nursery class okay and told Trevor I would see him after church. I turned from him to head down the hall in the opposite direction, but stopped short when I almost walked right into someone. I began an apology, but cut it off when I saw who it was- the guy who had been eyeing me in passing since my first Sunday here. My eyebrows rose in surprise.

"Hey, your social life is about to amp up considerably." Mr. Smooth's silky voice matched his designer suit and I leaned away as he leaned in and raised his arm to rest it against the wall above my head. I blinked and took a step back as Mr. Smooth continued. "I saw you the first week you were here, but couldn't get through the mob of women clamoring for my attention to introduce myself. I'm Andrew, by the way. But you can call me Andy." He thrust his hand toward me and flashed a polished grin.

"Sophie," I replied, shaking his hand. I pulled mine from his grasp when he held on longer than necessary and consciously refrained from wiping it on my skirt.

"That's the cutest drawl, little lady," he twanged, his hand creeping slowly down the wall toward my cheek. "Where are you from and what brings you to Oregon?"

"I'm the aunt turned nanny for a while until my brother and his wife bring their baby home from the hospital," I replied shortly. My skin was beginning to crawl.

"You'd be more than welcome in my pew," he hinted. I nearly choked when his knuckles caressed my cheek. I pulled away as he continued. "I'd save you a seat. Consider this your *personal* invitation."

He ran a hand through his highly gelled hair and favored me with another award winning smile. At what point is it not considered rude to abruptly end a conversation and skedaddle? I was ready to be as far from this guy as possible.

"My cousin works at one of the hospitals around here," Andy informed me, fingering a lock of my hair.

"Really?" I asked, flicking my head to remove my hair from his fingers. Only half listening, I searched frantically over his shoulder for my brother or anyone who could free me from this egomaniac.

"...a doctor."

I turned back to him. "How nice for your cousin," I said, cutting him off. "Thanks for the welcome, but I really need to get to Sunday school." I moved to walk around him, but he cut in front of me, blocking my path.

"So, are you going to ever agree to go out with me? I don't usually have to beg the ladies, but I'm not above begging if that's what it takes for you."

Blech. I tried not to cringe. *I think I just threw up a little in my mouth. This guy is beyond wrapped up in himself.*

"You know, I'm so busy right now with my nephews, I don't really have time for socializing." And that was just one of the reasons I wouldn't be sliding into his pew next Sunday. "Thanks for the offer, though." I managed to hold back a satisfied smile when his jaw dropped and I stepped around him, successfully this time, and went in search of the Sunday school room. I gave one quick glance over my shoulder as I went. Maybe I should have bee-lined it for the restroom. Certainly he wouldn't follow me in there. You never know.

James

"So, I really think you should make an effort to come to church with me next week." Andy said to me on the way to Kaley's house Sunday evening. "There's this girl…She's new, here for a while helping family or something, and I want to know what you think."

"For you or for me?" I asked warily, not ready to discuss women with him.

"Well, she does look like someone you'd go for. Long dark hair, amazing eyes… But I meant for me." Then as an afterthought he said, "You could get any girl you want. How do you do it?" He continued without waiting for an answer. "The better question is *why* don't you?"

I chose humor as a distraction. "It's the uniform. Women love a guy in uniform."

"They're scrubs, dude. I'm not sure that counts," he said, laughing.

"I'm just fine going with Kaley to her services. She could use the help with Mark's busy Sunday schedule. You know that." Andy had been bugging me since he moved in to attend church with him. But he liked to attract attention and I preferred the more laid back option of helping my sister wrestle two energetic young boys. "Besides, relationships are highly overrated." I shrugged.

"She was one woman in millions," he pointed out. I could hear the irritation in his voice. To my knowledge, Andy hadn't ever really been in strong *like* let alone love, so he couldn't understand how one person can ruin all future relationships forever.

"Make that one in billions. They all can't be that bad. You aren't ever going to give any of them another chance?" he asked incredulously. "Fine. You'll force me to break my no-setting-relatives-up rule and set you up on a date. You can double with me and Sophie," he suggested. "On second thought, I don't want you anywhere near Sophie. I've seen how you work your magic and turn women to mush. You're on your own. But get on it, man. You're not getting any younger."

"No time," came my somewhat lame reply. Truthfully? I was a little gun shy. Okay, a lot gun shy. As in not even allowing myself in the general vicinity. It's not worth all the hassle and definitely not worth the heartache. Been there, done that.

"Hey, do you remember that song Grandpa Anderson used to sing to us about marrying an ugly woman? How did it go?" Andy asked, attempting to hum a few bars of the 1960's-something classic.

"If you want to be happy for the rest of your life, never make a pretty woman your wife...' or something like that," I quoted, amused. I hadn't thought of that song in at least twenty years. "Do you remember how we used to laugh at grandpa like crazy when he sang that to us? The very idea of marrying in general set us off," I chuckled. "But apparently the song writer knows something we don't..."

"Just do like the songs says. Find an ugly woman and marry her and all your troubles will be over," Andy suggested. "That also clears the path for me to pick up all the beautiful women who fall all over you. Send them my way, please."

I laughed and held up my fist for Andy to bump. "They're all yours."

"Uncle James," my nephews screeched and burst through the front door and down the steps to wrap their arms around me. Landon is seven and Eli is five. Both could pass for my own with the same brown hair and eyes. Their pictures are almost identical to mine when I was their age. I reached down and scruffed Landon's hair and picked Eli up and swung him over my shoulder.

"How's school, Landon?" I asked as Eli wriggled to be put down.

"Good," came his usual response. "But I read a whole chapter book by myself." I grinned at his puffed out chest.

"Way to go, dude," I praised and held my fist out for knuckles. "And what about you Elijah?" I asked, lifting my free hand to tickle him, but stopped immediately when his squirming threatened to launch him off my shoulder and onto the ground. I set him down and opened the front door as he glared up at me.

"It's Eli," he grumbled.

"No, it's Eli-schmeeli," Landon teased him and ran ahead of us into the house.

"No, it's not," Eli screamed and tore into the house and up the stairs after Landon.

"Boys…" Kaley shouted after them, a warning clear in her voice.

"I swear…" she sighed. "Hey, James. Hey, Andy," she greeted us wearily. I chuckled as I gave her a hug.

"Leave them alone. They are just being brothers."

"If it were up to you, they'd do and get whatever they wanted. I'm the one who has to be the parent."

"What about me?" my brother-in-law complained even as he leaned in to give Kaley a kiss on the cheek on his way to the living room.

"How about you practice being the parent and go talk to your boys," she said wryly and then grimaced as a loud thump sounded above our heads from upstairs.

"Babe, the game's about to start," he whined, but turned and headed for the boys bedroom.

"Where is this sweet little lady you are introducing me to?" Andy rubbed his hands together in anticipation.

"I wasn't…" she looked between me and Andy in confusion and then her eyes narrowed slightly as they settled on me.

"Oh, no," she objected loudly. "You aren't getting out of this by pawning her off on Andy."

"I told you I would let you know when I was ready and I'm not. Why not let Andy have a shot? I'm just here for the food."

She brushed past us and grumbled all the way to the kitchen. I frowned and followed Kaley while Andy laughed and wished me good luck, punching me on the shoulder as he headed to the living room to watch the game.

"By agreeing to come here tonight, you agreed to give Lacey a chance," she pointed the gravy ladle at me. She lowered her voice. "She isn't right for Andy."

"There aren't many who are," I told her.

"Exactly. Which is why I was introducing her to *you.* " She smacked my arm with her free hand. "She'll be here any minute. What am I supposed to do?"

"You don't have to do anything except introduce us both to her and she can choose. I'll just let Andy work his magic and sway her to his side."

"Ugh," she groaned and rolled her eyes, turning back to the gravy boat. "That's what I'm afraid of." She lifted the gravy spoon, gravy dripping onto the counter, and pointed it at me. "Lacey is my friend. If you mess this up…" she threatened, flicking gravy onto the floor in front of my shoes.

"Hey, watch where you fling that stuff," I complained. I reached for a paper towel and leaned down to clean up the mess that barely missed my polished Belvederes. "I'm not going to mess anything up. And you should be thanking me for even coming since this was mainly to get Mom off your back."

She gave me a withering look as the doorbell rang. "Carry this to the table, will you?" She handed me a bowl of mashed potatoes and the gravy boat. "I'll get the door." She clutched her hands to her chest, walking backward, and pleaded, "Please, be the brother I know you can be."

I followed her out of the kitchen to the dining room and grinned wickedly. "Which brother is that?"

Chapter 7

Sophie

"How are you settling in?" Adri asked over the phone the next day.

"A well as can be expected, I guess. Jeran and I are getting along well and I'm getting used to dividing my time between the house and the hospital..." my voice trailed off.

"But?" Adri prodded.

"The guys here are worse than those in Texas," I admitted.

"How is that possible?"

"I mean, I know I'm not here for the guys, but I'd hoped to...I don't know," I sighed in frustration.

"Maybe you just need to take a little time for yourself. This is a huge change for you. You can only be around a toddler for so long before you feel like banging your head against a wall."

"And you speak from experience?" I asked, amused.

"Of course not. Get out and meet new people," Adri suggested.

"Well, there is this guy at church..." I thought over the brief conversation with the smarmy man and shivered. "Never mind."

"Noooo. You met someone and you didn't tell me?"

"It was too painful to recount," I told her.

"Come on. How can I help you if you don't give me anything to go on?"

"Fine," I muttered. "But it's only because I will be proving my point about guys in Oregon. I'll have to tell you about the doctor too, I guess," I said more to myself.

"There's a doctor?" Adri squealed. "You are not getting off this phone until you spill it. All of it."

I proceeded to replay in horrifying detail the whole uncomfortable church encounter and then the mostly pleasant encounters with Dr. Anderson. Until the most recent one, of course.

"He sounds pretty conceited," Adri agreed. "But aren't all the good doctors full of themselves? Maybe he can't help it."

"Don't defend him," my voice rose. "I know he's doing his job and my nephew is his priority, but he could work on his delivery. Trevor's never had a problem with him. Maybe he has issues with women."

"What did you say he looks like?" Adri wanted to know.

"He's kinda hot," I said, trying not to sound like a smitten teenager.

"How hot?"

"Like really hot," I admitted.

"Hot doctor is good. Who knew scrubs could be such a turn on," she mused.

"Not me. Until now." Sigh.

"You have to promise me that you will give people a chance. Maybe that church guy isn't so bad on further examination. Even if he is, he could introduce you to other dating possibilities."

"So I'm using him to find other guys? What's wrong with that picture?"

"Not *using* him. But when you are together, you'll happen to run into people he knows and he will introduce you. That could be helpful in the long run."

I still wasn't convinced. "Whatever you say," I told her.

"Just be open. That's all I'm asking."

"Fine."

"What casserole did you decide to go with tonight? Trevor asked, crossing the kitchen to muss Jeran's hair.

"Daddy," Jeran beamed and held up his arms for Trevor to hold him.

"Pickings are getting slim," I admitted. "So tell Daddy what we decided to go with, Jeran."

"Wish chicken," he reported and put both little hands on Trevor's cheeks. "When do we get to make a wish?" he asked and leaned forward until they were eye to eye, foreheads touching.

Trevor pulled back slightly and raised an eyebrow. "Wish chicken?" he mouthed.

"As in, I wish we didn't have to eat another chicken casserole," I told him. Trevor laughed. "Not really. It's Swiss chicken. We are just finishing up a salad, aren't we, little man."

"Yup," Jeran said with a pat on Trevor's cheeks. He squirmed to get down.

"I'm going to go check on my lovely wife. Call when dinner is ready." Trevor left the kitchen in search of Stacy and I scraped the chopped carrots and tomatoes into the bowl with the lettuce and spinach.

"Mix that around for us, sport." I turned to take the casserole from the oven and placed it on the table.

"Woo, woo, woo," Jeran sang.

I looked over my shoulder to see salad flying through the air and raining down like spring blossoms all over the counter and floor. "Whoa there, little chef." I stilled his hands with my own. "We can't eat the salad if it's on the floor."

"Yes we can. We could eat like puppies," he reasoned. "I want a puppy, Aunt Sophieeee."

"Well, not tonight. You'll have to talk to your mommy and daddy about that one." *Please no puppies.* "Why don't you go tell mommy and daddy that dinner is ready while I clean up our puppy salad."

I lifted him down from the chair he stood on at the counter and he ran out of the kitchen yelling, "Puppy salad. Puppy salad."

"I'm off to the hospital," I announced a short time later, standing from the table and taking my plate to the sink.

"We didn't wish yet," Jeran protested.

"I'll tell you later," Trevor grinned at Stacy's look of confusion.

"I wish that your brother would get better and come home soon." I said, planting a kiss on the top of Jeran's head.

"I wish fo a puppy," Jeran yelled. I laughed at the panicked look on Trevor's face.

"I'll let you two field that one," I told them as I left through the back door.

"Come here, little guy," I whispered to Dylan, lifting him from the incubator. I kissed his soft little head and held him as close as the tubes would allow. We settled into the rocking chair and I raised the bottle to his lips. "Song or story tonight," I asked. When the only response was noisy eating, I decided. "Story it is."

"A long time ago, fierce storms roared through villages and homes. Earthquakes opened the earth and swallowed people and buildings. Mountains fell and buried entire cities. For three days, darkness covered the earth. Candles couldn't be lit. Fires couldn't be started. People were sad and scared because the darkness covered them like a thick blanket. After three days, the darkness dissipated and the people who were still alive heard a voice from heaven. They didn't understand it at first, but after the third time, they heard and understood. It touched their hearts and all the crying stopped. A man came among them. He told them to bring their children to him. He healed them. All their pains. All their sickness and disability. He took it all away. He loved the children. Angels came down from heaven and surrounded the children. The children saw marvelous things from heaven. What do you think about that, baby? Did you know Jesus can heal you? He can."

"Do you really believe that?" Zeke asked quietly. I jumped at the sound of his voice.

"How long have you two been there?" I asked over my shoulder.

"Where'd you hear that story, girl?" Ms. Gina asked. "It's pure beautiful- Jesus comin' and blessin' them children. We could sure use some of that 'round here."

"My mother used to tell me that story every night before bed. She said it chased the bad dreams away because Jesus and the angels would watch over me in my sleep. It's in a book of scripture I have. I could bring it and show you if you'd like." I sat Dylan up and gently patted his back, encouraging a burp.

"That'd be real nice of you, Ms. Sophie. I could stand to hear that one again." She started back to the office. "Get to singin'. I'll only be a holler away if you should need anything."

Zeke moved over to stand beside me. "Do you really believe that?" he repeated.

I glanced up at him from the rocker. "Yes, Zeke. I really do."

"What's the point? With all the sh...stuff that goes on in the world? It's a nice story, but that's all it is."

"What did the world do to you to make you so bitter? And if you don't believe it, why the tat?" I nodded with my chin toward his arm.

"What? Oh, this one?" He glanced down into the eyes of a sorrowing Jesus, whose tear drops transformed into flames that shot down Zeke's arm. A faint blush crept up his neck. "A drunken accident." He shrugged.

"Whatever, Zeke. It doesn't make you less manly to believe in deity. There's a song I listen to on the radio, one of my country jams, that says, 'Real men love Jesus.'"

He snorted. "Tell that to the girls I go out with."

"Maybe you aren't going out with the right type of girls."

"Girls like you?" he snorted again. "Admit it. You'd never give me a second look."

How had the conversation gotten to this point? "Are you fishing for compliments or asking me out?"

"Maybe both." He grinned. The blush spread to his cheeks.

My promise to Adri to give guys a chance sped through my mind. Zeke was cute. "Then maybe I'd say yes." His grin widened. It was my turn to blush under his intense gaze. "Get back to work," I told him. He winked and chuckled as he walked away.

"Sophie, right?" Smarmy man sidled up to me after church the next week.

"Right," I replied tightly. Again I thought of Adri and I groaned inwardly. *You owe me, Adri.* "What was your name again?"

"Andy." I felt a little guilt at his surprised and wounded expression. *Sorry. This girl isn't falling all over you like all the others.* "You ready to put me out of my misery and agree to go out with me?"

"Sure am." Even I almost believed my faked excitement at the prospect.

Once the shock wore off, his face lit up like a clear Portland morning and I had to admit he was nice looking. "I knew you couldn't resist me for long." And then he had to go and say that. "Give me your digits and I"ll call you sometime." The nonchalant way he winked at me as he pulled his phone from his pocket and typed in my number as I recited it to him through clenched teeth attested to his practice in this area. He made it look cool, as if he had bestowed a great gift on me. Adri *so* owed me.

"I can't wait," I muttered to his retreating form.

James

"I keep running into you here," I said to Mrs. Mitchell near the hospital's Starbucks. After our last volatile, um, conversation, I was hesitant to approach her. I could be professional about this. I gestured to the vacant seat next to her and raised an eyebrow in a silent question.

She wiped her perfect mouth and quickly swallowed before looking around. I wondered if it was for an escape route. "Uh, sure," she motioned to the seat and took another bite of the delicious swirly bread-like thing on a napkin in her lap.

When the silence became awkward, I cleared my throat. "What are you eating?" I asked, knowing I should apologize for my previously unprofessional behavior. Instead, I settled for avoidance, and latched on to the first thought that entered my mind.

"The cinnamon swirl coffee cake. It's delightful." The last word came out as more of a moan and she closed her eyes. I quickly averted my gaze when she opened them again so I wasn't caught staring. This running into her wasn't a good idea. "Here," she said with a grudging sigh. "Try some." She broke off a piece and held it out to me.

Her forgiveness was a pleasant, if unexpected, surprise. One I wasn't sure I deserved." Thanks, but if it's as good as you say, I may be tempted to take what's left of yours."

She quickly pulled the offered piece back out of reach and turned her body away from me, hugging the cake possessively to her. "On second thought, go get your own." I couldn't help the grin that spread over my face at the teasing look she threw me over her shoulder. Time to go.

"I think I may just do that. Thanks for the suggestion. I'm glad I bumped into you today." As far as apologies went, that one stunk, but this was the perfect time to make my exit. Leave on a positive note. I stood as she turned back toward me. Something resembling disappointment flashed quickly through her eyes. Or maybe it was relief. She probably thought I was bipolar.

"Sure," came her confused reply. "Thanks, uh, for stopping to say hi. Have a good day."

I lifted my hand in a small wave and turned toward Starbucks. I'd better steer clear of Mrs. Mitchell because it was getting tough to tell which was more tempting, the cinnamon swirl coffee cake or her.

"Sorry, dude." Andy palmed the ball and headed for his gym bag on the sideline. "I gotta go."

"You're cutting out on our game?" I asked in disbelief. "What's up?"

"I've got a date, man. Can't keep the beautiful lady waiting."

"Who is it this time?"

"Sophie."

"She finally agreed to a date, huh? You must really like this girl to keep badgering her until you got an affirmative response."

"Yeah. She promises to be a pretty good time."

"Wow. Your enthusiasm astounds me."

"I just don't want her to be heartbroken when this doesn't last as long as she wants. I think she's pretty into me, but she is only in Oregon a few months to help family, and I don't do the long distance thing, so I kind of have to keep her at arm's length. Save her from herself and all that."

I snorted. "That's big of you. Who knew you were so selfless." I took a long drink from my water bottle.

"Yeah, well, somebody's gotta do it. Might as well be me. If it wasn't her I was saving, it would be some other beautiful female."

"They are just falling at your feet." I rolled my eyes. "See you later."

Sophie

"What's the name of the place we are going again?" I asked Andy as we pulled away from Trevor's house.

"You mentioned you'd like to see more of the city, so I thought I'd offer the best tour guide services around. Me. And the first destination on our list is the Portland Japanese Gardens. I've been there one other time. It's not the most interesting place on the planet, but I do what I can do for you touristy types."

I mentally rolled my eyes. How very kind of him to suffer through this experience on my behalf. "Hope we make it out alive," I said.

"You will just owe me one," he flashed me a grin that was calculated to weaken knees. It only succeeded in strengthening my resolve to get out a little more and meet other people.

"What do you like to do in your down time if it's not touring oriental gardens?" I asked him.

"I don't need to tell you about the gym because as you can see I spend quality time there." He tightened his grip on the steering wheel so that I could better appreciate the flexing of his toned forearms and biceps, I wanted to laugh, but didn't think that was the response he was going for.

"Do you do any running?"

"Only up and down a basketball court. Otherwise, running is pointless. But I take it from your question that you are a runner."

"I admit that I love it," I responded wistfully. "I haven't done very much of it since I've been here because I don't know the area well yet and I haven't had a lot of spare time."

"Well, there are miles of trails here. You shouldn't have a problem finding something you like. Or you could come to the gym with me. I'd take care of you." He winked at me.

"Oh, look. Is this the place?" I asked, equal parts hope and relief.

"Yup. Here we are."

The Portland Japanese Gardens was made up of five gardens which encouraged a sense of harmony, tranquility, and peace. The pink buds on the trees and the orange, black, and white koi fish swimming lazily in a pond were breathtaking surrounded by stone, water, and other green vegetation. The quaint bridges and rock steps and paths begged me to wander slowly in a carefree fashion with a smile on my lips and a song in my heart about God's creations and the promise of rebirth in springtime. Varying shades of green sprouting from spongy earth made me feel as if I was visiting a fairy land where magical things could happen.

I would definitely have to come back when I could take the time to really feel the gardens, soak them in. As it was, Andy appeared to be in a hurry, moving from garden to garden with little or no comment about the colors or beauty. I wanted to flit like a butterfly from flower to flower, drinking in the goodness, while he was more of a rampaging bull trampling serene thought and feeling. I wasn't entirely sure the Gardens were to be experienced in twenty minutes or less.

"Where is your favorite place to go..." my question died on my lips as we came to the sand and stone garden. I reached for Andy's arm as a soft "oh" escaped my lips. Moss covered rocks surrounded by waves of light grey sand reached for the blue sky; monuments of living gratitude for the sunlight. I could almost hear the cymbal-like crash of waves against rocky cliffs where tiny ferns and other plant life clung in symbiotic mist. The distant cry of gulls floated on the wind as cool, salty spray kissed my skin in teasing persuasion to join the ocean and discover its hidden secrets. Now I understood the Shinto, Buddhist and Tao philosophies of something more in water, stone, and plant than just the objects themselves. The sand and grey green stones presented to me gifts of peace and tranquility I had rarely experienced outside of church or at the ocean itself. My desire to remain in that spot and soak in the sense of calm was strong. On the tail of that was an even stronger desire to share this with someone who would love it as I did. Someone who would appreciate the sacred whisperings of the ocean to my soul. Someone...

"I've never understood how sand and rocks could be anything but boring. This is supposed to be a garden for contemplation, but the only thing I can contemplate here is no color. No life. No imagination." Andy interrupted my solitude.

I strangled the groan of disappointment that threatened to erupt from my throat. The images shattered in an instant robbing me of this perfect moment and taking my soft and private musings with them. "No imagination," I muttered. "You've got that right."

Misinterpreting my meaning, Andy asked,"Are you ready to get out of here? I'm starving. Let's go contemplate some food."

There were a few other things I was ready to contemplate in relation to Andy and food wasn't one of them. But maybe I was being too hard on him. He'd warned me beforehand that this wasn't his favorite spot. He would probably be a different person in a different setting. I could see all kinds of flaws in that line of thinking, but I couldn't kick one of the only friends I made here to this point to the curb just yet.

"I am hungry." I smiled at Andy. "Where's the best spot for grub in this city?"

Chapter 8

James

"Yeah. I'll meet you there. Wait. That's my pager. I've got to go," I told Andy. I pushed end on my phone, pushed the remote button to relock my car, and turned back toward the hospital. Looked like basketball was out tonight. I took the stairs two at a time and entered the NICU in a hurry. The flurry of activity told me that something was wrong. The loud monitors were beeping double time, adding to the confusion.

"What's going on, Ms. Gina," I asked loudly.

"Oh, thank the Lord you were still at the hospital, Doctor. His breathing is labored and his temperature is up. It sounds like there is fluid in his lungs," Ms. Gina responded with urgency.

"Okay little guy, what's going on?" I asked as I opened the incubator. "Ms. Gina, turn off that machine so I can think, please." Ms. Gina moved quickly to follow his instructions. Suddenly, the noise was gone and the confusion with it. Blessed quiet filled the room. "Pull up his chart." I warmed my stethoscope while Ms. Gina brought his chart up on the computer. "It doesn't sound good," I said to no one in particular. "Call over and tell them to get the TTE ready. I've got to get in there and see what's going on."

"What's wrong with him?" The sound of her voice jolted me. I hadn't even noticed Mrs. Mitchell standing to the side of the incubator, wringing her hands.

"We need to get an ultrasound to see if it tells us anything," I told her. "I'll let you know what we find. Sit tight for a few minutes."

"I'll call Trevor," Mrs. Mitchell said and left the room to make her phone call.

Mr. Mitchell must have broken land speed records to get here. I watched as he pulled Mrs. Mitchell in for a hug. I approached them and stuck my hand out. "Mr. Mitchell." He pulled away from the hug and turned to shake my hand.

"Dr. Anderson. What did you find out?" he asked nervously.

"It looks like we are going to need to take him in for surgery," I told them as I brought up the results of the ultrasound on the computer. "There appears to be a second larger hole in the lower chamber." I quickly sketched a rough picture of a heart on a piece of paper and made an 'X' on the lower chamber. "His lungs are pretty congested and he's headed for heart failure. I need to repair the holes in the wall between the two lower chambers here and here." I made two more 'X's' on the picture. "The surgery is pretty routine and he should be able to go home in less than a week." I watched Mrs. Mitchell fold her arms and bow her head while Mr. Mitchell said something about making a phone call. He left the room and I moved away from Mrs. Mitchell to go prep for the surgery.

A few hours later, I exited the OR and made my way to the waiting room where Mr. and Mrs. Mitchell sat next to each other, speaking softly. They stood as I entered and crossed the room to them with a smile on my face. "The surgery went without a hitch. We repaired both of the holes. He's still asleep, but a nurse will call you back in about a half hour to be with him when he wakes up. I'm really pleased with his response to the surgery so far. Ms. Gina will check on him throughout the night. She can get a hold of me in an emergency. I'll be back in to check on him in the morning. We will talk more then."

I took Mr. Mitchell's offered hand and looked to see Mrs. Mitchell with tears in her eyes. "Thank you," she whispered, and turned to Mr. Mitchell. "He's going to be okay."

I was shocked at the intense desire I had to pull her to me. I hadn't wanted any woman near me since Nicole. It had been years. Now I couldn't seem to do anything without thinking of Mrs. Mitchell. I was going to hell for sure. I shook my head to clear my thoughts and left the couple to get a few hours sleep before heading back for my rounds tomorrow.

Sophie

"There are two waterfalls about twenty-five to thirty miles from here along the Historic Highway within about three miles of each other," Andy informed me.

"I think I saw one from the freeway on my way here," I remembered.

"Probably Multnomah Falls," he confirmed.

"I'd love to see them up close," I told him, excitement already filling me.

"Well, let's go."

That's how I found myself in Andy's car- giving him another chance- and heading east out of Portland. "I can't believe how green everything is here," I commented as we entered I-84.

"What's it look like in Texas?" Andy asked.

"Relatively flat, dry, hot. Everything is so lush here. Look at the moss." I pointed out the window at the deep green trees with moss growing on their trunks.

The Historic Highway brought us in even closer proximity to the lushness that was Oregon. Ferns spread across the forest floor like lacey green umbrellas. Water droplets glistened off their fronds in the sporadic sunshine. I was even more amazed when we parked in a spot across from Horsetail Falls and felt the spongy ground beneath my feet. Mist from the falls carried across the road to us, drawing us to it by lighting on our faces like near-invisible, cool kisses, causing me to suck in my breath and shiver. It beckoned us to come and be wrapped in its beauty. I untied my hoodie from around my waist and pulled it over my head.

We stood near the waist high rock wall, watching. Because of the tree cover, the area seemed softer, muted, creating a peaceful feeling of being in an atrium bubble. I couldn't contain my awe. I noticed a set of about eight stairs to our left and moved in that direction. Taking care not to slip on the wet stone surface, I made my way down the stairs to the sandy section at the base of the falls. The wind and mist were stronger there and I wrapped my arms around myself to ward off the chill. Rainbows piggybacked on the mist as snatches of sunlight bounced through the trees, playing tag in the cool, moist air.

"I can't believe some places on Earth can be so lucky," I said wistfully, motioning Andy closer and raising my phone for a selfie of us.

"What do you mean?" Andy asked, wrapping an arm around my waist and resting his cheek against mine.

"Doesn't it seem like some places get all the beauty while others have to work for any small piece of it?"

Andy shrugged. "I guess I've never really noticed."

"What is the most beautiful thing you've ever seen in nature?" I asked, snapping another pic of the waterfall.

"Does the perfect arch on a three point shot- nothing but net- count?"

"Um...that's not exactly what I was thinking when I said nature, but I can see how a bunch of sweaty men chasing after a ball could be like a pack of wolves chasing a deer...or something. Cavemen, maybe? They lived in nature."

"Try this one then. The perfect set of reps increasing muscle mass and definition." He flexed a bicep and grinned at me.

I couldn't tell if the grin was pride in his muscle definition or because he was teasing about that being the most beautiful thing he'd seen in nature. Maybe he needed to get out more. Or maybe I needed to learn to broaden my scope of things to appreciate. Either way, we were not on the same page when it came to what constitutes beauty in nature.

I snapped a few more pics and we crossed the road and loaded back into the car, pointing the car back the way we had come, to stop at Multnomah Falls. My eyes drank in the rock walls and greenery that lined the

Highway, creating a quaint, olden day feel about the area; like a walk through the hills would reveal a venerable, forgotten cemetery lying beneath the dripping ferns, protected from mans' prying eyes and crushing, irreverent feet.

Although the frequent silence between Andy and me wasn't uncomfortable, we couldn't find much to say to each other. He appeared to be more of a grudging tour guide rather than a willing, enthralled participant. And while I didn't expect him to be as thrilled with the sights as I- he'd probably seen these falls a hundred times- I had a hard time truly enjoying the wonders around me when I felt like we needed to hurry the tour along.

Parking at Multnomah was at a minimum. The bustle of people coming and going from the lodge-type visitor's center/souvenir shop and various food carts made walking to the falls an adventure. But it was worth the effort.

I craned my neck back to see the top of the falls, passing the bridge that hung as if magically suspended in front of the falls on the way up. The combined din of people and rushing water made conversation difficult. But I don't think I could have found words for the beauty before me. I would have loved to have taken the quarter mile hike to the bridge that spanned the river running below, bringing tourists closer to the thundering falls, but Andy didn't want to brave the crowded foot path and bridge; especially when a light rain began to fall. As I waited for Andy to snap a picture of me by the sign naming the waterfall, I vowed I'd return to experience it myself one day.

"I wanted to let you know I GOT MY TICKET," Adri shrieked.

I laughed and pulled my phone away from my ringing ear. "I'm so excited. When do you come?"

"In three weeks. Start planning how you are going to keep me busy. You get one week to convince me why I should move to Oregon."

"No pressure. There are some beautiful waterfalls. Andy is a fair tour guide. I'm sure he'd be willing to help persuade you," I joked.

"Why would Andy be persuading me? What about all the persuading he's been doing with you?"

"I find I'm not easily persuaded. He's cute and his overbearing personality sort of grows on you, but I'm just not feeling it."

"You make him sound like a puppy."

"I kind of feel like I'm with a puppy sometimes. We've been out a few times now and it's all about him. He demands all the attention, plays like crazy if it's something he enjoys, but then loses interest quickly. The cuteness wears off and soon you are just left with the emotional clean up."

"Well, rub his nose in it and move on."

"I'm going with him to his cousin's birthday bash Friday night."

"Perfect time to cut him loose. How's the doctor?" Adri asked nonchalantly.

"I'm not sure. It's almost like he seeks me out sometimes, but then he pulls back mid conversation and I don't speak with him again for days."

"Maybe he's seeing someone. Or maybe he's one of those guys who lets work dominate his whole life."

"I don't know. Whatever."

"Well, I'm not moving there if you can't show me solid proof that the guys are worth it."

"I told you a month or more ago that they aren't," I defended. "Besides, you wouldn't move here for a guy anyway."

"You're right, but the idea of chasing a guy across the continent is romantic. Provided he makes enough money that I could have the gym for hours a day and excessive shopping."

"Could you be any more shallow? And since when are you a romantic? Hey, maybe you and Andy would hit it off. I'd be willing to part with the puppy for your more capable hands."

"What does he do for a living?"

"You know, I don't even know." Suddenly I was feeling bad that I didn't know more about Andy than I did. "Maybe I'm the one with the problem."

"We've always known that. But we love you anyway," Adri teased.

"Thanks. With friends like you..."

"I'll take a look at the puppy when I come," she promised. "Maybe he'll be so cute, I won't be able to resist."

"You'll fall in love instantly. Hey, I've got to go. Stacy needs to go feed Dylan."

"Speaking of Dylan...How is he?"

"He had surgery last night. It was kind of an emergency. I felt bad that Stacy stayed home with Jeran, but I was already at the hospital. It made more sense to have one of them come rather than wait til I got home so they could both go. I spent the evening in the waiting room with Trevor." I couldn't help the image that filled my head of Dr. Anderson and the almost tangible, compassionate look he sent me right before he left the waiting room. It left me wanting to crawl into his arms and stay there for good. I can't read men, I guess. I shook the image out and focused on my conversation with Adri. What had I been saying? Oh. "I did go home after the surgery while Dylan was in recovery and Stacy took my car back to the hospital so she and Trevor both could be with him. It was pretty emotional. But Dr. Anderson is good at what he does."

"I'll just bet he is," Adri commented.

I laughed. "You are terrible. I didn't mean it like that."

"I know. But just think about it. This hot- according to you-, rich doctor who saves babies lives..." she sighed. "What could be more attractive? He sounds like the ideal man. I'd definitely have a bad case of hero worship if I was in your shoes. Besides, there's no harm in dreaming."

As I hung up the phone, I thought about what Adri said and had to disagree. I'd been dreaming about someone like Dr. Anderson all my life and all it had brought so far was heartbreak. So yes, there was harm in dreaming. Trouble was, I couldn't control my dreams.

James

"Hey, you caught me on my break. What's up?" I asked Kaley the next day.

"Well, since you never seem to have time to call me, I have to be the better sibling and call you." She paused and then asked, "How's life?"

"Life's life. What do you want to know?" I asked.

"Why don't you come over for dinner tonight? The kids would love to see you." Kaley always used the kids as a lure. I wasn't biting this time.

"I'll see you in a few days at the party, remember?"

"Fine. If you don't want to spend time with your favorite sister, I'll just see you in a few days."

"Okay," I sighed in resignation. "There is something I've been wanting to talk to you about because you were there with the whole Nicole thing and…something weird is happening to me."

"Define weird," Kaley said.

"Well, there's this girl…" I barely got out before she squealed in my ear, deafening me.

"I've been praying that you would find someone after all this time. I'm so happy for you." I rolled my eyes and ran a hand through my hair. Oh, brother.

"Wait a second. Don't get too excited. She's… married." I held the phone away from my ear to avoid the tongue lashing that was spewing through the phone.

"…and if you think I won't say anything to mom and dad about this you are way wrong." I put the phone back to my ear figuring I'd missed the worst of the rant. She wasn't finished. "A married woman? Oh, James, you are worse off than I thought." She sounded like she was on the verge of tears. Time to intervene.

"Kaley bug, would you just hold on a minute and let me explain? I promise it's not as bad as you think." *At least I hope not.* I went on to tell her about seeing Mrs. Mitchell for the first time and the resulting slow but steady thawing of the unused organ in my chest. "But I haven't had feelings like this for *any* woman in years and there have been plenty that should have sparked something. Why would I have feelings like this now and for a married woman?" I finished.

"Maybe this is your sign that it's time to let go, James," she said quietly. "It was so long ago. You deserve to be happy. Not with a married woman, mind you, but really happy. I want that for you so badly. Take your heart out of deep freeze. It hurts to put yourself out there, but isn't feeling *something* better than going through life feeling nothing?

"I'm afraid," I said almost to myself. "I was so young and stupid. I made so many mistakes. I haven't allowed myself to feel for so long, that the thought of breaking down barriers terrifies me. I can't go through all that again." I heard the anguish in my voice and knew that Kaley couldn't have missed it either.

"You're a different person now than you were then. You've learned a lot from that experience. You will be more careful, take things slowly. Just promise me that you will be open to it. If you happen to meet someone, don't push her away. Allow yourself to feel something…"

"I don't know if I'm ready," I started to protest, but she talked over me.

"I'm not asking you to propose to the first woman you go out with. I'm just asking that you go out with someone and that you not push away any small feelings you may have. Let them grow, explore them, and then see if you can open up a little more."

After all the sacrifices she made for me, I couldn't deny her anything. "I guess," I said grudgingly.

"Thank you. I love you. I'll see you in a few days at the party."

"Thanks, sis. Love you too."

"I'm bringing Sophie to the party tonight," Andy informed me.

"Is this the one you swore never to introduce me to?" I chuckled.

"Yeah. But since you have sworn off women for the rest of eternity, I figure we are all safe. She spends time with her nephew in NICU most days of the week at your hospital. I can't believe you haven't already seen her. If she hasn't caught your eye yet, you'd better get them checked while you are at work one day."

"Yeah, yeah. There are quite a few women walking around the hospital. I'm supposed to know yours from the others? I gotta jump in the shower," I replied as I headed down the hall.

Chapter 9

Sophie

I parked in front of the upscale apartment building and looked it over, searching for Andy. "Hopefully Google hasn't failed me again," I muttered under my breath.

Andy promised he would meet me outside so I wouldn't have to walk in alone. I spotted him through the double glass doors. "Well, here goes nothing," I said getting out of the car and walking up to the building. *Remind me why I said I'd do this*, I silently berated myself as I plastered a smile on my face.

"You made it," Andy smiled and reached for my hand.

"Good ole' Google." I said, briefly squeezing his hand and releasing it. "Remind me who is going to be here tonight," I requested as he opened the door and gestured for me to walk through.

We headed for the elevator as Andy told me, "A few relatives, but mostly people my cousin works with at the hospital. You will probably know some of them since you spend so much time there."

That actually made me feel a little less nervous. The hospital was becoming a second home. I wondered which of the doctors or nurses was behind the door as Andy turned the knob and pushed the door open.

Laughter and music immediately bombarded my senses. I smiled as I took in the streamers and balloons. "Nice job with the decorations," I praised

Andy as we walked into the living room. I'm not sure he could hear me above the noise.

He leaned closer, his hand on my back, and talked directly into my ear. "There's food on the dining room table. Bathroom's down that hall," he pointed, "second door on the left. Find a spot wherever. I'm going to go find my cousin. Be right back."

I turned in a slow circle, taking in the party atmosphere, and smiled when I spotted one of the nurses from the NICU. She waved and I started across the room to say hello. I stopped short in the middle of the room like my feet were trapped in rapidly hardening cement. It couldn't be…

James

Andy found me on the deck and waited until I finished my sentence before inserting himself into the group conversation. "Sorry ladies," he apologized, "but I need the man of the hour to meet someone. Go get some food. Dry your tears. He'll be back soon." I was too grateful to Andy for getting me out of that conversation to do anything but let him drag me away while silently thanking him repeatedly.

"She's here. In the living room. I want you to meet her."

I was going to be forced to meet this girl. She must really be amazing. I'd never seen Andy like this before. He was all but gushing. Do men gush? I'm sure I never have. Disgusting. Pathetic.

As we moved into the house, I wondered why he kept going on and on about her when I couldn't hear anything he was saying over the music. It occurred to me that I really needed to turn that down before the neighbors complained. I dug deep and replayed in my mind what he had told me about her so I'd have something to say in case of any awkward pauses. Not that we'd be talking that long, hopefully. Texas. Nanny. Hospital. Got it.

The going was slow as I was stopped every few feet to shake hands or receive a pounding on the back from my friends and colleagues. Just when I thought we'd never get to this girl, it was like the parting of the Red Sea all over again and there she stood in the center of the room, still as a statue and staring at us with an expression I'm sure mirrored my own. I felt a slight sinking in my gut and jerked my arm out of Andy's grasp, stopping dead in my tracks. *Oh no. It couldn't be...*

I grabbed Andy's shirt collar and pulled him to me so I could hiss in his ear. "What is Mrs. Mitchell doing here? You do know you are dating a married woman, right?"

Andy stared between me and Mrs. Mitchell, the disbelief plain on his face. He grabbed my shirt sleeve and dragged me to the middle of the room. Confrontation time.

Sophie

"You're *married*?"

"You're… married!"

"You're the cousin?"

Our voices rang out in surprised unison, but Dr. Anderson's accusation was the only one that really registered in my shocked brain.

"Married? Why would you think I'm married? To whom?" I asked, truly puzzled.

Andy looked back and forth between his cousin and me with a slightly worried expression. "I thought you said you had never met her."

"The doctors and nurses call you *Mrs.* Mitchell," Dr. Anderson spoke to me over Andy's accusation. "You and Mr. Mitchell are together at the hospital all the time. I even saw you together," -he made a hugging motion with his arms- "in the hall a few weeks ago…" His voice trailed off and he looked at the floor, obviously embarrassed. "So you're *not* married to Mr. Mitchell?" Was that relief I heard in his voice? Interesting.

I couldn't keep myself from laughing behind my hand at the irony. "No. Thank heaven. He's my older brother. Can you imagine us married? That would be more than awful." I shuddered. "I don't know how my sister-in-law does it…" I rambled on and then stopped when I looked back and forth between Andy and the Doctor, curious.

They were having a silent conversation with their eyes that I wasn't privy to. Andy's face held a mixture of pleading and defeat. He looked at me, then back at his cousin, closed his eyes and exhaled, and suddenly called out, "Hey everyone, it's time to sing to the birthday boy!" He shoved past James and headed for the dining room table and the cake. What just happened?

I allowed the wave of people heading to the dining room to pull me along with them. I recognized Zeke moving with the flow and ending up next to me. "Hey, Zeke. How'd you get the night off?"

"Ms. Sophie," he grinned as he looked me up and down. I grinned back at him. He wasn't subtle, but he was harmless enough. I think he teased me simply because he could. "Good to see you. I'm supposed to snag Ms. Gina a piece of birthday cake in exchange for her covering for me for a few. You know, representing the night shift and all that."

"Gotcha." I nodded. "Besides you and Andy, I hardly know anyone. Who are all these people?"

"Some staff from the day shift, other doctors at the hospital, the doc's sister and her family…" He pointed out each group to me.

I looked to where he pointed to see a pretty woman about my age standing with a man- her husband?- and two boys. I never would have guessed she and Dr. Anderson were related. They looked nothing alike except for their hair color.

"…Happy birthday to you," Zeke and I joined in for the last strains of the traditional birthday song.

"Everyone load up," Andy called over the cheers and well wishes. I watched as Dr. Anderson's sister disappeared only to emerge from the kitchen wielding an ice cream scoop and two containers of ice cream. She started to call out to her sons who beat a hasty path to the table to be first in line for the cake, when Doctor Anderson put a hand on her shoulder and leaned closer to tell her something. I watched her sigh in resignation while he smiled adoringly at his nephews.

"We're up." Zeke shoved me gently from behind toward Andy and the cake.

"Do you want some help?" I asked Andy above the din.

"Between Kaley and me," he gestured with his head to the lady next to him manning the ice cream, "I think we got it covered. Have a piece of cake and I'll come find you when I'm finished."

I grabbed a plate and held it out to Andy. He winked at me as he slid a thick piece onto my plate and stepped back so the doctor's sister could drop a scoop of ice cream on it.

"I'm Kaley- Andy's smartest and prettiest cousin- and James' favorite sister." She smiled at me and then laughed lightly when Andy snorted, "Only because you are the only sister."

"I notice he didn't correct you on the prettiest part," I smiled at Kaley.

"That's because he knows it's true." Doctor Anderson appeared next to Kaley and slung an affectionate arm around her shoulders. My gaze settled on him, my heart melting just a little at the obvious love between siblings. "Too bad she couldn't say the same for Chia, here." He pointed to Andy. I looked at Andy with a puzzled expression and Andy glared at the doctor and then Kaley.

Kaley laughed, shaking her head as she said innocently, "Don't look at me."

She laughed louder when Dr. Anderson squeezed her shoulders and said, "Now, now, Kaley bug…" I smiled at the exchange. I really liked this girl.

Kaley's smile turned to worry when we heard a crash coming from the kitchen. She quickly surveyed the room and groaned, "I'd better go make sure my boys aren't redecorating your kitchen in a chocolate cake theme." She handed off the ice cream scoop to Dr. Anderson and hurried into the kitchen. With Kaley gone, awkwardness settled around the table like deflating helium balloons.

"I'll scoop the ice cream," I told Dr. Anderson. "The birthday boy shouldn't have to work."

"It's no big deal," he said. "I'll just mingle as they come through the cake line."

I took the scoop from him and shooed him away. "Go mingle. You're adoring fans are waiting."

"Thanks, Mrs. Mi...I mean...thanks." I grinned as he stumbled over his words. He was adorable when he was flustered.

My eyes followed him across the room to a group of doctors and nurses. What would it be like to stand next to him in a room, my hand in his, or his hand resting lightly on my back?

A plate in front of my face startled me from my thoughts. "You looking to sample other dessert, Ms. Sophie?" Zeke teased. I glanced up at him and blushed furiously when I realized he was watching me watch Dr.

Anderson. My gaze flew to Andy. He was watching also, but unlike Zeke, he didn't look amused.

"You're holding up the line, man." Andy told Zeke.

Zeke glanced over his shoulder and then stepped forward. I plopped a scoop of chocolate ice cream on his plate. "I'll save you a seat," he said with a wink.

"No need," Andy told him tightly. Zeke chuckled under his breath and moved past us to find a seat. "I don't like that guy," Andy muttered when Zeke was out of earshot.

"Ignore him," I said and plopped another scoop of ice cream onto a waiting plate.

Kaley eventually returned from the kitchen and told me she could take her job back. "My husband, Mark, is going to take the terrors home before they can redecorate the whole apartment," she said with a sigh. I laughed lightly and gladly handed over the ice cream scoop.

I took a plate of cake and watched as she dropped some ice cream onto it. Andy handed me another cake-filled plate. "Hang on to that for me will you, babe? I'll be over in a minute."

Babe? Ugh. I took the plate and surveyed the room, looking for an empty seat. I caught Zeke's eye and he pointed to the empty seat next to him where Ms. Gina's piece of cake sat getting dry. I walked in his direction and caught the triumphant smirk he threw Andy's way.

"You've finally been granted work release, I see," he commented, moving Ms. Gina's cake to the floor so I could sit.

"Thanks," I told him as I sat beside him. I gestured to the cake now waiting patiently at my feet. "You might as well eat that and get another piece for her on your way out."

Zeke paused for a moment in his dessert consumption as if the thought hadn't occurred to him and bent to retrieve the cake. "Might as well." He shrugged and tucked his now empty plate under Ms. Gina's. I watched him dig in and took a bite of my own.

"So what's up with you and the doc?" Zeke asked around another bite.

"What are you talking about?" Genuine surprise laced my voice. "I'm dating his cousin, Andy. The guy you love to give a hard time." I nodded in the direction of the dining room where Andy still slaved away passing out cake. How many people were at this party anyway?

"Does the doctor know that?"

"That I'm dating his cousin or that you tick Andy off?"

Zeke laughed. "Jealous, is he? You should not have let me in on that little secret. This is too much fun."

"Oh, leave him alone."

"Let him be a man about it. He looks like he can take care of himself."

This time I laughed. "Because you are looking?"

Zeke snorted in disgust and returned to his original question.

"Of course he knows Andy and I are dating." At least he did now. I cringed remembering the embarrassing face-off right before Andy called for singing and the cake.

"Maybe you'd better make sure. He's spent more time studying you tonight than he spent studying the heart all through med school," Zeke laughed, a piece of chocolate cake shooting out of his mouth and onto the floor in front of us.

"Gross, Zeke," I giggled. "You'd better clean that up."

"Can't. I have to get another piece of cake for Ms. Gina. I've been gone too long as it is. With the drive back, she'll think I skipped out. She wouldn't be too happy with me if she didn't get her piece of cake. And between you and me, this party is a snooze fest." He stood to go, but I grabbed his arm.

"Don't leave me here, Zeke," I pleaded. "I don't know anyone. With Andy doing the cake…"my voice trailed off as I turned pleading eyes on him.

"You don't have to cling to me, Ms. Sophie. What would your boyfriend and the doc say?" I frowned up at him. "Besides, I'd go anywhere with you very willingly. You don't have to drag me."

I stuck my index finger in my mouth and faked vomiting at his cocky grin.

"Here, let me help you get to know the crowd." He stood quickly and faced the room. Before I knew what he was doing, his shrill whistle sounded through the apartment and the once boisterous crowd fell immediately silent. "Everyone," Zeke called out. I made a futile swipe at his arm to draw him back down to his seat. "Thanks for coming to the good doctor's party tonight."

"Zeke," I hissed.

He waved me off and continued. "I have a close friend of the doctor's with me. Sophie stand up here." He put his arm around my shoulders and proudly presented me to the room of strangers. "Sophie would like to lead you all in a game. Listen up while she explains the rules, and you all have a good night."

I'd kill him.

His arm dropped from my shoulders and I watched, seething, as he sauntered to the dining room to grab Ms. Gina's piece of cake. My murderous glare was lost on him. I, however, didn't miss the smug grin he shot me as he passed by on his way back through the room, cake in hand, to the front door.

"That ought to liven things up a bit," he said over his shoulder, pleased with his interference. I wanted to run after him and drag him back by the hair on his head.

I closed my eyes and groaned with the closing of the door. I felt my face heating to the color of a tomato and Dr. Anderson's once delicious birthday cake threatened to make a reappearance. I opened my eyes and slowly turned back to the room. Every eye was on me. Expressions varied from mild interest to humor to pity. Okay, here it goes. I took a deep breath and opened my mouth. True to form, that's all it took.

"I'm new to your great state, so I'm gathering all the information I can about this place. We are going to play an Oregon State trivia game. Dig deep and brush the cobwebs off the files. There will be prizes for anyone who can tell me five useless trivia facts about your great state in thirty seconds or less." I paused and scanned the room for any volunteers. No one would meet my eyes. They all looked around at those standing next to them, poking and nudging in silence to get someone, anyone, to begin the game and put me out of my misery.

Thankfully, Andy chose this moment to finish with the cake and I turned pleading eyes on him. Surely he would bail me out. Or not. He gave me an almost imperceptible shake of his head and gestured to the cake on the table. Oh, please. At least his expression showed minute remorse.

You know that painfully awkward silence that fills the stadium when your boyfriend of one week catches you off guard with a marriage proposal on the JumboTron in front of thousands and you cringe at the suffocating boo's from the crowd as you pull your ball cap lower to cover your eyes and slouch in your stadium seat? Or how about that time at your cousin's wedding when the pastor asks if anyone objects and someone objects? And you wish the pastor would go on with the wedding anyway because the dumbfounded shock has everyone shifting nervously in their seats. Or maybe it's the hushed whispers behind hands when you fall off the stage on your way to the podium for your big 'Employee of the Year' acceptance speech. That awkward tension happens at birthday parties, too.

Just when I thought I'd have to break into an embarrassing and rather bone jarring tap dance, I heard Dr. Anderson's voice floating toward me as he walked to the center of the room. "If I win," he stood next to me and smiled mischievously, "you have to go to dinner with me." I glanced quickly at Andy. "On Zeke."

My eyes shot back to Dr. Anderson. On Zeke sounded perfect. I smiled and looked at my watch. "Ready... go!"

"Ummmm...Oregon is home to the world's tallest barber shop pole," he threw out, holding up one finger. "People are banned in Portland from whistling underwater. The Nike "swoosh" logo was designed by an Oregon State University student. There are nine lighthouses along its coast. It's the only state to have an official state nut—the hazelnut. That's five. Is my time up yet?" James quickly asked, sucking in a huge lungful of air.

"No! You've still got fifteen seconds. Give me more," I cried, bouncing up and down a little on the balls of my feet while staring at my watch. The crowd had moved in around us, some checking their watches, others yelling encouragement.

"Okay. Wow. The pressure's really on. Ummmm....Oregon and New Jersey are the only two states without self-serve gas stations. It's legal to smoke marijuana on your own property even though you can't buy or sell it here."

"5...4...3...2...1," I called, raising my arms up and down to get everyone's help. We all chanted together as James tried to get one last fact out there. "There are more ghost towns than in any..."

"Time's up!" I yelled, exhaling loudly. "Holy cow! You know your Oregon trivia," I said, honest amazement laced my voice. "I'm impressed. And those were totally useless, too," I informed him. "Well, except two of them."

"Two?" James questioned. "Which two?"

"The one about pumping my own gas, of course. Now I won't look like a tourist from Texas. And good to know about the marijuana," I said with a somewhat straight face.

James just looked at me for a moment with a half- smile on his face. *Man, I wish I could read his mind right now*, I thought.

"You're something else, *Ms.* Sophie Mitchell," he told me as the smile grew on his face until it reached the corners of his eyes and crinkled there, holding me mesmerized. I could almost feel those laugh lines under my fingers. They itched to explore not only the lines, but all the contours of his perfect face. He had totally bailed me out tonight. I owed him and I couldn't wait for the chance to pay him back.

Chapter 10

Sophie

"You said your cousin was a girl," I accused as Andy walked me out to my car after the party. What had previously promised to be full fledged humiliation had turned out surprisingly well, but I was still unsettled about Andy and Dr. Anderson being related. Admittedly, the game had loosened everyone up and Dr. Anderson's colleagues had felt almost like old friends by the time the night ended. But I'd never tell Zeke that. Maybe my nervous tendencies could be a positive thing after all. Doubtful.

"No…And I knew you weren't really listening to me that day," Andy shot back.

"Well, can you blame me?" I asked. "You *were* a little smarmy." I congratulated myself for holding back a shudder at the memory.

Andy reached for my hand to pull me to him. I squeezed his hand, but didn't move into his arms. I saw his disappointment before he masked it completely. *I know*, I sighed inwardly. *But I can't help that I'm half in love with Dr. James Anderson, who is actually your male cousin.*

"So he's the reason," Andy sighed. Maybe he could read minds.

"The reason for what?" I asked, trying to sound all innocent as if I didn't know what he meant. But I hadn't told anyone about my little crush on the doctor. Could Andy sense the tension I felt between James and me whenever we were together?

"The reason you're keeping me at arm's length. I think we could really have something if you'd give us a chance."

"I haven't encouraged you from the first day," I gently reminded him. "And I did give us a chance…" Kind of. What had we been doing all these weeks if it hadn't been giving each other a chance?" I paused to let him interject if he wanted. When he didn't, I continued. "This has nothing to do with your cousin." At least not in the way he thought. "I think you wanted to parade me around like your latest arm candy or trophy or something. I put you off and put you off. It's like you now have something no one else could get."

"Ego trip much?" he asked.

I snorted at the irony of that statement. "You know I don't feel that way about myself." Hoping to soften the blow that would come next, I put my hand on his shoulder. "Can I be painfully honest with you? You come on too strong at the outset. I like this Andy-the one who isn't trying so hard to make himself appear that he's God's gift to women. You don't have to do that. It turns people off. You are an amazing man. You don't want people to see it, but I notice how much you care about them. Take the party you threw for James, for instance...You have his back. I like that about you. So just be…you."

"So let me get this straight. You don't feel anything for me?" I cringed at his bluntness and the touch of hurt I heard in his voice. "How in the world can that be possible? You said so yourself- I'm suave."

I couldn't help but laugh. "You had me going until you said that. And for the record, I didn't say you were suave. That would have been a compliment. I gagged and said you tried to be Mr. Smooth." I laughed again and punched his arm. But then I paused and really looked at him. "You know we aren't a good fit."

"The only reason I took you to all those zen/peace, nature, and harmony places is because I knew you liked that kind of thing."

My heart softened toward him a little. "See. You really are an amazing and caring person. You sacrificed the things you enjoy for something you knew I'd like. But all that you just said proves we having nothing in common. I don't even know the real you. What do *you* like to do?"

"Well, I know what I don't like. It's all the wandering aimlessly looking at plants, water, and trees. You've seen one, you've seen them all. It bores me to tears. I need a little more excitement in my life than that. And a gym."

"Admit that this damages your pride more than anything else." I sincerely hoped that was all it damaged. I couldn't read him very well.

Finally he sighed; which still didn't give me a good read on how he really felt. "We aren't the best fit," he admitted. I felt relief, though a very little.

"Despite what you think, I love being your friend," I confided in total honesty, even though I knew that guys cringe when a girl throws the friend card around. But I really wasn't trying to be *that* girl. "You are a good friend. My first here in Oregon." I gave him a one-armed hug. "Thank you for that."

James

"I like her James. I mean, really like her." Kaley stood in the doorway of the kitchen, a dish towel in her hands. "She is smart, quick on her feet, funny…" She pushed my legs off the couch and sat down next to me.

"You forgot beautiful."

"Yes, that too." She slapped my arm proudly. "Speaking of which, It was pretty smooth how you got a date out of her."

"You noticed that, did ya?" I chuckled at my cleverness.

Kaley laughed a short laugh. "Not so smart on your part, though, that you have a chaperone named Zeke tagging along."

I groaned at that. "Don't you worry. I'm working on that one small snag."

She shook her head having no doubt that I could come up with something. Then she sighed, "Poor Andy."

"Poor Andy? Why?" I asked, confusion manifest in the furrowing of my brows.

"Because he doesn't stand a chance with her now that you know she isn't married." She laughed again. "That was pretty funny tonight." She thought for a moment and sucked in a surprised breath. "She's the one you told me about on the phone." I watched as her eyes lit with understanding as she made the connection.

"The same one," I replied with a shake of my head. "You were ready to hang me from the highest tree."

"Or turn you over to Mom and Dad so they could take care of you." She laughed. "You really didn't know she was single, huh?"

"No. I thought everyone at the hospital was calling her Mrs. Mitchell when they were saying *Ms*. I felt so guilty being attracted to a married woman. I almost had a heart attack when I saw she was the one Andy has been bugging me for weeks to meet." I shook my head, feeling stupid.

"That's a great story. Leave it to you… At least I don't have to tattle on you to Dad and Mom," she teased.

"Thanks for all your help tonight. It was really thoughtful of you and Andy to put it all together."

"And it turned out better than we planned, thanks to Sophie. Did you know that she was going to open a sports therapy clinic in Texas? Had a place in mind and everything, but dropped it all to come here and help her brother and sister-in-law with the baby and their other son? She doesn't even know how long she'll be here, but she put her life on hold for them. I can't help but be impressed by that."

"How do you know all this?"

"We talked." She threw me a sly look.

"What does that mean?" I asked warily. "When did you talk?"

"Tonight." She shrugged a shoulder and then patted my leg. "I'd better go. I need to make sure the hubby was able to wrestle the boys into bed."

"I feel bad that you stayed to clean up when you could have gone with them when they left."

"We drove separately anticipating that I would stay the whole time and the boys would need to be relocated before the night was over to decrease the risk of disaster. Sadly, we didn't get them out before the whole kitchen remodeling project began."

I laughed and walked her to the door. "Well, thanks again. And tell your ever patient husband thank you for me. He puts up with a lot from our family, but especially from you."

She huffed in offense. "Watch it. I'll call Sophie and share some more secrets about you."

"You even have her number? Wait… some *more*?" I was actually getting a little worried. "What exactly did you two talk about?" She patted my cheek and smiled, walking past me to the elevator. "Can I at least have her number?" I called down the hall after her.

"Good night, James. Happy birthday." She laughed and waved. "Good night, Andy."

I grumbled as the elevator door closed behind her and turned to see Andy coming through the door from the stairwell.

"What was that all about?" Andy asked jerking his thumb over his shoulder in the direction of the elevator.

"Just Kaley being Kaley." We went into the apartment and closed the door. "Hey, thanks for the party, man."

"No worries. That's just the kind of guy I am."

I chuckled. "I never doubted it."

Sophie

"So, when's dinner, Nurse Zeke?" I walked toward him with purposeful strides the next evening.

"Ms. Sophie," he drawled, "Lookin' good." He held out his arms to me. "Sure. I'll go with you to dinner. It's about time you asked." I stopped in front of him and swatted his arms away, then folded my own arms across my chest. A hug was the last thing he was getting. Although his actions the previous night directly resulted in my getting a date with a certain doctor, I couldn't let him off the hook that easy.

"Uh, uh, Mr." I took a step back. "If you think-"

"Hey, Sophie," James smiled, joining us at the nurses station.

I stopped mid-sentence and turned, the sight of him forcing the words I was going to use to fillet Zeke completely from my mind. "So it's Sophie now, is it?" I tried unsuccessfully to keep the grin off my face.

"If that's okay with you?" His tentative answer was also part question.

"I suppose so. We are going out to dinner, after all." I looked pointedly at Zeke.

"Hey, I thought you just asked me to dinner," Zeke interrupted, sounding offended. "What's the deal?"

"You *are* going to dinner with Sophie," James told him. "But since you threw her under the bus at the party last night, and I won the game you introduced, *you* are buying. For both of us. It won't be as cozy as you hoped, but that's life." He shrugged. "You two work out the details and let me know. See you tomorrow, Ms. Gina," he called into the office on his way out the doors.

"So when are you free?" I asked Zeke, smiling brightly as I made my way over to Dylan's incubator. His glowering look made me laugh. He looked just like a little boy who was used to getting his way and now, for the first time, wasn't getting it.

"If I go catch the Doc, we could go tonight. I know this great little place right here in the hospital just a few floors down." I rolled my eyes at the victorious smile he shot me as he whirled around and jogged toward the doors. They opened before him and he was soon enveloped by the hallway as the door shut behind him.

"Last of the big time spenders," I muttered, opening Dylan's incubator and gently lifting the infant out. "Hey, little guy," I crooned and settled into the rocker. "You ready to eat? Aunt Sophie is here to fix you right up. You have to eat so you can get big and strong." He rooted around until he found and latched onto the bottle nipple, then he was all famished business.

"What song shall we sing tonight?" I whispered and planted a soft kiss on his head. I breathed deeply and sighed with happiness. His delicious baby smell was intoxicating. I looked at his little hands and feet, so perfect. Babies were a miracle that I would always be in awe of.

I pushed off the floor with my toes to set the chair in motion, and began humming a children's song from church. By the third song, I figured Zeke hadn't found James and I would be going home to another casserole. I had just started into a rousing rendition of On Top of Spaghetti when a noise caused me to turn my head. There, standing just off the nurses station with their arms folded across their chests, were James and Zeke, listening and looking quite entertained. "Oh, I didn't know you were back." Blast the heat rising in my cheeks. I would have quit a long time ago had I known I had an audience. In my embarrassment, I blurted the first thing that came to my mind. "Speaking of spaghetti, did you know there was a chef in New York who used his wife's breast milk to make cheese and served it in his restaurant?" James' eyes grew huge and Zeke choked on a laugh. I closed my eyes in humiliation. The situation had gone from bad to worse. "Dylan's almost finished eating." I said quickly. "Do you mind waiting another minute or two and then we can go?"

"Uh, no. Take your time. We'll just be at the desk when you are finished." James told me, a small smile playing around the corners of his mouth.

"I'll actually be thawing milk to make cheese for our dinner," Zeke laughed and headed down the hall behind James.

"You're hilarious, Zeke," I called after him, making him laugh harder. Sheesh.

With Dylan taken care of and sleeping comfortably, James, Zeke, and I walked down halls and caught an elevator down to the third floor of the OHSU hospital and our final destination: The Marquam Cafe. "This is so nice of you, Zeke," I teased, taking my place in line. "Hmmmm…What do I want?" I studied the choices displayed behind the sneeze guards.

"How about some spaghetti and meatballs?" James suggested with a chuckle, referring to my earlier performance in the NICU.

"Good one, Doc," Zeke encouraged.

"You two are really quite funny. Have you ever thought of standup comedy? Or maybe a ventriloquist act? But then which of you would be the dummy?" I put my finger to my lips thoughtfully.

"Whoa ho," Zeke laughed at the same time James muttered, "Ouch."

"She got us there," Zeke elbowed James. "But it would definitely be the Doctor who'd be the dummy."

"That's where you are wrong, my friend," James argued. "Who's had more schooling?"

"Yeah, but can you talk without moving your *lips*?" Zeke wanted to know.

"No, but doesn't the dummy just sit there doing nothing? You practice that every day on your shift."

"All right, boys," I intervened before it got ugly. "That kind girl is waiting on us." I nodded to the pretty girl working behind the counter.

"You forgot to mention beautiful," Zeke said seductively and winked at the girl. I smiled when she blushed and lowered her gaze.

James snorted and moved around us in line to grab a plate piled deliciously high with honey glazed chicken and rice pilaf. I chose an oriental salad and followed him to the register where we told the lady that Zeke would pick up the bill and then to a table near the back. We both shook our heads as we watched Zeke flirt with the girl behind the counter.

"Poor girl," I said, picking up my fork full of salad.

"Oh, come on. You know you'd love to get your hands on someone like Zeke." James glanced up at me as he cut a piece of chicken and brought it to his mouth. I gave an indelicate snort and shoved another forkful of salad into my mouth.

"Yeah, right." I chewed slowly. "Me, Zeke, and hands should never appear in the same sentence. He's a nice guy, from what I know of him, but he's not really my type. Too...I don't know... egotistical, maybe?"

"And you're dating my cousin?" James asked incredulously, raising an eyebrow.

"Yup," I mumbled. I wasn't going to tell him that Andy and I didn't have a lot in common and had basically called it quits the other night. I shrugged and took another bite as Zeke made his way to our table. "Your food is probably cold," I told him as he pulled out a chair and sat down next to me.

"It was totally worth it," he grinned in satisfaction. "I think she likes me."

"How could anyone resist you?" I laughed. He wiggled his eyebrows at me and dug into his lukewarm food.

"Andy mentioned after one of your dates that you are into running," James said on our way to the elevators. Zeke had gone on ahead of us a few minutes before to get back to work so we were alone.

"Yeah. Andy is more into weightlifting, I guess. I have gotten in a few good runs around my brother's neighborhood, but I haven't strayed too far."

"There are some famous running trails around here, if you ever want to go with me," he said hesitantly, looking at me out of the corner of his eye.

I pushed the up button on the wall. "That's right. You run." I turned my head to look at him as the elevator doors slid opened.

"Mostly up and down a ball court, but yeah. This is a beautiful place to run."

"When do you want to go?" I asked excitedly. "I'd love to get out and explore."

"What are you doing tomorrow evening?" he asked, putting his hand out to keep the elevator doors from closing.

"Running with you?" I grinned up at him.

"Sure." He smiled. "Meet me here about this same time?"

"Okay. See you tomorrow. Be ready. I'll run circles around you."

He laughed. "You wish. See you tomorrow." He moved his hand from the door and waved in farewell then turned to walk in the direction of the parking lot and his car. I watched him walk away until the doors closed and I couldn't see him anymore. I leaned against the wall and sighed happily. Spending time with the doctor sounded like a fantastic idea.

Chapter 11

James

"Next basket- I win," Andy hooted.

"Yeah, yeah," I rolled my eyes and dribbled the ball down the court. I slowed up at half court and casually asked, "How are things between you and Sophie?"

Andy's eyes narrowed as he swiped at the ball. "Since when do you care about my relationships?"

"Man, that hurts," I faked a pained look and put my free hand to my chest. "I always care about your life and happiness."

"Uh, huh," Andy said knowingly. He swiped at the ball again. "How long has this been going on?" He raised an eyebrow and didn't look pleased.

"What?"

"You and Sophie?"

"It hasn't," I promised. "We've only talked a few times at the hospital. But I know you've taken her out and I wanted to find out how serious it is." I stopped dribbling and held the ball loosely at my side.

"You think you have a shot with her?" Andy asked with a laugh.

"Not if you are serious about her," I replied honestly. I'd never dream of moving in if he was serious about pursuing a relationship with her even though it left a hollow feeling in my gut.

"I wish I could say that I'm totally into her and you even asking about her has me so bent that I'm gonna punch you in the face. But that would just be an excuse to punch you in the face," Andy said with a laugh. He faked left, grabbed the ball and sank a three pointer.

"That's how it's done," he bragged, his hands high in the air in victory. I high fived him and went to grab my stuff.

"I swear it, James. It's good. We didn't click. Though I can't figure out why." He shrugged. It's totally possible that I'm too much man for her. She can't handle it." I shoved him and he laughed. "Really," he said, "She's all yours."

"Thanks, I think," I said slowly, my eyebrows pulled together.

"There are too many other women fighting over me to go after the one that keeps pushing me away. I learned a long time ago about repeatedly banging my head against the same old wall. I'm over it," Andy said as he wiped his face with the bottom of his shirt and took a swig out of his water bottle.

"Don't think I missed the slam about being too much man for her," I said as I headed for the door. "Moron," I threw back at him over my shoulder.

Andy laughed and choked on his water. "Just trying to tell you that everything's cool between us."

Good, I thought. *Because I am going running with her tomorrow.*

Sophie

I hesitated outside the NICU. My stomach felt like it was going to erupt all over the hospital floor. I kept telling myself that I didn't need to be nervous. I had spent time with James yesterday and had been fine. *Yeah, except Zeke had been there as a comedic buffer.* I took a deep breath. I could do this. I peeked through the window on the door and stepped into the room with a sigh of relief when I didn't see him.

"Hey, Ms. Gina." I waved as I passed the nurses station and made my way to Dylan's incubator.

I had just begun my first song when James came up behind me. "How's the star of American Idol doing today?"

I looked up with a smile that instantly died on my lips. I'd only ever seen James in a shirt and tie or scrubs. While both outfits did good things for him, the t-shirt that hugged his biceps and showed off his chest muscles and basketball shorts did spectacular things for him in a dressed down kind of way. Casual looked good on James. I blinked and cleared my throat. "You and Zeke must sit up all night thinking of as many references to singing as you can."

"Trust me, I have a lot more where that came from."

"That's what I'm afraid of," I said wryly.

He chuckled then asked, "Is the little guy almost finished?"

"Yeah. A couple more minutes and we'll be good to go. Where were you thinking?"

"There are quite a few nice trails not far from here with amazing views. Nothing too strenuous. Or we could head east and end up at the Willamette. Then you'd have the hill to contend with on our way back. Pick your poison."

"Let's go to the river, if that's okay," I suggested. "I'm not afraid of a little hill. Unless you don't think you can make it." I gave him a sly smile.

A slow grin spread over his face. Man, he was hot! "Your concern is touching," he said with a hand over his heart. "But I think I'll be okay. Drag me up the hill behind you if I fall behind." I laughed. Spending time with the doctor was going to be very enjoyable.

James

I let her set the pace as we ran down SW Campus Drive away from the hospital. We didn't go as fast as I was used to, but she kept a steady pace and we were to the river before I knew it. I watched her from the corner of my eye while she watched the boats on the water.

She made a pair of running shorts look good. Her long, lean, tan legs attested to her love of running in the sun. I was drawn to her in a way I hadn't allowed myself to be drawn to a woman in years. Since that first night in the NICU, listening to her sing, I had been captivated. I'd need to watch myself around her, or I'd fall for her. I couldn't let myself get distracted by her even if she was beautiful and intriguing. A little bit of Texas sunshine right here in gloomy old Oregon.

"What?" she asked when she turned and caught me staring at her.

"You seem fascinated with the river. Why?"

"I'm not sure. There's a certain sense of peace that accompanies water for me. It's hypnotizing, don't you think? This is nothing, though. You should see me at the beach."

I smiled as she sighed happily. "Oh, yeah? I grew up at the beach, basically. My parents live a little less than two hours from here in Tillamook, and we were less than ten miles from the beach."

"I'd love that." I heard the wistfulness in her tone.

"You ready to head back?" I asked.

"We'd better. I could stay here all night."

Sophie

"I'll race you back up," I said as we stepped through the sliding doors into the hospital lobby.

"Nine floors?" He huffed in disbelief.

"Sure. We'll take the elevator to twelve from there. What are you afraid of?"

"Not a little thing like you. That's for sure." He told me at the stairwell door. "You're on." He grabbed my arm to hold me back and pushed past me.

My outraged voice echoed through the stairwell. "You cheated, Doc."

I sprinted to catch up. We both slowed to a jog about the fifth floor, and to a walk by the seventh. By the time we made it to the ninth, I was huffing and puffing, using the railing to drag myself up the remaining flight, and trying not to laugh in order to conserve valuable oxygen.

James opened the door for me and I fell to the ground dramatically, crawling on my hands and knees the last foot into the hall. James leaned over with his hands on his knees, his attempts at catching his breath hindered by his laughter.

"Boy, are you ever out of shape," I panted from the floor where I lay on my back spread eagle.

"Be right back," he called over his shoulder as he dashed off down the hall.

Where was he going in such a hurry? I guessed I'd better get up. The hospital floor probably wasn't the greatest place to take a nap. I rolled over to my knees to push myself to my feet, when I felt a shock of freezing water on my back. I let out a startled yelp, jumped to my feet, and spun around to face a grinning James holding a cup now half full of ice water.

I glared at him through squinted eyes and walked toward him menacingly. "You shouldn't have done that, Dr. Anderson," I growled good-naturedly.

His response was a laugh as he threw the cup back and took a swallow of the cold refreshment. "I'm not afraid of you, Ms. Sophie. Maybe you should cool off." He extended the cup out to me. "Need a drink?" I suddenly had the insane urge to kiss the smirk off his handsome face.

"No, thank you," I sniffed and turned toward the NICU. "Watch your back, Doctor Anderson," I warned over my shoulder. His laughter followed me all the way to the NICU.

"How's the baby?" Adri asked me over the phone later that night.

"His body is recovering well from the surgery, but he developed an infection. He's on antibiotics now and doing a little better. Thank heaven James is the best."

"Who's James?"

"I mean, Dr. Anderson." I told her and closed my eyes against my slip. I knew she'd latch right onto it and she didn't disappoint.

"Are most people on a first name basis with their nephew's surgeon?" she inquired.

I flinched slightly and swallowed a groan. "No."

"Wait. Is this the hot doctor you told me about? The one with the ego?"

"Maybe," I mumbled.

"So…"

"So what?" I squeaked.

"Oh, no. You aren't getting out of this one. You went out with him and you weren't even going to tell me!? That hurts." She sniffed dramatically.

I laughed at her. "Oh, stop. Okay. I didn't say anything because you know my track record with men and I didn't want to make it into anything more than it is. And we had hardly talked before the party Friday night-"

"But…" I could picture her with her hand out, palm up, moving it in circles to get me to continue.

"Not but, *and.*"

"Okay, *and…*" she said, exasperated.

"And he is Andy's cousin." I laughed when I heard her choke.

"But wait a minute. I thought Andy's cousin was a girl."

"I know. I did too, but Andy took me to his cousin's birthday party and she is actually a he and actually Dylan's doctor from OHSU."

"What are the odds? You do things the weird way."

126

"I know," I sighed. "We didn't get along at first, but that's mostly because he thought I was married to Trevor."

"What!?"

"Yes. You heard me correctly. Married to Trevor."

"Gag."

"Exactly."

"So, when are you going out with him again?" I could just picture her rubbing her hands together, a grin on her face. I paused a little too long. "You are going out with him again, right? And I can't believe you didn't call and dish right after. What kind of best friend are you?" she sniffed.

"I'm sorry, Adri," I apologized. "Don't be mad. It wasn't really a date. The birthday party was kind of a disaster and so the nurse, Zeke, took us both to the hospital cafeteria for dinner." Adri snorted a laugh." It all kind of happened so fast. So it wasn't really a date," I insisted. "We've just gone running together."

"I am coming up there," she reminded me. "Only two weeks to go. You'd better not be so stingy with the details from now on."

"I won't," I promised. "And I can't wait for you to come. I've missed you."

"I need to check this doctor out for myself. You are probably messing things up without me there to help."

"Yes, because the last five plus years of dating have worked out spectacularly under your constant supervision."

"Ungrateful. I'll pretend I didn't hear that."

"I love you."

"Uh, huh. I love you too."

Chapter 12

James

"What's new with Sophie?" Kaley started right in on me.

"What makes you think there is even a Sophie to report on?" I asked, irritated at her presumption. "She's dating Andy, remember?"

Kaley laughed. "Right. What was I thinking? You are too scared to make a move. That's okay. I was just going to tell you to bring her to dinner this Sunday. But if you aren't seeing her, I'll invite someone else." She had me and she knew it.

"You love doing that, don't you?"

"Doing what?" she asked, all innocence.

"Exerting manipulative sisterly power over my life. You can't keep out of it."

"I love you and I want you to be happy. I think Sophie could bring you happiness, so…don't think of it as a date. Think of it as I want to get to know her better. She doesn't know how to get to my house and you do. So play chauffeur and bring my friend so she and I can hang out."

I shook my head. "Whatever. I'll see if she has plans. Don't count on her. And maybe I don't want you two to become BFF's." That had potential disaster written all over it. I wasn't sure how comfortable I was with that idea.

Kaley laughed. "That's the problem with you, James. You are still stuck in junior high. Fine," she said as if it didn't make a difference to her. "I'll just call and invite her. While we are enjoying a delicious Sunday dinner, you can sit home with the Chia Pet and eat whatever isn't molding in your refrigerator. I'll make her a *BFF* on my own. Love you, brother."

I pushed end and growled at the phone. I wasn't comfortable with this. Not at all.

Sophie

"Hey, Zeke." I smiled as I walked to Dylan's incubator.

"Ms. Sophie..." He grinned. No matter how ridiculous Zeke was, he could always make me smile. Even as I rolled my eyes at him.

"What do you hear from Miss Cafe?"

"Not much. We went out and there was no connection, you know? She's cute, but I need something more." He looked at me and I had the distinct impression I was the 'more' he was talking about.

"Zeke," James called from across the room, "I need you to get another IV bag for the Carter baby."

"It's not empty yet," Zeke pointed out. "Do you want to change the solution?"

James skewered him with a look. "Yes. I'll write the order."

"On it, Doc. Catch you later, Sophie."

I studied James as he worked, but quickly glanced away when he looked over. I concentrated on feeding Dylan and was startled when a shiny pair of dress shoes appeared in my line of vision.

"Are you busy tonight?" James asked.

"Possibly. What did you have in mind?"

"So if it's not a good enough offer, you have to wash your hair or something?"

I laughed, somewhat embarrassed. "No. Sorry. I would love to do something with you tonight. What did you have in mind?" I tried unsuccessfully to keep the blush from my cheeks.

James grinned. "You said that you love water. I wondered if you'd had a chance to go to the beach yet?"

"Are you taking up where Andy left off with playing the tour guide?" I asked, amused.

"Sure." He shrugged. "Someone has to keep you entertained."

"And you think you are the man for the job?" I teased.

"No. I am, Ms. Sophie. I'll take you anywhere you want to go," Zeke told me as he walked past carrying a bag I presumed was for the Carter baby.

"Thanks Zeke. I'll let you know." I turned back to James. "I've been dying to go to the beach."

"So have I," Zeke informed us on his way past again. "I'll round some people up. Where do you want to meet?"

James threw Zeke a confused look. He stood dumbfounded as if trying to figure out what he'd missed. He was probably wondering, as I was, how Zeke managed to insert himself into our plans. His sincere confusion was so comical that I couldn't help the giggle that came out. James looked at me and grinned sheepishly then shrugged his muscular shoulders.

"Don't you have a shift to finish?" I asked Zeke.

"No. I worked the day shift. I'm almost off." Zeke grinned. "A trip to the beach sounds perfect." Well, isn't that just... perfect.

"Why don't we all meet here in two hours," James suggested. "I'll grab Andy and we'll caravan to Cannon. It's closest."

"Sounds good," Zeke and I said in unison. Zeke grinned and pointed a finger at me then winked. I just shook my head and laughed.

"Thanks James." I hoped he could hear the sincerity in my voice.

He smiled. "You're welcome. See you in a few." Then he was gone.

I squeezed Dylan close and grinned. "I'm going to the beach, baby," I whispered excitedly.

I threw a towel and hoodie into my bag and slipped on my flip flops. "Are you two sure it's okay that I go?" I called to Trevor and Stacy as I thumped down the stairs. "I probably won't be back until late."

"We are good. Go have fun playing doctor," Trevor said with a wicked grin.

"He means playing *with* the doctor." Stacy wiggled her eyebrows at me.

I felt my face heat up, but laughed. "It's not like that, and you know it."

"Drive careful," Stacy said. "We'll leave the door unlocked for you."

"Bwing me somethin' good, Aunt Sophie," Jeran called after me on my way out the door.

I spotted Zeke, James, Andy and about ten or fifteen other people I'd never seen before as I pulled into the parking lot and found an empty stall. Zeke hadn't been kidding when he said he'd round some people up.

"I think everyone is here," James announced. "We are headed to Cannon Beach, so ride with someone who knows how to get there. See you there."

"Ms. Sophie," Zeke draped his arm around my shoulders, "There's a spot next to me in the car with your name on it."

I shot a questioning look toward James. He was the one that had planned this thing, after all. Zeke had basically invited himself and half of Portland along, it appeared.

"She's with us, Zeke," James called over his shoulder on the way to his car.

I shrugged out from under Zeke's arm in relief. "Thanks anyway, Zeke. I'll see you there." I jogged to James car and yelled, "I've got shotgun," as Andy opened the front door. "Thanks." I slipped around him and into the front passenger seat. "I saved the back seat just for you." I smiled innocently up at him and gestured with my thumb over my shoulder. James laughed and started the car. "Or I happen to know that Zeke has a spot next to him in his car. I bet he'd be happy to let you ride with him."

"You are such a comedian, Sophie. You'd better watch out. Scary things come out on Cannon Beach at night." I turned in my seat to grin at him and blushed when he winked at me.

Ten minutes into the hour and a half drive, I turned to James. "I'm bored." I made sure to make my voice extra whiny. "Entertain me." James rolled his eyes and signaled to change lanes.

"Yeah, James. We're bored," Andy whined, taking up where I left off. "Why don't you tell us about the time you peed your pants on that date with...what was her name?"

I snorted and turned to James expectantly. He shifted in his seat, looking extremely uncomfortable. "It wasn't like that and you know it," he defended himself, throwing Andy a warning glare in the rear view mirror.

Andy answered the glare with a smug look. "Then tell us what it was like," he insisted. "Sophie is dying of curiosity now. We both are."

"Fine. But only if you tell her about the time you threw up all over that girl at Prom." I didn't miss the gloating tone in James' voice. Two could play this game and they both had ample ammunition apparently.

"Great," I said settling back into my seat. "This is exactly what I was looking for. I'm ready. Entertain me."

"So, right after we graduated from high school, a semester or two into college, Andy and I asked these girls out. I had liked this girl for forever and finally got the nerve up-"

"Only because you were headed out of the country soon," Andy interrupted. "And if it turned out to be a complete disaster, you'd never have to see her again. Oh, how prophetic," Andy laughed.

"Anyway..." James continued, "We decided to take them to Cape Meares which is less than twenty minutes from Tillamook where we all grew up. I had been up studying all night the previous night for a final and had thrown back a ridiculous number of energy drinks to keep me awake for this date. We had a picnic at the beach, walked around the lighthouse, and found some pretty cool sand dollars and stuff. It was dark by the time we left and I didn't think anything of a wet seat when we got back into the car. We had, after all, been at the beach. When Andy pulled up to the girl's house, I got out to walk her to the front door-"

"Being the gentleman that you are," I supplied.

"There was never any question," James agreed. "So, I was walking her to the front door when I heard Andy calling to me from the car. I turned around to ask what he needed, but decided not to worry about it when he fell back into the car with convulsions of laughter. The direction of the look he had given me before he got back in the car ran through my mind and I glanced down. I shifted in my shorts, remembered which seat I sat on, and closed my eyes. If the girl hadn't been watching me, I would have slapped my forehead with my hand. I felt like such an idiot."

Andy took up the story from that point, barely containing his laughter. "In the porch light, I could see that James had a problem. I was just trying to help a brother out. The only thing was, my date could see he had a problem too, and got this horrified look on her face. That started me laughing uncontrollably. My date got all mad because instead of helping James out, I laughed at him. She was worried that he had a serious medical condition and I was being *insensitive.* I couldn't stop laughing long enough to tell her that I had spilled a bottle of water on the seat when I was transferring stuff from the back seat to the trunk before our date. I had told James about it so he watched where he sat on the way to the beach. He was too caught up on this girl to remember about the wet seat on the way home and sat in it." Andy couldn't go on with the story. He was laughing so hard, he was wiping tears from his face.

Although James was laughing too, he took up the story from there. "I'm not sure if my date even noticed, but I'm positive her friend recounted my disgrace in painful detail to her later. Andy's date didn't talk to either of us for the rest of the drive to her house. And when we got to her house, she ran to the door without a backward glance. Needless to say, I was relieved that I was leaving the country soon and wouldn't have to face that girl again."

"I didn't even care that my date never spoke to me again because I couldn't have looked at her without remembering James and his wet pants and not laugh," Andy admitted. "It was so worth it."

"Did you know that if the muscles around your bladder are weak, it can lead to stress incontinence?" That sent Andy into another fit of laughter.

"Thanks, Sophie," James muttered under his breath.

"So what you are saying is that James didn't actually sit on a wet seat. He was so nervous about the doorstep scene that he peed his pants?" Andy was lying down in the back seat, holding his stomach, and laughing. "I knew it wasn't my fault. All these years..." Andy said in between laughs.

I glanced apologetically at James, but couldn't help it. In the end, my laughter mingled with Andy's. James' brooding next to me and my knowing that I had inadvertently caused the brooding only made me laugh harder. Finally, when my stomach couldn't take anymore, I wiped the tears from my face and sighed.

"Sorry, James," I tried. "I really am."

"Man, I'm not," Andy said. "That story will now go down in history as the best pee story ever."

"Okay, you two," James said sternly, "That's enough." But I grinned when I saw his lips twitch. I reached over and nudged his shoulder. He glanced at me and I felt the smile he sent me all the way to my toes.

The beach was just as breathtaking as I'd hoped. We couldn't have arrived at a more perfect time. The sunset turned the water a shade of peach that I had never seen before. The way the last of the sun's rays reached out to Haystack Rock, cast its shadow to the side and made the monolith appear even bigger. I watched in reverent awe.

I felt someone come up from behind me and stand a foot or so away. We stood in silence for a few moments and then I snuck a glance out of the corner of my eye. James. I should have known. Zeke or Andy wouldn't have been capable of such contemplative silence. I appreciated that about James.

I felt my breath catch when I recognized the look on his face. It matched mine when I watched the majesty that was the ocean. Here was someone who understood me.

"Thank you for bringing me here, James," I whispered softly, reaching to squeeze his hand. I couldn't stand the thought of noise ruining the moment. He turned his hand in mine and flashed me a slow smile as he returned the pressure on my hand.

"Hey, you two," Andy called from a few feet away. James let go of my hand and we turned toward Andy in unison." We are walking down the beach a ways to get closer to the Haystack."

"Oh, shoot. I promised Jeran I'd bring him something," I remembered out loud as we followed Andy.

"There's a nice piece of seaweed," Andy suggested, pointing to our right. "Or a mangled sea slug."

"That looks disgusting." I wrinkled my nose at the slimy, twisted thing with brown, oozing yuck and James and Andy laughed. "I'd really like to find a cool shell or a sand dollar. Jeran would love that."

"Good luck with the little light we have left," Andy called back to us over his shoulder.

We caught up with the rest of the group and got as close as we could to the dark monolith rising from the ocean without getting our clothes soaked. Zeke sauntered over to us and grinned wickedly. "Afraid of a little water, Sophie?" He kicked some water up at me with his bare foot. I sucked in my breath when the cold droplets hit my skin. It was almost time to break out the hoodie. Without warning, he came at me and easily lifted me into the air, threatening to throw me into the water.

I wrapped my arms around his neck and squealed, "I'll take you with me."

"You are so scary, Sophie." He pulled me away from his body like he was going to launch me. I scrambled closer, tightening my grip around his neck. He paused and looked down at me. I realized how close our faces were and immediately loosened my hold around his neck.

"Please put me down," I told him and turned my face away.

Zeke gently lowered me to my feet. He pulled me to his side with the arm that remained around my waist. "I don't bite, babe," he teased in a low voice.

"Don't make things weird between us, Zeke."

"Don't worry, beautiful. I'll wait until you are ready."

I pushed him away and took a step back. "Don't hold your breath," I muttered as I turned to find Andy and James. Zeke's laughter followed me. I rolled my eyes. I knew Zeke was harmless, but he had just enough ego that he thought he was entitled. It would be a cold day in...well, Texas, before I was ready to take him and his ego on.

James

When it was too dark to enjoy the monolith, one of Andy's groupies started a fire and broke out a guitar. I took a seat between Andy and Sophie and tried not to stare as she slipped her hoodie on.

"It's freezing," she shivered.

"Nahhh. Temperature is perfect," Andy said.

"If you are an arctic fox or polar bear," she argued.

"What part of Texas are you from?"

"San Antonio. Home of the Alamo," came her practiced reply.

"What would the temp be in San Antonio right now?" I asked.

"Eighties, easy," she replied, hugging her arms to herself.

"No wonder you are cold. Here. Take my jacket. I have an extra." I unzipped my jacket and took it off, draping it across her shoulders. "I'll be back." I stood, brushing sand from my jeans, and jogged up the beach to my car to get my other jacket out of the trunk.

I couldn't believe I was actually at the beach with Sophie Mitchell, Ms. San Antonio herself, and it was legal. I wasn't breaking any commandments or anything. I wondered what it would take to make our jogging trips a regular thing. Start out nice and slow. Just a friendship type of thing where no one was too invested. No one gets hurt. Besides, she had enough other guys on her trail. She could date them and we could hang out.

Her nephew was scheduled to go home next week and then she'd be heading back to Texas. No strings.

But it sure didn't feel like no strings when I approached our little party to see Zeke cozied up next to her. In my spot. I clenched my hands at my sides and took the empty spot on the other side of Andy. Not getting invested was a good idea in theory. I closed my eyes and let the rhythmic strumming of the guitar weave itself around the soothing sounds of the ocean, wrapping around each other, pulling me gently into the waves and then pushing me back to shore. Pushing, pulling, pushing, pulling. Like the tentacles a certain Texan had managed to wrap around my heart almost from the first time I saw her. The pull I felt from her caused me to push her away or give in and be pulled out to sea without a lifeline, drowning, no escape, and carrying me away from myself to darkness.

Sophie

"You and the nurse looked awfully cozy tonight," Andy said in the car on the way back to Portland.

"Zeke is...I don't know what Zeke is, but I'm not worried. He'll lose interest in a few days when some pretty thing like Cafe Girl comes along."

"Or maybe he's the type that loves a challenge," James inserted himself into the conversation. "I'll talk to him for you if you want."

"Thanks, but no. I can take care of it myself. And besides, everything will be back to normal between us tomorrow." At least I hoped so. I tried to steer us to another topic. "I believe we were about to be favored with another hilarious, if mostly disgusting, story about Andy."

James took the hint. "Okay," he said by way of apology. "I'll back off."

Andy chimed in. "I will too. But I could take him if it became necessary," he reassured me. I laughed at their gallantry. "Enough about you, Sophie. Let's talk about me." Andy grinned and rubbed his hands together. I could tell he loved telling this story. Actually, talking about himself in general. He and James were as opposite as day and night.

"Let's go back about twelve years," he began. I turned in my seat so I could see his face. "James and I were in high school. I had asked the girl I was going to marry to the Prom." James snorted, but Andy continued. "Another Harry Potter movie was due to be released in theaters the following month. So, we decided to have a Harry Potter movie marathon to be up on all things Harry Potter by the time the new movie hit theaters."

"I'm surprised," I interrupted. "I don't see you as a Harry Potter fan."

"After all the time we've spent together, I'm beginning to think you don't know me at all," Andy faked offense.

"I think you're right about that." And I really did. Shame on me for not getting to know him better before I broke things off. Had I ended it prematurely and made a mistake? I wondered. But it didn't feel like a mistake.

"You don't love the gym, so we could never work out," Andy told me. Well, there was that.

"Anyway, back to my riveting story. We were sprawled out with pillows and blankets all over one of my buddy's family room floor. I'd been stuffing myself with popcorn and candy for close to five hours when suddenly, I knew I was in trouble. I excused myself to go to the bathroom, but it didn't help. Things were getting serious, but I couldn't leave. We were going to be parting soon to get dressed for the dance anyway. I could wait it out, I thought, right?" I nodded. "Wrong." He pointed a finger at me for emphasis. I put my hand to my mouth to muffle my laugh. It wouldn't be so funny except Andy was one dramatic story teller.

"I could tell I was getting ready to blow. You know how it feels when it's creeping up your throat and you get the mouth sweats?" I nodded again, going for serious. "That's what was happening to me. I looked around frantically for a garbage can, a bowl, a bag, anything, but there wasn't one in that whole big room. Not even so much as an empty shoe lying around. I stood to make my way to the bathroom again, but all I could see stretched out in front of me was a sea of bodies. It was like that Frogger game where you have to jump on passing logs to get across the river. Except I had to find space between all our friends to get across the room to the bathroom. Wasn't happening. I turned to my date to tell her I needed to leave, but no words came out; only licorice, popcorn, soda-"

I fake gagged and held up my hand. "I get it, thanks."

"-All over her," he continued as if I hadn't interrupted. "Man, the stench..."

At that point in the story, James started laughing. "I've never seen anything like it," he choked out. "One minute, we're all watching Ron complain about giant spiders or something, and the next minute Andy shoots to his feet, turns green, and erupts like a geyser. Stuff spews from his mouth

143

and nose with a ferocity unlike anything I've ever seen before or since." That was saying a lot considering all he had probably seen in his profession. Their description was so real, I didn't know whether to laugh or do a dramatic reenactment and toss my cookies all over James' beautiful car.

"You okay, Sophie?" Andy asked earnestly, eyeing me.

James' head snapped in my direction, a look of horror on his face. "I'll pull over," he offered. "Just say the word."

I reached over and cracked my window, taking a few deep breaths. "I'm good. I promise. Keep driving."

"Skip to the end, Andy," James ordered in exasperation.

"Ah, come on. It would have been hilarious if she'd lost it all over the seats of your baby," he laughed, picturing the drama. "Look at us, making our own memories."

"Finish the story," James and I said together.

"Fine. So all the girls started screaming. It triggered a chain reaction and one after another, people started throwing up all over the place." Andy watched me closely and waved his hand. "But you don't need to know all the stinky details. I'll just skip to the end." I smiled when James rolled his eyes. "I apologized and made a beeline for the door. Needless to say, we didn't go to the dance later that night. The end," he finished proudly. I shook my head in amazement and laughed.

"The truly sad part of that story is I couldn't marry her. She never would have agreed to be stuck with me forever after that."

"A shame," I agreed. "Instead you are here regaling us with all the gory details so we can pass it on for generations to come." Andy sat back and crossed his arms over his chest, satisfied.

"Did you know that vomit produced by sperm whales is used in perfume?"

"Why am I not surprised you know that?" James laughed.

"Can you imagine how much paper this girl would rack up in Jeopardy or Who Wants to be a Millionaire?" Andy asked. "You could make us very rich, Sophie."

"I'll try to remember you when I become rich and famous."

"You owe us anyway," Andy said.

"How do you figure?" I frowned over my shoulder at him.

"We've taken you in as one of our own. Shown you our beaches. Given you play by play highlights of some of our most memorable life experiences."

"You two are true friends," I said humbly, pretending to get teary-eyed. "I don't deserve you."

"Well, no need to get all dramatic. We'll still let you hang with us." Andy patted me on the shoulder.

I dozed off sometime after that. James' voice startled me awake.

"San Antonio, we're at the hospital."

"Sorry I fell asleep." I smiled up at him groggily and rubbed my eyes. "Thanks for the great time." I turned to include Andy in my gratitude. I reached down on the floor by my feet and grabbed my bag. "See you guys." I opened the car door and stepped out. James quickly jumped out and jogged around the car after me.

"Did I forget something?" I asked, looking over my shoulder at his car and then down at my bag.

"No." He pulled something from his jacket pocket. "Give this to your nephew," he said, holding his hand out toward me where a sand dollar rested in his palm.

"How did you find this?" I whispered and took it reverently from his hand.

"I stumbled on it while you and Zeke were busy," he told me with a shrug. I felt my cheeks redden and was grateful for the dark night.

"Thank you, James. You have given me a perfect day." I went up on my toes and kissed his cheek.

"We'll have to go again. To Cannon Beach, I mean. But when it's low tide so we can study the tide pools and get closer to the monolith," he stumbled over the words.

I smiled. "I would love that. Running Friday?" I asked.

"Yes. Good night, San Antonio."

"'Night, James." I watched him walk around his car to the drivers side. Andy waved as they drove away. I slipped inside my car and set the sand dollar on the seat next to me. As I brushed its scratchy surface with my fingertips, an odd sort of warmth wrapped itself around my heart.

Chapter 13

Sophie

Zeke cornered me just outside the NICU the next evening. "How is your balance?" he asked.

"How do you mean?" I had to admit my curiosity was piqued.

"A bunch of us are heading downtown to do one of those segway tours on Saturday. Do you want to come along?"

I laughed in surprised delight. "How many years have you guys lived here? What don't you know about Portland?"

Zeke grinned. "We know everything there is to know about Portland. We just haven't ever seen it by segway. You game?"

"You better believe it," I told him and laughed again as Zeke swiped his badge and we pushed through the NICU doors. "I've never been on a segway, so I'm not guaranteeing we'll all come out of this alive. But if you feel like living dangerously..."

"Dangerous is my middle name, right Doc?" Zeke raised his voice so James could hear us across the room.

"What?" James looked up from an incubator. I felt myself blush when a smile lit his face at the sight of me.

"I was just telling Ms. Sophie that dangerous is my middle name. We are doing a segway tour Saturday afternoon. You and your cousin should come."

James glanced at me and then back at Zeke. "I'll check and see if Andy is game, but count me in. Thanks."

Saturday would be a little more fun now. I grinned and turned to go feed Dylan.

James

"So, what are your plans Sunday?" I glanced quickly behind me as we ran the Marquam Nature Park Loop the next day.

"Uh, well, church," she puffed.

"My sister wondered if you wanted to join her and her family for dinner on Sunday." I felt a little prick at the way I made it sound. "Passing on the left," I called to an elderly man up ahead.

"I'm not sure how to answer that," she finally said. "That's really nice of your sister, but I don't want to be in the way. You know, if you weren't planning on an extra person tagging along." Yup. She had taken it exactly how I'd intended it to be taken. I felt like there was a constant battle going on inside me. Let her in a little, don't let her in at all. Friends or not?

I stopped off the side of the trail and pulled her to a stop next to me. "Sorry for the way I made that sound," I said around a huge intake of air. "I would really like a friend to go with me to my sister's house for Sunday dinner." I squeezed her hand. "Please don't make me face her alone."

"She doesn't seem that frightening, but if it will help you out," she sighed dramatically. "I guess I could go." She looked at our hands, the beginnings of a smile peeking from the corners of her mouth.

I bent forward to make eye contact. "I appreciate you condescending to spend time with me. That's really generous of you." I smiled.

She grinned and shrugged a slender shoulder. "That's just the kind of person I am."

"No wonder my sister wants to get to know you. The more I'm with you, the more I realize you'd be good friends. You both are all sorts of humble and stuff."

"Yeah," she laughed and then smacked my shoulder. "Beat you back," she called sprinting up the trail.

Sophie

"Thanks for letting me hitch a ride with you," I told James and Andy as I jumped into the car Saturday afternoon.

"You've become quite the freeloader. We expect you to drive next time," Andy said from the back seat.

"So like tomorrow for dinner?" I asked.

"He's kidding," James beat Andy to a response. "I'll pick you up around four if that's okay."

"Yes. Now tell me about these segways. I've suffered through the movie Mall Cop, but that's my only experience with them. Did you know that in some hospitals, admission rates for segway injuries are higher than that of pedestrians being hit by cars?"

"I was wondering when you would favor us next with some off-the-wall-meant-to-be-helpful-but-actually-isn't trivia that makes me fear for my life just a little bit more." Andy leaned between the seats and glared at me.

"I'm sorry," I apologized sheepishly. "You guys know how I get when I'm nervous. I don't even know how I remember such ridiculous and unhelpful information."

James grinned at me. "It's not *all* unhelpful information, San Antonio. Andy is more scared about this adventure than you are. He just doesn't have enough brain power to make his fear interesting for the rest of us."

I laughed, a little more at ease now with the teasing, as Andy growled behind us.

"We won't let anything happen to you, San Antonio," James assured me.

"James won't, but I'm not promising anything," Andy still glowered in the back seat.

"Come on, Andy," I laughed and turned around to look at him. "Just think, if something does happen to us, we have a doctor on the premises and you can tell us 'I told you so' for years to come. That will be fun, right?"

"*Heart* doctor," Andy grumbled.

"Well, heart doctor or not, we're here. Strap on your courage, boys. Let's go see Portland." I jumped out of the car and hurried over to Zeke and his friends. I recognized some of them from the beach the other night and greeted them with smiles and hellos.

We moved into the tiny office and listened with rapt attention to the safety spiel. I tried to listen, anyway, but Zeke's constant whispering about keeping me safe accompanied by his hand moving slowly up and down my arm and then my back in a possessive way affected my ability to listen closely.

"Hey, Zeke, keep it down," someone called from behind us.

"Yes, please," the middle-aged worker paused in his instruction giving. "This is the most important part of the tour. Safety first." There were a few snickers as the worker smoothed down his comb over and continued.

What before had seemed life threatening with the segways was looking to be a reprieve from Zeke and his hands now. I looked around the group, wondering how difficult it would be to navigate the people in these close quarters in order to make my escape. I shifted away from Zeke and eyed the door.

"You're that anxious to get started, huh?" a voice whispered close to my ear from behind me, sending chills all the way to my toes. I could feel the slight pressure of his strong chest pressing against my back as he leaned in to keep from interrupting the safety instructions. I grinned on the outside and sighed on the inside. James.

"It's a little crowded in here. My bubble is being invaded," I turned slightly to whisper back, nodding casually in Zeke's direction.

James' eyes flicked to Zeke and back to me with a knowing grin. "I think the instruction part is wrapping up. As soon as you can show you can keep your balance on one of those things, you should be good to go."

"No problem. I'm all about balance. Let's get going."

Although I wouldn't beat any land speed records on a segway, I held my own. What a delightful way to see the city. I was really glad Zeke had suggested this. The weather was perfectly overcast, but not too cold. A slight breeze coming off the Willamette had me putting on my hoodie, but no rain fell. I laughed as Andy zoomed in and out of the group, almost crashing numerous times.

"I was kidding about using the on-site doctor," I called to Andy as he went barreling past. He turned back to grin at me and veered into a enormous planter filled with flowers, throwing himself over the top of it and into oncoming traffic. I screamed out a warning and James increased his speed to get over to Andy. Cars honked and swerved around him as he rushed into the street to stop traffic and helped Andy off the ground. Andy seemed a little dazed as James directed him to a bench nearby. Zeke and some other guys got the segway out of the street and traffic continued on with a few disgruntled looks and single finger waves from the drivers.

"We should probably take him to the hospital just to make sure he doesn't have a concussion or something," someone called out.

"I'm fine." Andy shrugged James off. "That's why they make us wear helmets. Once I get the rocks out of my palms, I'll be good as new."

"They can remove those at the hospital while they do a CT," James said, hauling Andy to his feet. He turned to Zeke and asked, "Can you guys get the segways back?"

"No worries, bro."

I watched Andy from the back seat on the way to the hospital. He said he was fine, but he favored his left hand and rode with his eyes closed. James met my gaze in the rear view mirror and offered me a weak smile, but I could see the worry in his dark eyes. I'm sure they reflected the worry in my own.

Four hours and a finger splint later, we pulled up to James' apartment building and helped Andy inside. He fussed the whole way up to their apartment about not needing anyone to hold his hand, but when he half stumbled to his bedroom, I was glad James had insisted. I watched from Andy's bedroom doorway as James threw a blanket over Andy and told him he'd return in a while with his prescription. I liked that they took care of each other even though to me they seemed like a very unlikely pair.

I stayed in the car while James ran into a pharmacy and paid for the prescription. We stopped for Chinese take-out and pulled up to Trevor's house soon after.

James put the car in park and turned to me. "Sorry I can't stay to eat this with you."

I grabbed my order out of the bag and opened the door. "Please don't apologize. We didn't even need to stop for the food anyway."

"Andy needs to eat to take the pills," he reminded me.

"You'll let me know if there's anything I can do?"

"Yup. I'll see you tomorrow afternoon."

"You think he'll be okay if we still go?"

"Yes. Because it was only a mild concussion, he'll be fine. He just needs to rest and he can do that whether or not I'm there. We'll just have to give him a few days before he's back on the basketball court with that finger."

"It could have been worse." I could see the relief in James' eyes. "You're a good friend," I said softly. "See you tomorrow." I offered a small smile and took my cashew chicken and egg roll into the house. I was confident Andy would be bragging about being one of the segway statistics before we knew it.

Chapter 14

Sophie

"I know I shouldn't be, but I'm a little nervous," I admitted to James as we drove the couple of miles to his sister's house. Not only was he looking great in a white button down shirt, sleeves partially rolled up to reveal muscular forearms, and a tie, which had my mouth watering, but I'd only met Kaley briefly at his birthday party.

"You definitely don't need to be nervous about Kaley. She told me on the phone that she just wants to get to know you better. It's really not that big of a deal," he reassured me.

"Did you know that sixty-five percent of mothers and seventy percent of fathers show a preference for one child over another? So which are you?" I pressed my lips together in an effort to not fill the silence with my nervous chatter.

James laughed a little and glanced at me briefly across the car before returning his eyes to the road. "Need you ask? I'm the favorite, of course."

"Would your sister agree with that?"

"You bet. So you don't need to ask her. Take my word for it, San Antonio, that I was and always will be the favorite child."

It was my turn to laugh. "Whatever you say, golden boy." I shook my head and reached out a hand and fiddled with the radio until I found a country station. "What do you usually listen too?" I asked when James shot me a questioning glance.

"Talk radio or, most of the time, nothing."

"Talk radio? Snore. Once you convert to country, you'll never go back." I turned up the volume and sang along to Sam Hunt.

"That's assuming I'd convert."

I threw him a devilish grin.

"This is classified as country?" James asked after he'd listened to a few measures. "I'm not sure what I expected, but this has more of a pop feel to it."

"Country is going through an evolutionary phase," I admitted. "I'm partial to more of the old school, but I like a little Luke Bryan and Lee Brice."

"At least it's not Willie Nelson. He's one I've heard of and never want to hear again."

"He's a classic," I argued. "Mamma's don't let your babies grow up to be cowboys," I twanged.

"Ugh," James cringed. "Please tell me you don't really listen to Willie."

"Okay. I don't actually like his stuff," I admitted.

The music and a steadying breath calmed me until James announced we had arrived at Kaley's house. We walked up to the porch still debating the merits of 'my' music when I saw a little face peek through the curtains of the front window. I smiled and waved and the face disappeared. Seconds later, the door opened and two boys launched themselves at James. He gathered them both up with a surprised laugh and carried them into the house.

"This is Landon," James informed me, lifting the bigger of the two boys a little higher. "And this is Eli." He nodded to the other boy and instructed, "This is San Antonio. But you can call her Sophie." They obediently called out a hello in unison and Eli added, "I'm five."

"Nice to meet both of you." I smiled at them then addressed Eli. "Good thing you're five so you are big enough to wrestle your uncle."

"Show her your muscles," James told him sending a grin my way.

Eli lifted an arm up and made a fist. "See my guns?" he asked proudly.

"You are so strong," I agreed, my eyes wide with amusement. Adorable. "I knew it. You too, Landon. Both of you take your uncle down."

"Hey now…" James objected. Then, "Kaley, we're here," he called as we made our way to the living room where he threw the boys on the couch and collapsed on top of them. Kaley came into the room amidst squeals from her boys and greeted me with a hug.

"Sophie, it's good to see you again. Glad you could come."

"Thank you for having me. It's good to see you again as well."

"How is Andy?" She asked James.

"Sleeping," he chuckled.

"So, in other words, he's doing great," she interpreted.

"At least he thinks he is for the next couple hours 'til the meds wear off."

"Are you sure it's safe to leave him alone?"

"He's only on something a little stronger than Tylenol. Because of the concussion, they can't give him anything too strong. But he promised not to operate any heavy machinery. He wouldn't be able to anyway with that splinted finger. We won't stay here too long though."

"Well, there are just a few more things to finish, then we can eat."

"What can I help with?" I asked.

"It's just about ready, but come with me. I'm sure I can find something for you to do to save you from the madness in here." She looked pointedly at James and shook her head then motioned for me to follow her. I laughed and stepped into the kitchen where delicious smells were coming from the oven.

I breathed in deeply. "Something smells delicious." My stomach growled loudly in agreement and I placed a hand on it and blushed as Kaley laughed.

"We'd better get some food in that stomach before you die right here on my floor. Will you put these breadsticks in that basket?" she asked, pointing to the basket on the counter. "And there is a salad in the fridge. I'll get the chicken parmesan out of the oven and we'll be ready." I placed the salad and breadsticks on the table as James came into the kitchen.

"Where do you want us?" he asked Kaley.

"Will you please round up the boys and get them in here?" I watched as she began fixing plates for both of her boys and wondered where her husband was.

As if she read my mind, Kaley glanced up from the plates and said, "Sophie, you can pick any seat. Mark won't be here for a while. He's still at the church doing his clerk stuff."

I chose a seat and unfolded my napkin on my lap when laughter erupted from the hall and James stomped into the kitchen, a nephew sitting on each foot, small arms wrapped around his legs. He lifted a leg and set it on a chair one at a time so each boy could slide onto his chair in turn, then he took the seat next to me. Kaley asked James to offer a blessing over the food and we dug in.

"How is your nephew doing, Sophie?" Kaley asked when everyone was eating and the only sound around the table was happy chewing.

I lifted my napkin to wipe my mouth and answered, "He is doing so well, thanks to James." I smiled up at him.

"He's a strong boy," James said, easily transferring credit from himself.

"Modesty is new for you," Kaley observed. "It looks good. Surprising, but good."

"Come on now," James objected. "I'm the most humble, modest person you know. Admit it."

"Right after she admits that you are the favorite child of the family?" I asked mischievously.

James leaned close. "We weren't going to mention that, remember?" he said in a stage whisper. Kaley scoffed at him while simultaneously grabbing a napkin to mop up Eli's spilled milk.

"Oops." I put my hand to my mouth. "I must have forgotten."

"Sure you did. No dessert for you."

"I'll give you extra for bringing this favorite child fact to light," Kaley conspired with me.

"Always trying to score points…" James rolled his eyes.

"I'm trying to win her friendship. It gets lonely around here being the only female in a house of boys." Then she turned to me and whispered, "What will it take? Double dessert and I've got lots of dirt on James if that will put me in the lead."

"Okay, now…" James protested at the same time I laughed and rubbed my hands together.

"Dirt on James would definitely put you on top."

James narrowed his eyes at me good naturedly, but I briefly saw true panic there. He watched me, but spoke to his nephews. "Isn't this dinner delicious, boys? Tell mom that she needs to be a good girl and eat hers. Right now." He turned his glower on Kaley. "Really, Kaley. Now would be a good time to put food in your mouth." Kaley must have sensed the seriousness beneath his teasing tone too because she looked at James apologetically and changed the subject. Curious.

"Boys, finish eating and carry your dishes to the sink. Then you can take Sophie into the living room and pick a movie while Uncle James helps me clean up."

"I don't mind helping," I told her. But the boys quickly shoved another bite into their mouths and popped up from their chairs with their mostly empty plates. After depositing them into the sink with a clatter, they hurried over to me. "Come on, Sophie," Eli encouraged.

"I get to pick the movie," Landon called over his shoulder as he raced out of the room. Eli frantically grabbed my hand and pulled me after Landon, calling, "No. I get to pick it."

James

"What was that?" Kaley demanded as soon as Sophie was out of earshot.

"What was what?" I stood from the table and carried a stack of plates to the sink. I leaned against the counter facing her and crossed my arms over my chest.

"We were just teasing, James, and you got all bent out of shape. When are you going to let it go and move on?"

"I'm not ready to confess any deep, dark secrets to Sophie yet. It's not like she and I are in a relationship. We are just friends."

"Well, she wouldn't have even known you had something to hide if you hadn't freaked out. If you were trying to not get into it with her because she's just a *friend*, you blew it just now. All you did was pique her curiosity."

I blew out a breath and ran a hand through my hair. "You're right. Sorry I got so upset."

"I think if you ever decided you wanted to share that part of yourself," Kaley said gently, "it would be safe with Sophie."

"We haven't even known each other very long. Aren't you kind of pushing this?"

"You haven't been *friends* for very long, but you've been interested for months. I remember what you told me about the first time you saw her."

"That was just a fluke. It had more to do with the feelings her singing invoked, not her personally."

"Keep telling yourself that."

"Can we just agree to disagree before I get upset again?"

"Sure. Go save your *friend* from my crazy boys."

My heart stopped when I saw Sophie on the couch nestled between the two boys. She smiled at something Landon said and wrapped an arm around Eli so he could snuggle closer. They had really taken to her. I understood the feeling. I shook my head to dislodge the thought. Kids are fickle with their emotions. They'd latch on to anyone who would pay them attention. It didn't mean they wouldn't be the same with any other girl Kaley invited over. Except I knew them and I knew that wasn't true. I suppressed a frustrated growl. I didn't need another reason to be attracted to her. Friends. I needed to remember to repeat that over and over. And over.

Landon glanced up. "Uncle James, we picked Despicable Me. Come watch it with us.

"That's one of my favorites," I told them, taking a seat on the floor with my back against the couch. Just then, Sophie shifted and her knee brushed my arm. Maybe this wasn't the best spot for me to sit.

Sophie

"Thanks again, Kaley," I said, returning the one-armed hug she gave me at the door. "The food was delicious and your boys are adorable."

"Thank you for sacrificing your Sunday to spend time with us. Next time, you won't even have to bring James. We could just get together during the week. Lunch or something."

"Lunch would be great if you don't mind making a picnic of it so my nephew can burn off some energy."

"A picnic sounds perfect. I'll give you a call." She reached up and affectionately mussed James hair. "Thanks for bringing her, brother."

"Anything I can do to help you make at least one friend. Where would you be without me?"

"Yes. I couldn't survive."

James' mocking grin turned to annoyance as she reached out and mussed his hair again. James grabbed her wrist and pulled her hand away from his head. "I know it needs a trim. I'm going for the longish version of sexy." He sent her a smoldering look.

"Yeah, the hair isn't helping you achieve sexy. I don't know what will help you with that. Good luck though." She laughed and stepped part way behind the door as he took a playful swipe at her. I laughed at their sibling banter all the while silently disagreeing with Kaley. James Anderson didn't need any help with sexy. He invented sexy. Shaggy hair and all.

"Thanks again for coming today," he said as we drove away from his sister's house. "I hope it wasn't too painful." He glanced at me and flipped his head to get his hair out of his eyes.

I reached up and mussed his hair like Kaley had done moments before. It barely brushed the top of his collar in the back. It would be so fun to run my fingers through. "It was fine, Uncle James," I teased, but pulled my hand back quickly when the flutters exploded in my stomach from the innocent contact.

"Kaley," he said ruefully as he shook his head. "I know it's longer than I usually wear it, but I haven't had a lot of time lately with picking up Dr. Harmon's patients."

"And then you've been running with me..."

"If I hadn't been with you, it would have been basketball with Andy. It's a good outlet."

"I could do it for you right before our run on Wednesday."

"Do what? You cut hair?" he asked skeptically.

"I used to give Trevor haircuts all the time before he got married. I'm a little rusty, but I wouldn't shave you bald."

"Name your price."

"Hmmm," I pretended to consider.

"The lady in Chinatown even gives massages. It's all included in one amazing low price."

I laughed. "Definitely no to the massage. If you are that sore after our runs, I could go easier on you."

"Ha, ha. Just the haircut then."

"You could always get a massage from the nice lady in Chinatown when you have to go back and get my butchering job fixed."

"You offered, don't try to back out now." He said, flashing me chocolate puppy dog eyes. I couldn't help but laugh as I shook my head. "So you'll do it?"

"Only because you asked so nicely and I did offer. But promise not to hate me if it turns out badly."

"I have complete confidence in your abilities."

"We'll see..."

Chapter 15

Sophie

I tried to keep the nervous grin off my face as I carried a kitchen chair out to the front lawn. A glance at the sky told me that the weather would cooperate with this madcap idea I'd had. Three days ago, the haircut had seemed like a nice way to help a friend out. Today it felt different. My heart rate accelerated with every car that drove through Trevor's neighborhood. I took a calming breath and jogged into the house to get the cape, clippers and scissors. James would arrive any minute.

James

So this seemed like a really good idea three days ago, but I wasn't feeling so sure about it now. I'd told Sophie I had complete confidence in her abilities and I hadn't been lying for the most part. I didn't, however, have complete confidence in my ability to keep her at arm's length. *Especially when she looks like that,* I thought as I pulled up to her brother's house and parked. I took in her running shorts and fitted t-shirt and shook my head. Her smooth dark hair was pulled up into a ponytail and the tip of her tongue rested softly on her top lip in concentration as she fiddled with some electric hair clippers. She looked up and smiled as I climbed out of my car. I mentally rolled my eyes at my body's reaction to her. This wasn't a good idea.

"Hey," I called as I strolled toward her.

"You still think this is a good idea?" she questioned.

Absolutely not. "Of course. You're not trying to back out on me are you?"

"Nope. Have a seat." She gestured to the chair in the middle of the lawn. "I thought the weather was nice enough that we could do this out here." She secured a hair cutting cape around my neck. "That way, you don't have to clean up Stacy's floor when we are finished."

"Oh, *I* would have to clean it up, huh? I'm not even getting a massage out of the this and I'd still have to be on clean-up?" My incredulous tone was all for show.

"You forgot to mention that instead of a massage, you get the pleasure of my sensational company during the haircut and then again on the run that will follow." I could hear the grin in her voice.

"You are right. My apologies. Who needs a massage?" I shrugged.

"That's what I thought," she said and raked her fingers through my hair. She picked up a comb and a water bottle. "I'm going to spray you down a little. It may be cold."

I sucked in a breath and she laughed when the water hit my head and neck." You did warn me." She finger combed through my hair again and then took the comb and scissors and got to work.

"You have really nice hair," she said softly. "Did you know that hair is the second fastest growing tissue in the body? Can you name the first?"

"Easy. Bone marrow," I replied with a cocky grin. "Doctor, remember?"

"Alright, smarty pants, who were the first people to remove unwanted body hair?"

"The Romans?"

"Nice try, but not correct," she told me. "I'll give you a hint. It starts with an E."

"Eeeethiopians?"

"Wrong again." She grinned.

"East coasters?" That startled a laugh from her.

"Easter Islanders?"

"Do people even live there still?" she asked around a laugh.

"Are you telling me, O Goddess of Trivia, that you don't know if it is still inhabited by people?" I tsked, throwing her a look of disappointment.

"Do you want a hint?"

"No. A few more guesses." I pretended to think for a minute. "Okay. Ego maniacs, equestrians, Equal Rights activists?" Laughter bubbled from her just as my phone rang. I checked the ID and said, "I need to get this. Sorry."

"Hey, Andy," I answered the call on the third ring. "Who were the first people to remove unwanted body hair?"

I brushed Sophie's hand aside with a grin as she exclaimed, "Hey, no cheating!" and made a grab for my phone.

I tipped the phone away from my mouth and whispered with a grin, "This is my phone-a-friend."

My grin widened when she rolled her eyes and went back to cutting.

"Hello. I'm still here," Andy complained in my ear.

"Sorry, man. What's your answer?"

"My answer is- who knows and who cares?"

"Harsh, dude," I told him with a chuckle.

"Aww, man, now I forgot the reason I called," Andy whined.

I laughed out loud. "Sorry. Call back." I pushed end and told Sophie, "One more guess." I paused, considering. "Egyp.....tologists." I guessed with a twinkle in my eye.

She slapped my shoulder. "You knew it was the Egyptians the whole time," she accused.

"Maybe. Maybe not," I shrugged. "I guess you'll never know."

"You are one bad monkey," she said. But I could hear the grin in her voice.

A comfortable silence surrounded us. I closed my eyes as the rhythmic motions and sounds of combing up and then cutting lulled me into a zen state. Who needed a massage. Had a haircut ever felt so relaxing?

"You aren't going to fall out of the chair on me, are you?" She came around to stand in front of me and continued cutting.

"The sun and the calm of just sitting are putting me to sleep," I admitted. If she ran her fingers through my hair a few more times, I'd be out.

An annoying tickle on my nose had me scrunching it up and down to find relief. It would take too much effort to drag my hand out from under the cape and up to scratch it. I sneezed violently and Sophie's cutting stopped.

"Oops," she laughed as she reached up and brushed some hair off the tip of my nose with her soft, slightly damp fingers.

"What do you mean, oops?" I drawled lazily.

"Never sneeze when your hair is near scissors."

"You're very funny, San Antonio. Has anyone ever told you that?"

"I'm not the one who is funny. Well, at least not funny looking."

"Ouch. I don't know if that speaks more of my looks or your hair cutting abilities."

"Touche," she laughed. The more I was with her, the more I found she could joke with the best of them. She could dish it out and she could also take it. She was quick. I liked that about her.

"Where did you learn to cut hair?" I asked, curious.

"It was one of those phases teens go through."

"Ah, you went through a destructive phase," I teased knowingly.

Her laugh brought a smile to my face. "No. It was my creativity phase," she said, all mock self-importance. "My friends and I wanted haircuts, but couldn't afford salon prices, so we mustered up some courage, dug deep and channeled our inner cosmetologist, and made freaks of each other." She laughed at the memory.

"It was that bad, huh?" I laughed with her.

"No. Not really. But we definitely improved with practice. When I felt brave enough to venture out on my own, I talked Trevor into being my guinea pig. It must not have been too bad because he came to me every time he needed a trim after that. It's just a fun little skill I picked up."

"What about the sports therapy? Kaley said you were getting ready to set out on your own."

Her grin turned into a full blown smile. "Yes! I found a spot and have some patients I am taking with me. I won't be big to start out, but I *am* starting out. Finally." I could feel pride, happiness and satisfaction bouncing off her in waves. I knew how she felt. Being a doctor put that look on my face more than once in the past.

"I am happy for you." And I was. Doing something you love makes all the difference. "It takes courage to go out on your own. But if your determination to make haircuts work is any indicator, you will do well."

"Thank you, James."

We both fell into a comfortable silence as she continued combing and snipping. The sunshine and Sophie worked their magic and I had just reached that fully relaxed state again when I felt Sophie shift. Suddenly my senses were on full alert. My sleepy state vanished instantly and I felt ready to bolt.

I opened my eyes to see what had caused this awareness that raised the hair on my arms only to see her face level with mine, mere inches away. Her eyes were trained on my hair, her concentration complete. Her subtle scent of coconut and some flower swirled around me and filled my senses creating a kind of tunnel vision where all I was aware of in that moment was Sophie. I studied her pink lips, wondering if they felt as soft as they looked. The hand that felt like lead ten minutes ago inched with surprisingly little effort toward the edge of the cape. It took conscious effort to keep my hand at my side and not raise my fingers to her lips. To trace them. Her smooth, flawless skin looked slightly kissed by the sun, and her eyes were this indescribable combination of grey, green, and blue.

"What color would you call them?"

"What?" she asked quietly and glanced down at me. I hadn't realized I'd said it out loud.

Her hand stilled as our eyes met. I felt a pull from her as I gazed into those questioning eyes. Could she feel it too? My eyes moved to her lips of their own accord. Her hand brushed my cheek as she lowered it from my hair to her side. I felt myself lean toward her, helpless to stop the forward motion.

Sophie

"Hey, Soph!" I jumped at the sound of my brother's voice. "Why do you have my son's doctor tied to a chair?" Trevor called across the yard to me as he slammed his car door.

I released a breath in a whoosh and blinked. It was telling that I didn't even hear him drive up. "Stay away and he won't get hurt," I told Trevor in my most threatening mobster voice, flashing my scissors at him.

Trevor put his hands up in a placating gesture and backed toward the front porch. "Please, don't hurt him. He has the hands of a surgeon. We need him. And..." he grasped for something dramatic to say, "I don't want blood on my... front lawn."

A loud burst of laughter spewed from me. "Watch it, or you'll be next."

"Careful, Doctor," he warned James. "My *wife* clearly isn't stable." I snorted at that and Trevor grinned as he reached a hand out to open the front door. He stepped back abruptly when the door opened on its own.

"Your wife isn't stable, huh?" Stacy gently shoved Trevor in the chest.

He grabbed her hand and brought it to his smiling lips. "Just talking to Dr. Anderson about Sophie."

Stacy glanced across the yard and grinned when she saw James. "Ahhh. I see. Hey *wife*," she called to me, "think you could give Trevor a haircut after you are finished with the doctor?"

"I think I could manage that," I said around my hand that was unsuccessful at holding back my laughter. I was surprised that even with

James' more olive coloring, his deep blush was so noticeable. I should have felt bad about his obvious discomfort, but I couldn't muster the sympathy.

"Carry on then," Stacy laughed and took Trevor's hand to lead him into the house.

I watched them look at each other, so much love evident between them, and smiled wistfully. Someday, I hoped to have the kind of marriage my brother had.

"I can see that I'm not going to live that down anytime soon," James muttered and wiped a hand over his red face.

"Probably not," I admitted with another laugh. "I'm pretty much finished with you. Not a lot more damage I can do without shaving the rest of it off. There are only one or two really uneven parts. At least it will grow out," I managed a straight face until a look of horror crossed his.

"The really scary thing about all of this is that I can't tell whether or not you are serious. Do I even want to look in a mirror?"

"You do if you want a decent chance of fielding any questions that are sure to come." A groan was his only reply." You can brush off out here and then go change in the house if you are still up for a run."

"I guess before I answer you one way or the other, I need to ask if I'm okay to be seen in public."

I looked him over, shrugged, and said, "You'll do." I commanded myself to breath normally while shaking out the cape. "Tell Trev I'm ready for him, please. And the bathroom is straight down the first hall on the right." I watched him enter the house and put a hand to my chest. I didn't think anything could make him look better than he had since the day I met him, but that haircut...wow. I was in big trouble.

"You okay?" Trevor asked as he made his way across the lawn and sat in the chair in front of me.

"Yeah. Why do you ask?" I asked nonchalantly as I stepped behind him and secured the cape around his neck.

"You looked a little...faint... just now." He craned his neck to look up at me. "You wouldn't be drooling over the doctor now, would you?"

I cinched the cape tighter around his neck and leaned over to whisper, "No more talking. I have scissors and your cosmetological fate is in my hands, remember?" I brushed my hands across his shoulders, smoothing the cape dramatically, and whispered, "Good," at his fake choking sounds. As long as we understood each other.

I was almost finished with Trevor's hair when James met us back out on the front lawn. I'm pretty sure I'd never get used to the way he made clothes look good.

"Just one more cut," I announced. "There." I removed the cape from Trevor's neck and brushed the little hairs off his ears and the collar of his shirt.

"Thanks, Soph," Trevor said as he bent over and brushed quickly at his hair and the back of his neck. "I'll take the chair and stuff in so you two can go. See you around, Doctor."

We both watched as Trevor grabbed the chair and headed across the grass to the house.

"Which direction?" James asked when the door closed behind Trevor.

"Let's go left today," I suggested and started out at our normal pace.

"You had me going for a minute, San Antonio." James glanced at me.

"Had you going how?" I asked, returning his look.

"This is the best haircut I've ever had, but with the way you talked, I thought bald would have been the painful next step for me."

"Well, I figured you missed out on the massage, so I'd better make it worth your while."

He laughed. "Massage or not, you realize I can't ever go back to Chinatown now, right?"

"It will be tricky for me to cut your hair from Texas."

"Yes. Texas. I had forgotten about that. I was hoping I could talk you into staying in Portland indefinitely so I wouldn't have to go back to Chinatown."

"You are going to go and give me a big head." I blushed. Curses.

"Well, it can't get much bigger than it already is, actually."

"Is that your professional opinion or simply an observation?"

"Well, since my professional opinion would deal primarily with your heart..." *Heaven help me* "...it would have to be an observation."

"Based on what, may I ask?"

"Based on the fact that I can't even get my arm all the way around your swollen cranium when I do this." He reached out and snagged his arm around my head and pulled me to him. I shoved him away and ducked out from under his arm. "Or maybe it's that my muscles are so big, when paired with your enormous head, it's impossible to reach all the way around."

"Enormous head, huh?" I growled and launched myself at him. His laughter poured out around us as we fell onto the grass of a random home. "Enormous head?" I repeated as he rolled off of me and sat up, his laughter decreasing to a chuckle.

Still lying on my back on the grass, I gazed up at him through partially lidded eyes. My heart swelled in my chest until it was almost painful. He was so beautiful on the inside and out. I loved spending time with him. I loved who I was when I was with him. What was he thinking about right now? He always seemed so unaffected by me. Why couldn't he feel even a fraction of what I felt for him? I quickly stood up and offered my hand down to him before I did something stupid like cry. I wouldn't cry over one more man. I could keep this thing on the friendship level because I was going back to Texas to become the person I had worked tirelessly for years to become. I was not getting hung up on another man.

James

I'd decided I'm not exceptionally adept at keeping my distance from Sophie. Today alone had been disaster after disaster waiting to happen. I tried not to even think about what would have occurred if her brother hadn't interrupted us during the haircut. Now the whole arm around her head and falling to the grass with her thing... I shook my head to clear the image. It was like I had to be in contact with her whenever she was within arms length. Even now as I mentally flogged myself, I knew if I looked at her there on the grass, I wouldn't be able to look away. Why was I so affected by her? I quickly shook my head again. A traitorous voice in the back of my mind whispered that I didn't want to think about these missteps because I would like where they would lead if I allowed them to play out.

I startled when a hand appeared in front of my face. I had been so caught up in my thoughts that I hadn't seen Sophie stand. I stared for a second at her hand and felt incomprehensible anger rise in me. I wouldn't let myself fall for this girl, but I couldn't deny the intense pull I felt whenever I was with her. That I couldn't reconcile the two feelings made me angry.

I waved her hand away and stood. "Wasn't I just telling you about my incomparable muscles? It would be unthinkable to accept your offer of assistance when this admirable physique is so capable." I wanted to take her hand, but I knew how it would have felt, so I stepped behind my self-erected, solid wall and teased her instead.

"Even with my enormous head, I almost couldn't make sense of what you just said. You are so weird." She shook her head and started off at a jog, leaving me behind to squelch the feeling of loss at not touching her.

I sprinted to catch up to her and asked, "When do you want to head back? I thought we could get some dinner." She looked at me quickly. "I mean, it's the least I can do for the haircut. If you're not busy."

180

"Sure." She seemed surprised by my offer. I guess aside from the jogging, we never did anything together alone. There had always been some annoying co-worker or roommate too eager to join us. "This road loops around and we'll end up back at Trevor's. Let me just check with him to make sure he doesn't need me tonight and then I could meet you somewhere."

"Did you get a haircut?" she asked as soon as we were seated in the classy Peruvian restaurant. The innocent look on her face was comical.

I'd play along. "Sure did. How does it look?" I raised a hand and smoothed my hair then made a show of turning my head left then right for her to get a good look. "Are you speechless at my hotness?" I grinned at the slight pink coloring that rose on her cheeks.

"Well, not exactly," she hedged. My grin died. "I mean it looks *okay* on you." My grin turned down to a frown as she eyed me critically. "I was wondering more about the amazing cut and style." I raised an eyebrow at her in disbelief. "I can't get over how masterfully artistic the cut is," she continued. "Who's your stylist?"

"She's this sassy little thing with a gargantuan head." I held my hands up on either side of my head to give her a visual. I bit down on a smile as she rolled her eyes because her lips also twitched. "I'd highly recommend her except she's a lie and a cheat. Doesn't even give a massage when you go for the haircut." My grin surfaced at her indignant gasp.

"Yeah, well, I don't even know what to say to that. So there."

She was so unexpected that a loud laugh burst from me before I could check it.

"Would you mind keeping it down?" she hissed. Merriment sparkling in her eyes belied her tone. "I'm starving. I worked really hard for this dinner and I'll be pretty upset if your unruly behavior gets us kicked out of this place."

I grinned at her as I apologized, "You are right-"

"As usual," she interrupted.

My grin widened. "-as usual. I'm sorry I stressed you out with the thought that you would be deprived of a meal."

She sniffed. "That was a pretty good apology. Thank you. I'll take it." It was all I could do to not reach across the table and run my fingers across her smooth cheek. She was so adorable.

"In all seriousness," I began, "thank you for the haircut. I appreciate your time." I gave in and reached across the table and squeezed her hand.

She smiled and said, "In all seriousness, you are welcome. I was happy to do it. And... I guess if we are being serious, I can admit that it looks really good and not just because I'm the one who cut it."

"Well, that didn't hurt much, now did it?" I squeezed her hand again. "Even if it was said grudgingly." I grinned at her, but was saved from what was sure to be a sarcastic reply when the waiter stepped to the table to take our order.

The food was almost as good as the conversation with the beautiful girl across from me. I couldn't remember a time when I felt more comfortable around a woman. The other restaurant goers, soft wind and percussion music, and clinking of dishes faded into the background. All I saw was Sophie. The way her eyes- blue tonight- lit up when talking about a particular patient's success or one of her family members. The way her laugh filled my lonely soul to overflowing. The way she wrapped a lock of hair around her finger or bit her lower lip self consciously. All these Sophie-isms stealthily threaded their way into my heart and took up residence there almost against my will.

A sense of overwhelming panic immediately rose up to choke out the serenity I felt. The sights, sounds and smells of the restaurant crowded back in, shattering my contented bubble with their volume-over stimulating and insistent. I took a long drink of ice water to steady myself. I needed space and distance in the worst way. After our run Friday, I'd head for Tillamook and take a break from all things Sophie.

Chapter 16

Sophie

"Hey, Sophie. This is Kaley, James' sister."

"Hey, Kaley. How are you? How are those cute boys?"

"We are good." I could hear Kaley's smile in her voice. "I was wondering if you wanted to get together at a park for a picnic today? I'm needing some girl time."

"Sure," I answered, surprised and pleased by the invitation. "That sounds fun. If you don't mind that the girl time will include a little stinker two year old."

Kaley laughed. "I don't mind. There's a pretty nice park not too far from me. I'll put something together and meet you there. I'll text you the address of the park.

"Sounds good. But I can pack a lunch for Jeran and me," I told her.

"It was my invite. I've got this. I'll let you pick it up next time," she said. "See you in a bit."

After checking in with Stacy, I buckled Jeran in and headed for the park. We were starving by the time we arrived and sat down at a table near the playground. Jeran ran for the toys, hunger momentarily forgotten, while Kaley unpacked our feast. I watched Jeran climb the stairs and disappear into the red plastic tunnel.

"So girl time, huh?" I asked, opening the container of blueberries and stealing one before I set the bowl on the table.

"I wouldn't trade my three guys for anything, but sometimes it gets lonely surrounded by men. You know? Growing up, I always wished I had a sister. Don't get me wrong. James is the best brother. He wasn't even that bad to have around when we were younger. My friends seemed irritated by their little sisters tagging along a lot of the time, but it just looked fun to me." She shrugged.

"I know what you mean. Trevor is my only sibling. It's fun having his wife, Stacy, for a sister," I told her. "But until the past few months, we haven't had a chance to get very close, living in different states and all."

"With James' track record, it looks like I won't even get that," Kaley lamented. I wanted to ask what she meant by 'his track record', but didn't want to pry.

"How long have you and Mark been married?" I asked instead.

"Just over twelve years," she said. At the look of surprise on my face she confided, "It took a few years to finally get pregnant. There was a time when we didn't think it would ever happen. We are grateful to have the two we got."

I called Jeran over and sat him next to me at the table. A little digging in my purse produced a package of wet wipes and a bottle of hand sanitizer and I scrubbed as much of the playground off of his hands as I could.

"It's funny to think that you are only a few years older than I am and you've been married for twelve years and have two boys. Life is definitely interesting in that it never happens the way you plan."

"Everyone has their own story. For sure." She paused to take another bite of her lunch. I could see an internal debate going on in her eyes.

"Just say it," I told her, inserting a straw into the top of Jeran's juice box and handing it to him. He took a long drink and slipped from the bench. I watched him toddle back to the playground.

"Don't be mad?" she asked. " I just wondered if you ever want to get married. Or are you too busy opening your therapy clinic to worry about that right now?" She cringed, afraid she had offended me.

How much to tell? She had told me about her trouble getting pregnant. I could give her a little. "I was engaged once," I admitted softly.

It was Kaley's turn to look surprised. She leaned forward and put her hand on my arm. "What happened?" she asked gently.

Just then, Jeran shot down the slide and landed with a bump on his rear end at the bottom. With a grin on his face, he jumped up and ran toward us. "Aunt Sophie," Jeran interrupted. "I wanna swing. You push me?"

"Sure. Come on, buddy. I'll race you." I motioned for Kaley to follow me so we could continue our conversation as I stood from the table. Jeran paused, ready to bolt, and grinned up at me. "Ready. Set.-" I began.

"GO!" Jeran shouted, his little legs already propelling him across the grass as quickly as they could. His squeals made me laugh and I reached out to tickle his back, making him squeal even louder and push harder to get to the swings. When we were a few feet from the swings, I picked him up under his arms from behind and swung him into the air. I placed him in the swing on his way back down.

"I flied," he laughed. "Push me, Aunt Sophie. Unda doggie."

"Under doggie, huh? Ok." I pushed him above my head and ran underneath the swing. I turned and pretended to growl at him.

"Yay. Yay!" he called.

When Jeran was settled into a steady rhythm, Kaley spoke from nearby. "You were telling me what happened with your engagement."

"Right. Kinda hoped you'd forget. So, we dated for over a year when things started to get a little tense between us. Then one night, he- Daniel's his name- just out of the blue, asked me to marry him. I was so surprised because I had been bracing for him to end it that I said yes. We started planning and ordering. You know. All the pre-wedding things. Then two weeks before the wedding, he took me for a walk at the Riverwalk. He told me he couldn't marry me because he was in love with someone else." Kaley gasped and put a hand over her mouth. I continued, "He said he had tried to fight it and that's why things had been so tense right before he asked me to marry him. He said he thought if he went ahead with the marriage, he would be able to get over the guy."

Kaley choked. "Did you say *guy?*"

I laughed wryly. "Yeah. I guess I can be glad he had the decency to tell me in person instead of a phone call or even worse-- just not showing up the day of. I lost myself for a little while after that. I'm a little gun shy since then, but I do date. I ran into him a year or so later and he and his, uh, husband...whatever, are very happy."

"Good," Kaley stuttered. "He could have left you after you were married..."

"That would have been worse. I know," I agreed. "Anyway, in hindsight, I can see that he'd had reservations throughout our whole relationship." I sighed. "I just haven't met anyone worth the risk since."

"I guess in some ways you can feel good that it wasn't for another woman. I've always thought I'd wonder what she had that I didn't if Mark ever left me. Was she prettier, thinner, smarter, more successful? This way, you know it's not anything you did or didn't do."

"I guess. Way to find the bright side."

Kaley laughed. "Seriously though, I think you are great. James hasn't been this happy in a long time." I blushed when she mentioned James.

She laughed knowingly. "He's pretty great even if he is my brother." I blushed brighter and then her wicked grin turned contemplative as if she'd had a revelation. "Come to think of it, you're the first girl he's dated in yea...uh, quite a while." A look passed over her face that I couldn't identify.

"We aren't really dating," I told her. Unless you counted dinner the other night. But I didn't think James would. "We've only gone running and then with an unbelievable number of people to a few other places. He even told me yesterday that if he didn't run with me, he'd be playing ball with Andy. I've only been a stand in for his cousin. A way to switch things up." I was pleased that I could keep the despair out of my voice.

"He told you that?" she asked incredulously. "Maybe he's not so great after all," she said as I laughed. "Don't give up on him." She shook a finger at me. "No matter what you two say, I have a feeling about this."

"No matter what feeling you have, I'm only a visitor here." She frowned at my words. But then so did I because the excited seabirds that took flight in my stomach when Kaley said she had a feeling about James and me landed abruptly and made a home deep in my gut at my reminder of returning to Texas.

Jeran eventually tired of the swing and asked to get down. We wandered down a path and looked at flowers and played 'spot the banana slug', but Jeran's interest waned and his footsteps became slow and heavy. I picked him up, gently pressing his head to my shoulder.

"Someone is getting sleepy," I murmured as I rubbed his back and smiled at Kaley. "You've played hard, huh, buddy. Should we go home and find out which piggy makes the best house?"

Jeran rubbed his eyes and nodded. "Will the wolf get them this time?" he asked through a yawn.

"Let's go see." And we headed to our cars.

"Can you tell Kaley thank you for the yummy lunch?"

"My mouth is too sleepy," he mumbled.

Kaley laughed and gave me a one-armed hug as she spoke to Jeran. "I'm glad you liked it. And I'm glad you brought Aunt Sophie to play with me."

He lifted his head and looked at her through half closed eyes. "You not swing."

"No," she laughed. "But we talked while you were pushed on the swings. That's close enough."

"Aunt Sophie to big fo the swings," he agreed.

"Too many cookies." I smiled and kissed the top of his head as I buckled him into his car seat.

Kaley smiled. "Thanks, Sophie. Let's do this again soon. And remember what I said about you and James. I think you'll find he's worth the risk."

I waved her off and smiled as I buckled my seatbelt and pulled away from the park. I had worried that our picnic would be a little awkward because I didn't know what to call my relationship with James. And besides James' birthday party, I'd only spoken with Kaley at dinner the previous Sunday. But the picnic had been fun. If I wasn't returning to Texas sometime in the next month or so, I could see us becoming good friends.

We left Stacy with her little guy at the hospital and I led out in the direction of the waterfront. I loved getting out and seeing the city. And the view next to me wasn't bad either. I snuck another peek at him and smiled. Sunday had been so good. And then the haircut and dinner Wednesday were even better. With all the time we had been spending together, I was falling for him. I couldn't help it.

We headed down the hill and I was really digging this change in elevation. Who knew hundreds of feet could make running that much easier. No pun intended. I tried not to laugh at my own stupid joke. "You know, pretty soon, I'll outpace you and may have to trade you in for a new running partner." I held back a smile as he looked at me and grinned.

"Oh yeah? You think you're pretty fast? Care to put that to the test?"

"Go!" I shouted and took off down the hill. We sprinted past buildings and pedestrians, flying. When we got to the waterfront, I leaned over, gasping for air.

"We really need to talk about your tendency to cheat," he puffed next to me. I tried not to stare at his abdomen as he lifted his shirt to wipe his forehead. Holy moly. "What is it they say, San Antonio? Cheaters never prosper?"

I blinked and looked up at his grinning face. "Well, *they* were wrong because I kicked your trash."

"Kicked my trash? Such talk from a demure Texas gal."

I snorted. "Demure? I guess it's good to aspire to something." I paused as if thinking and then said, "Here. Would this help the image?" I looked up at him through my lashes, fluttered them a few times, and said in my best Texas drawl, "Ah kicked yo-wuh trash, Doctuh."

He laughed. "Doesn't matter how you say it. You lie as well as cheat. I may have to trade *you* in for a new running partner because there is no way you beat me in that sprint." He slung an arm around my shoulder and turned me back the way we had come.

"I'll give it to you this time if it makes you feel better," I allowed. He chuckled and gave my shoulders a quick squeeze.

A few minutes later, I broke the companionable silence. "What is the one thing you most regret from your past?" I instantly felt him stiffen next to me. His arm dropped from my shoulders. Not good.

"You first," he said, looking up at the buildings surrounding us. Anywhere but at me.

"I asked you first," I teased and bumped him with my hip. "Come on. There has to be something. Everyone regrets something, right?"

"What kind of a question is that?" He stopped and turned to me, his voice hard.

I frowned. "It's a pretty simple question." I paused for him to answer the question. When he didn't, I relented. "I'll go first then."

But before I could speak, he demanded, "What did Kaley tell you?"

"What?" I asked, confused. "Nothing. What are you talking about?"

"Things were going well." He gestured with a hand back and forth between us. "Why do you always have to go and get all personal?"

I felt my eyes widen. "Personal?" What did he want it to be if it wasn't personal? "It was just a question, James. Don't answer it then. Why are y'all making such a big deal out of nothing?"

"You don't need to know everything about everything." He glared at me, his hand low on his hip, his whole stance screaming *threatened*. My eyes widened even further, if that was possible, at his words and body language.

"James…" I lifted a hand to touch his arm, but he stepped back out of reach. I felt like I'd been slapped. "Okay…Y'all know what? I've got to go." I turned from him and sprinted in the direction of the hospital. I didn't look behind me to see if he followed. I didn't even slow down on the hill. My anger fed my pace and I flew up the hill without breaking stride. *And they say women are hormonal and difficult to read. Aghh, men!*

I texted Stacy from the parking lot to let her know I was back from my run and ready to head home whenever she was. What had James meant about always getting personal? What did he think Kaley had told me? What was he trying to hide?

I reached into my hoodie pouch and pulled out my phone. Adri wouldn't be home from the gym yet. Maybe Kaley could provide some insight into her brother's psyche. After the fourth ring, I heard, *"Hey. This is Kaley. I'm probably wrestling my darling boys and can't get out of the WWE hold to answer my phone. Leave a message and I'll call you back when I get some down time. Probably when they are asleep."*

"Hey, Kaley. This is Sophie. Would you give me a call when you get a minute? Thanks." I pushed end and sighed. Maybe I'd see if Stacy and Jeran were up for a trip to the beach tomorrow.

Chapter 17

James

"Mom, Dad?" I called as I pushed through the front door. I decided not to wait until tomorrow and made it to Tillamook in a little over half the time it normally took. The drive hadn't improved my mood and it looked like my parents weren't even home. I ran a hand through my short hair in frustration, but that only reminded me of Sophie again. I clenched my fists and growled.

"James, is that you?" My mom entered the family room and crossed to give me a hug. "I didn't know you were coming. Are you staying the whole weekend?"

I planted a kiss on her cheek. "I didn't know I was coming either. Where's Dad?"

"He's out tinkering. Have you had dinner?" she asked as she made her way down the hall to the kitchen.

"No, but I'm fine. I'm going to head out to the shop."

I jogged down the steps and across the backyard to Dad's shop. Sawdust met me at the door and I breathed deeply. The scent always managed to calm me. It probably had to do with all the years of working alongside Dad to finish one Scout project or another.

Dad looked up as I closed the door behind me. "Hey, son. What brings you to town?"

"Just needed to get away for a few days. What you working on?" I moved to stand beside him.

"Some shutters for the far upstairs bedroom. Your mom has been on me about it for a while now. Says the paint and bedding are fading with the sun exposure."

"They look like they are coming along. I really like the grain." I reached out and ran my hand along the cool, smooth wooden slats. "Are you staining or painting them?"

"It's up to your mother. This is her project. I'm just the workhorse." He looked at me and grinned.

I returned his grin. "You love every second of it. Admit it."

"Not too loudly or your mother will add to the already lengthy honey-do list and I'll need my meals and pillow delivered out here." I watched as he applied wood glue to a strip of wood. "You never told me why you are here." I saw his suspicious glance.

"Do I need a reason to visit?" I turned and brushed some sawdust off the shutter frames.

"How is the hospital? Hold this for me here, will you?"

I moved back to his side and held the wood where he indicated. "The hospital is good. Busier than usual since I took on some of Dr. Harmon's little people. But what can I say? I love what I do."

My dad patted my shoulder, pleased, and asked, "How is your sister?"

"The boys are running her ragged. That reminds me. I need to talk to mom, tell her to lay off. When she hounds Kaley about one thing or another, Kaley rides me." I blew out an annoyed breath.

"It's enough to drive a person crazy." Dad chuckled.

"I don't know why you are laughing," I grunted.

"Don't you dare go saying anything to your mother. She has to be involved in someone's life. If it's not Kaley's, it's mine. No. Don't say a word to your mother."

I laughed out loud. "In other words, we suffer so you don't have to," I interpreted.

"Why do you think I encouraged having children?"

"It's all making painful sense to me now. I never thought of you as cruel until this moment."

Dad laughed and I soon joined in. This was what I needed. Dad. The shop. Wood. A couple more days of this and I'd be able to return to the real world.

"What are your plans for today?" my mother asked the following morning over breakfast.

"I thought about giving Dad a hand out in the shop. See if we can't get your shutters finished and hung. Maybe head to Oceanside later this afternoon." I shrugged. "I haven't really planned farther out than that."

"Well, plan to go to church with us tomorrow. There's a darling girl I want you to meet."

I shot my dad an exasperated look, shoved the last bite of pancake into my mouth, and carried my dishes to the sink. "Take your time, Dad. I'll be out in the shop."

I slipped quickly out the door, but not before I heard my mother say, "You know, Max, I've been thinking that that back bedroom could use..." I grinned and walked faster. Poor Dad.

"Hold it right there while I set this screw," my dad instructed, raising the drill.

With one shutter remaining to hang, the ocean was calling to me. It was like an itch that I couldn't scratch until I was standing on the beach with the waves lapping around my feet. The distant cry of birds and rhythmic crashing of waves spoke to me in an indescribable way, not unlike the wood and sawdust in Dad's shop.

"I think that's got it." Dad sat back with a satisfied smile and admired our work. I would also admit to a certain amount of pride in the completed job.

"I'll take the tools back to the shop and then I'm heading out for some sun and surf." I grabbed the drill and turned to leave.

"Hold up there a minute, James. I need to ask you something."

I turned back with a sigh. "Yeah?"

"Now don't go getting all riled. Oceanside isn't going anywhere." Humor laced his voice. He lifted his hat and scratched his head, leaving his hat askew. "You know, years ago your mother and I had an argument. I don't even remember now what it was over, but it was the worst argument we'd had up to that point in our marriage. I said some things. She said some things. I probably said some more things because I often can't keep my mouth shut and leave well enough alone. We walked on eggshells around each other for days. Most miserable and lonely days of my life."

I spent lots of time thinking. That was all there was to do. I saw for the first time, very clearly, what mattered most. I came to the realization that our friendship, our marriage, mattered to me. It was more important than some petty disagreement over who was right and who was wrong. I loved your mother deep into my bones. I loved being with her even when we weren't doing anything in particular. I loved how I felt when I was with her. Everything seemed brighter and happier and more hopeful when she was around. Not having her around wasn't worth whatever stupid, insignificant thing we had disagreed on. I groveled. You can bet I groveled. But I also promised myself that I wouldn't let what mattered most be pushed aside for what seemed to matter right then."

All these years later, I still ask myself, 'what matters most?' I've found we can work through anything when we step back and look at the bigger picture of what will matter five, ten, twenty years from now. And it's not how we spent our money or who took the garbage out last. It's that that beautiful woman downstairs shares my bed with me at night and wants me around tomorrow. I need her, son. Our love forever is what matters. She is what matters most." He straightened his hat, gathered the rest of the tools, and silently made his way down the stairs.

I stepped over and around rocks in the entry portal to Tunnel Beach. The ocean sat perfectly framed by dark, jagged rock that was the entrance. I breathed in deeply and closed my eyes, listening to the sounds of the beach. The receding salt water took the last of my irritation and anger out to sea. *What was I left with now?* I wondered.

I walked down the beach, stooping to pick up a rock here or a piece of driftwood there. When I had a handful, I faced the ocean, selected a rock, and threw it as hard and as far as I could. What mattered most? I threw another rock. What mattered most? I hurled the driftwood. What mattered most? What mattered most?

"Welcome back, roomie," Andy said on his way into the bathroom early Monday morning. "How are your parents?" He yawned and scratched his head then closed the door.

"Same old." I checked the time on my phone. "Are we still on for basketball tonight?" I called through the closed bathroom door.

"Yeah. Man, you missed out on some good grub yesterday," he called back. The toilet flushed. "I didn't realize that Kaley and Sophie were so tight."

I thought I heard the shower turn on. Or maybe that was just the blood pulsing through my head. I ran a hand over my face. "Sophie was at dinner yesterday?" I called through the bathroom door again. I checked the time on my phone. When Andy didn't answer, I banged on the door with my open hand.

"I'll be finished in a minute," Andy yelled.

I didn't have a minute. I snatched a banana off the counter and took the stairs two at a time down to the parking structure.

"Hey, Doc," Zeke greeted me as I walked into the NICU.

"Hey Zeke. How was your weekend?" I asked, taking the clipboard he extended to me.

"Perfect. Ms. Sophie is a great time." My head snapped up and he grinned. *You've got to be kidding me.* "Yup. You heard me. I took Ms. Sophie to dinner Saturday night. This time without a chaperone. I do believe I like it better that way. All the charts are up to date." He handed me a clipboard. "I'm outta here. Have a good one, Doc." The sound of Zeke's happy whistle followed him out of the NICU and down the hall. I suddenly had an inexplicable urge to throw the clipboard across the room. It was going to be a long day.

I dribbled the ball down the court, glancing quickly over my shoulder to see how close Andy was. I put on speed and took it in for a layup. When the ball hit the backboard and bounced off, I dove for the ball to put it up again, tripping Andy in the process.

"Hey man, that's a foul," Andy protested. "And watch the finger. What the heck?"

"Quit whining," I told him and threw the ball to him with more force than was necessary. I was playing angry today. No wonder none of my shots were going in. How many points was I down now? Too many to count. And the thing was, I knew I'd play angry every day until I talked to Sophie.

She'd gone out with every guy I knew over the weekend, it seemed. Had I expected that I was her only link to a social life? I knew that couldn't be farther from the truth. It just rubbed me the wrong way that I couldn't get her off my mind all weekend and she hadn't had any problem focusing on everything except me. Now it rubbed wrong that I even cared. But I did. I had missed her like crazy this weekend. I had missed just having someone to talk to. I had missed connecting with someone the way Sophie and I always seemed to connect so effortlessly. I had missed laughing.

I knew I needed to apologize for overreacting. I had decided to apologize somewhere between the talk with my dad and Tunnel Beach. I should just call her. But what about keeping her at a distance? That's one reason for the nickname. It kept things from getting personal. She was just one of the guys when I called her San Antonio. Well, that was what I kept telling myself, anyway. It was such a fine line between buddies and something more. And I was having a hard time remembering that friends was where I wanted to keep our relationship. As soon as I was with her, I needed to get closer. I needed contact. The line became non existent and that scared me. Terrified me, really. That made me angry and I had to work hard to not growl out loud.

Andy looked at me with a raised eyebrow as he slowly brought the ball down the court. In a quick move, he pulled up in three-point range and let the ball fly. I shook my head in disgust as it sailed through the basket. Nothing but net. I grabbed the ball while Andy crowed over his lead and blew past him, flying down the court. I pulled up at the three-point line and let it go. It was way wide and I ran up on it, elbowing Andy out of the way. I pulled up for a little two-pointer and watched as it bounced off the rim right back to me. In frustration, I chucked the ball with one hand at the basket. I growled as it missed by a mile. *Forget it.* I waved the ball off and went to get my water bottle. *Dang it, Sophie!* I thought. *Women...* I shook my head with a frown and sighed.

"I know I will regret this," Andy said coming up behind me and bending over to retie his shoe. "But...something on your mind?"

I grunted in response as I held the bottle out and squirted a stream of water into my mouth. "Why do you ask?" I wiped my mouth with the back of my hand and tossed my bottle back onto my bag.

"Uh, I don't know. Maybe because I'm wondering what the ball ever did to you. You're playing sloppy ball, man," he pointed out then shrugged. "So I just gotta wonder what's up."

"Enough yammering," I told him and swiped the ball off the floor. "Next basket wins."

"Nice try," Andy laughed, grabbing the ball from me. "You're so far behind, we'd have to play for the rest of today and maybe tomorrow for you to catch up. I don't have that kind of time. I've got a date tonight."

I rolled my eyes and gave him a shove. "Whatever, Romeo. Fine. Paybacks next time," I promised as we grabbed our stuff and headed out.

"Only if you show up to play next time," he snorted. "There are too many ladies, too little time to waste on you when your head's not in the game."

"Speaking of heads…how do you even fit on the court with your head that size, bro?"

"Yeah, yeah," he taunted. "You can try to change the subject, but you still lost." I punched his arm and his laughter followed me as we walked to our cars.

"It won't happen again," I called to him before he drove off. And it wouldn't. I would apologize to Sophie so I could get over this craziness that had become my life for the past few days.

Chapter 18

Sophie

It had been six days since I'd spoken to James. I missed him more than I thought possible. I looked through the windows of the NICU doors as always. I just wanted an undetected peek. There he was, checking his watch. My breath caught at the sight of him. Oh how I missed him! As he moved to look through the windows, I quickly stood back, out of sight. I knew I had over reacted the other day, but after so many surprises when it came to men, I was ready for straightforward honesty. I wasn't ready to face him yet, so I found the nearest restroom and hid out for a while until I was sure he would be gone.

Ten minutes later, I squirted some hand sanitizer on my hands and went into the NICU. Ms. Gina was in the office, and seeing her was like seeing a ray of sunshine through dark clouds.

"Ms. Gina." I smiled. "How has your day been?"

"Well, Ms. Sophie…" she said from her cozy office chair. "I didn't know if you'd be in today or if Mrs. Mitchell was coming to sit a while. I'm still getting used to this new rotating schedule you people have worked out."

"You and me both," I laughed. "I'd better get out to the baby. No one should have to wait on dinner."

"If I'm not out there when you leave, come tell me goodbye, you hear?"

"Yes, ma'am. I promise."

I had just settled in the rocker with my tiny bundle and a bottle when I heard the main doors push open. I turned my head to see who came in and froze. James.

"San Antonio?" He asked, coming toward me. "How did I miss you? Did you take the elevator?"

"No. The stairs," I answered hesitantly.

"But I took the stairs. How did we not run into each other?" I hung my head, guilty, and wouldn't meet his eyes. I couldn't take whatever I would see there as understanding dawned. I didn't want him to know that I'm so immature I had been avoiding him for days; hiding in the bathroom like a child. Apparently my silence was a life sized arrow pointing out my guilt.

I heard him come closer and closed my eyes. I sucked in a breath when I felt him lean over and plant a lingering kiss on the top of my head. "I'm sorry," he whispered. He stood silently with his forehead resting on top of my head. I couldn't move. Then he softly said into my hair, "I will tell you someday. I promise. It just needs to be on my terms." Then he was gone.

I sucked in a ragged breath and buried my face in Dylan's blanket. I squeezed my eyes shut to hold the tears at bay. I wouldn't cry, but I would fix this.

"I can't believe you are really here," I squealed and hugged Adri close.

"I can't believe it either. That three hour layover in LA was the pits."

"I'm pretty sure one week won't be long enough for all I want to show you. Let's get your luggage. The carousel is this way." I turned to lead the way through the writhing mass of travelers, hoping she could keep up and we didn't get separated.

"Do you want to stop by the hospital on the way to Trevor's or do you feel airplane gross and need a shower?" I asked as we waited for her bag to ascend from the bowels of the airport.

"I'm really gross and I could stand a meal," she said, standing on tiptoes to find her suitcase.

"Is it the zebra print one from college?" I asked craning my neck around a woman toting a child, stroller, and carseat.

"Yup. Oh, hey, I see it," she said pointing and bouncing a little on her toes. "I may need some help lifting it off."

"Holy cow!" I grunted as I attempted to drag her suitcase off the carousel before it moved away from me. "Are you sure you are only staying for a week? What did you put in this thing?" I tugged hard and felt a vein in my temple bulge. "Adri, are you helping me?"

"Sorry. I couldn't get past that huge guy. We'll have to wait til it comes around again," she said in annoyance.

"You will be staying in my room with me," I informed Adri in the car. "Dinner won't be for a while. Are you hungry? We could stop somewhere," I offered. "They even have a Voodoo Doughnut here. Who did you tell me wanted to have their wedding there?"

"Me," she said. "But I was just a little girl. My taste in wedding venues has changed dramatically since then."

"Well that's a relief," I said with a laugh.

"Speaking of weddings," Adri said, "What's new with the doctor?"

"We haven't spoken for almost week," I admitted sadly. "Until today when I saw him for like thirty seconds.

"What? All I've heard from you for over a month is, 'James this and James that'. Blah, Blah, Blah. It's been disgusting," she said in mock annoyance. "What about running and dinner and the haircut? What about the beach and the sand dollar?"

"That day was…I can't even describe how that was the best day of my life." My voice took on a dreamy quality. "It was perfect. Then I went and ticked him off," I admitted.

"What happened?" Adri asked sympathetically.

"I just asked him a question and he went crazy. I was embarrassed, wounded pride and all that, so I didn't stick around to fix things. Then I've been avoiding him at the hospital. Until today. Adri, I think I'm in love with him."

James

"What's up with you today, man?" Andy asked as he dribbled the ball down the court.

"What do you mean? I've made every shot," I reminded him as I took a swipe at the ball. I got enough of a hand on it to knock it loose and we both dove for the ball. I came up with it and easily took it in for layup.

"*That's* what I'm talking about." Andy gestured toward the basket. "You've made every shot. You are all over the place. I'm ready to call the game."

"Can't take the heat today, huh?" I teased, then called a timeout and jogged off the court when I heard a text chime in.

"Hey, where you going? You can't leave the game for a text," he whined. "Wait. Is it a girl?"

I waved him off and picked up my phone. I couldn't help the grin that spread over my face when I saw Sophie's name.

Sophie: My friend, Adri, is in town.

James: Oh?

Sophie: Can we get together? I'd like her to meet you.

James: I think I could fit you in. :)

Sophie: Gee, thx. When?

James: Tonight.

Sophie: We'll come to you.

James: That's what all the ladies say.

Sophie: Ha, ha. I thought I was txting James, not Andy.

James: Ouch.

Sophie: See you at 7?

James: Perfect.

I pocketed my phone and grinned. It had been seven very long days. "Hey, Chia, Sophie and her friend, Adri, are dropping by the apartment in a couple hours. You gonna be around?" I grabbed my bag and gestured toward the door. The game was over anyway. There was no way he was making a comeback today.

"Another lady to add to my collection?" Andy grabbed his stuff and followed me. "Sure. I'm game."

"Nice, Andy. And you wonder why Sophie ended it."

"I thought she ended it with you, too, by the way you've been moping around the past couple days. I won't even put you through the embarrassment of mentioning the game the other day where I mopped up the floor with you. What happened with her?"

"She knows I'm keeping something from her and she asked what it is. I freaked out on her. It wasn't pretty."

"Are you going to tell her?" Andy asked after a long pause, trying to sound casual. "I mean, 'cause if you are, that's big."

"There is something about her that has me doing things I swore I'd never do again," I admitted and ran a hand through my sweaty hair already thinking about the shower I needed to take before I saw Sophie. "I don't know. I told her I would tell her. Maybe sometime in the future. If I don't chicken out."

"Admitting she may still be in your near future is huge for you, you know," Andy pointed out, looking down at his shoes. He was trying to make it seem like it wasn't a big deal when we both knew this was a colossal step for me.

"Who are you anyway? Dr. Phil?" I shoved him good naturedly.

"Okay. I've said enough. Just sayin'…"

Sophie

"I'm so nervous," I said to Adri on the way to James' apartment. "It's like first date jitters. I may throw up."

"Oh, stop. Take a deep breath and tell me about his cousin."

"Andy is hot. Like GQ hot. But he knows it and that's the turn off for me. I like a guy with confidence, but just enough insecurity to be humble. That combination of humble and confident means they can lead, but they aren't afraid to be wrong sometimes. That makes them strong enough for me to break down on, yet soft enough to make my breath catch when they touch me. That's way hotter in my book." *Like James*, I thought and sighed inwardly. I couldn't wait to see him.

"So is he built?" Adri asked.

"Who?"

"Um, Andy? Who did you think?"

I gave a self-conscious chuckle. "Oh, Andy. Of course. Yes. He's like those guys on the Calvin Klein commercials except not as skinny looking. Bulkier, maybe. Not that I've seen him without a shirt on or anything. You can just tell with the way his shirts hug his muscles...Never mind. You'll just have to see for yourself." *Oh brother*. "We're here," I said brightly.

Adri laughed all the way up the elevator and to their apartment door. She knocked quickly and then rolled her eyes when she saw my fists clenched stiffly at my sides. "Would you calm down and breathe. You look like you are going to pass out," she whispered as the door knob turned. "At least if you do, there's a doctor in the...Oh my..." she gasped softly when the door opened to reveal a very polished Andy.

"Ladies," Andy's smooth voice shook me out of my stupor. "Come on in." He stepped back with a sweep of his arm. I threw Adri an I-told-you-so look, but movement over Andy's shoulder caught my gaze and

I focused on James. Adri and Andy were temporarily forgotten. My heart started pounding in my chest. Hard.

James flashed me an adorable grin. "Hey."

"Hey." I managed. We stood there grinning at each other until Adri's giggle caused me to turn toward the sound. She was sitting on the couch next to Andy, laughing at something he was telling her. When had they moved to the couch? I blinked and walked toward them.

"Adri," I interrupted and waved James over. "This is James. James, Adri."

James moved across the room and around the couch to shake Adri's hand. "Nice to meet you, James," Adri said, and then turned to Andy. "Andy here was just telling me about this Asian garden that's almost a spiritual experience." I had to work hard to not roll my eyes. James put a hand on my back and bit back a grin. I felt myself leaning back into his open palm. How had I survived the past week without his touch? I looked up at him and saw he was watching me.

"San Antonio and I are going to go get Trivial Pursuit from the closet," he said, taking my hand and leading me down the hall. As soon as we were out of sight, he stopped and pulled me to him with a tug on my hand. I wrapped my arms around his neck and sighed as his arms tightened around my waist. "I'm sorry," we both said at the same time.

"I've missed you," James whispered in my ear.

"I've missed you, too," I told him, squeezing tighter. I could stay like this all night. Too bad we had to get back to Adri and Andy.

He pulled me closer for a second and then stepped back, his hands still on my waist. "Want to run tomorrow? I haven't been in a few days and I need to."

"I haven't been either. I'll meet you at the hospital tomorrow at the regular time."

He nodded a reply and then his gaze turned serious as he searched my eyes. I was just about to ask what he was thinking when he leaned down and planted a soft kiss on my forehead, lingering there for a minute. I closed my eyes and concentrated on him, his touch. This was what I was trying to tell Adri about in the car- strong, yet soft. It couldn't get much better than this.

He kissed my forehead again and stepped away. "Let's get that game before we stay in the hall all night. I wouldn't mind, but Andy needs to be knocked down a few notches and you are just the girl to do it."

"I get San Antonio on my team," he called out, grinning down at me, as we walked back to the living room. Adri and Andy groaned.

James

"That's my girl!" I shouted as Sophie answered yet another trivia question correctly to win the game. It was a shutout. An embarrassment really.

"That's not fair," Andy complained. "No one could beat her."

"Why do you think I wanted her on my team?" I put my arm around Sophie's shoulders. "She's my secret weapon." I pulled her close, grinning like an idiot.

"How about Monopoly?" Andy asked. I glanced at my watch as Adri yawned.

"We need to get Adri to bed," Sophie announced, standing up from the floor. "But how about a rematch some other time?"

I put my hand on her back and walked with them to the door. Adri reached over and lay her hand on Andy's arm. "So, let me know when you want to take me sightseeing."

"I'll call you," he promised with a flirtatious smile.

I reached for Sophie's hand. "I'll see you tomorrow." I smiled thinking how good it felt to touch her again. She squeezed my hand.

"Rest up. I'm going to run you ragged." She smiled up at me. I laughed.

"Adri, are you coming running with us?" I invited, looking over at Adri and Andy.

"Sophie knows how I feel about running, but if there's a gym around here you'd recommend, I'm there." I smiled when I saw Andy perk up at that news and they were off making plans for tomorrow.

I turned back to Sophie. She looked up at me, searching my eyes. "Thanks for letting us come over."

"Any time. We should try to get Adri to the beach while she is here." I smiled when her eyes danced at the suggestion. "How long is she here?"

"Only a week. Not nearly long enough to even make a dent in all there is to see and do," she sighed.

"You've missed her," I observed.

"Like crazy. We've been friends for seven years. This is the longest we've been apart. She's more like a sister, you know?"

"We'll just have to fill every day she's here. What about Cannon Beach Saturday morning?"

"Early enough for the tide pools?" she asked, hands clasped together in hope.

"Early enough for the tide pools," I chuckled. "You do know that means we'd have to leave at six a.m., right?"

"It will be worth it," she promised. "Thanks, James." She impulsively threw her arms around my neck in her happiness. When she moved to pull away, I wrapped my arms around her waist and pulled her back to me. I buried my face in her hair and breathed in her flowers and coconut scent. I'd have to thank my dad for his story the next time I drove over for a visit.

"I think Adri is the real thing," Andy called down the hall after me as I walked to my room.

"Good night, Andy," I said. And for the first time in days, it would be.

Sophie

"I'll hand it to you. James is attractive," Adri admitted back in the car.

"Attractive? Are you blind? He's way more than attractive."

"Well, it's not in the model way like Andy is, but he seems almost normal. Maybe Portland has changed your unlucky streak with men," she speculated.

"Keep praying for that, would you? I need all the help I can get." Then, "You and Andy seem to have a lot in common."

"Yeah," she sighed dreamily. "I think he loves the gym almost as much as I do. We'll see tomorrow."

"Who knows," I told her. "You may decide Portland has changed your unlucky streak too.

Chapter 19

Sophie

The next day dragged like the stuffed animal Jeran pulled around behind him through the house. Luckily, I had laundry and a two year old to keep me busy.

"We goin' to the zoo today, Aunt Sophie?" Jeran asked as I pulled another armful of clothes from the dryer.

"No," I replied. "Not today."

"We goin' to the pahk?" He climbed in the laundry basket and laughed when I buried him with another armful of warm clothes.

"No. But if you will help me fold these clothes, we can make cookies after."

Jeran's muffled cheer reached my ears right before clothes flew through the air as he erupted out of the basket and ran past me to the living room couch. He looked up at me with expectant eyes as he waited for me to drop the pile of clothes and pick out a shirt to fold. He chose one of his own and I hummed softly to myself while mentally counting the hours until I would see James again. I looked down at the dwindling pile when Jeran's voice broke through my musings. I watched as Jeran wadded up another shirt and set it with the other crumpled shirts in his pile on the couch and announced that he was all finished. I laughed at his pile of crumpled clothes next to my own neatly folded piles and kneeled down next to Jeran.

"Hey, buddy, can you help me with this next shirt?" I asked and demonstrated how to fold it in half. With his help, we folded and refolded all of the clothes and separated them into piles to take to each bedroom. Jeran walked proudly in front of me, holding his clothes carefully, to his room where he unceremoniously dumped the pile onto the floor in front of his dresser and turned around and put his hands on his hips.

"Which woom next?" he asked with self-importance, looking very much like a miniature version of Trevor.

"Mommy and Daddy's," I whispered. "But we have to be really quiet so we don't wake mommy up from her nap." I reminded him as we turned to walk down the hall to Stacy and Trevor's room.

"Mommy will be gwumpy, huh, Aunt Sophie?" Jeran stage-whispered. I laughed softly and gently nudged the bedroom door open enough to peek inside.

Stacy's back was to us, but I could tell with the slow rise and fall of her shoulder that she still slept. I exaggerated a tiptoe in hopes Jeran would follow my example and set the pile of freshly folded clothes on Stacy's dresser.

I whirled when I heard Jeran in his stage whisper say, "Mommy, we had to fold the clothes and be quiet so we can make cookies."

"Jeran," I hissed and watched with a resigned sigh as Stacy's eyes slowly opened and she blinked. She gave Jeran a sleepy smile when he patted her cheek and kissed the tip of her nose then turned and charged out of the room and down the hall to the kitchen. Who could stay upset at that sweetness?

"Sorry," I told Stacy softly. "I even prepped him."

Stacy laughed and yawned. "I guess you have to consider the age of the audience when you hand out instructions. Are you going running tonight?" she asked.

I couldn't help the shiver of excitement that skittered down my arms at the thought of spending time with James. "Yes," I grinned. "In about an hour. I'll hitch a ride to the hospital with you, if that's okay."

Stacy grinned back knowingly and laughed, "I've never seen anyone so excited to pound pavement." I ducked my head and blushed, making Stacy laugh even harder.

"Trust me when I tell you that you'd be excited too if you got to run with a hot guy."

"I've tried running with Trevor and it doesn't matter that he's the hottest guy I know. I still don't get all gooey over running."

I shrugged and grinned at her again before making a quick escape into the hall. "Tell James hello from us," she called as I made my way to the kitchen to make cookies. Hopefully my little cookie monster hadn't started without me.

We had one cookie sheet in the oven when Adri breezed into the kitchen dressed in the latest in gym wear. "You are smokin' hot," I told her. "Andy won't know what hit him."

"Let's hope so." She tightened her ponytail and grabbed her bag.

"I'll meet you back here after our run," I told her as the doorbell rang. I smiled as I watched Jeran race Adri for the door, squealing all the way. "Have fun," I called to her.

James

I glanced from the clipboard to my watch and then the NICU doors to see her lovely face framed in the window. Right on time. My heart skipped a beat at the smile she sent my way and I walked toward the door and her. Was it just me or had she gotten better looking in those shorts in the seven days since I'd run with her?

Zeke looked up at the sound of the door and glanced my way to make sure I was paying attention. Nope it wasn't just me. "Ms. Sophie…my favorite visitor," he smirked.

Stacy waited a beat and then acted insulted. "What am I, nurse Zeke, chopped liver?"

"No, ma'am," he said embarrassed. "I'm just hoping Sophie will come to her senses and drop the pretty boy doctor so I can have a chance." He smiled smugly at me and I narrowed my eyes. Sophie laughed and my eyes narrowed to almost a squint when she gave Zeke a one-armed hug.

"Oh, Zeke, but who would all your admirers flirt with if we got together?"

It wasn't exactly the emphatic rejection that I was hoping for, but our relationship was a work in progress. Sophie laughed again at the blush that crept up Zeke's neck and she gave him a little squeeze. Time to go.

"I'm going to change. San Antonio, why don't you go sing to the babies while you wait." I didn't miss the funny look Sophie gave me or Zeke's obnoxiously triumphant laugh as I headed for the office. Nothing like subtlety…

Sophie

"Which way?" I asked as soon as we stepped out of the NICU and headed for the stairs.

"You choose," James told me, slinging an arm around my shoulders. I wrapped my arm around his waist, loving being close to him.

"I choose the river route," I told him and let my arm fall from his waist. "If you think you can keep up." I bounced down the stairs ahead of him.

"The river route it is." He scrambled behind me. "And we'll see who has to work to keep up." I smiled back at him and increased my pace. I had missed this.

I set out at a steady pace and neither of us spoke as we took in the cars, people, and buildings surrounding us. I was beginning to love this place. The often dreary weather took a little getting used to, but I could get hooked. I threw a glance at James beside me. I was well on my way to hooked already. I almost stopped mid-stride at the sudden thought that came next about what it would take to set up my clinic here instead of Texas. I wasn't ready to think permanence yet.

"My parents only have a couple months left on their humanitarian mission. I'm trying to talk them into coming for a visit when they get released."

"I can't imagine that it would take a lot of convincing with a new grand baby," James replied.

I smiled. "You're right. It will be so good to see them again. It's been too long." We crossed the street. "What about your parents?" I asked him realizing that aside from his sister and her family and Andy, I didn't know anything about the rest of his family.

"What about my parents?" He gave me a sidelong glance.

Was he being obtuse on purpose? "Do you see them often?" I asked in exasperation. Getting any amount of personal info out of him was as difficult as getting Jeran to potty train.

"Yes, they still live in the house I grew up in. So, not close enough to see every day, or even every week. But we get together for holidays and sometimes more often than that. I was just there this past weekend. Maybe I'll take you to meet them one day." He glanced at me. Judging my reaction, perhaps? "We could take in the ocean at the same time," he suggested with a smile.

"Now, you know I could never say no to the ocean. You don't play fair."

"Who said anything about fair?"

"You know my weaknesses, but you never tell me yours." I paused to look out at the river stretched in front of us. It always filled me with excitement to see the busyness of the waterfront; like ants or bees continually on the move to create and maintain a way of life.

"It's my secret plan to discover and exploit your weaknesses. Use them to my advantage," he teased in a mysterious voice as he came to a stop beside me and looked out over the water also.

"I figured as much. Just know that if I meet your mother, I plan on discovering some of your secrets so I can return the favor. Blackmail is such a fun word. Don't you think?" I said brightly.

"I'm not afraid of you, San Antonio," he said as he took a step closer, punctuating his words and closing the gap between us, and causing a tingle to crawl up my arm where it brushed his.

I looked over at him trying to decipher the subtle change in his voice. A slight breeze ruffled his hair and I had to tamp down the urge to brush it back into place. With eyes still focused on the water, he reached for my hand, interlacing our fingers.

I bumped him with my shoulder and said, "You would be afraid if you knew what was good for you."

He turned his head to look at me then and smiled. "Oh, believe me. I know what's good for me..." I blushed at his implied meaning and his smile broadened to reach his eyes and transform his face.

We stood quietly at the water's edge for many peaceful minutes, although, I could no longer concentrate on the picturesque scene in front of me. I looked at James out of the corner of my eye, incredibly aware of his every breath. My senses were heightened and tuned directly to him whenever he was around. Anything on the periphery was hazy and I could only see him. Us.

James glanced at his watch and released my hand to sling his arm around my shoulder and turn me in the direction of the hospital on the hill. "We should probably get back. It looks like rain."

"I wonder how Adri and Andy are getting along," I said as we started away from the river.

"Do you have plans tonight? Or do you want to see if they'll meet us somewhere for dinner?"

"I'll text Adri when we get back and we can go from there. I'd like to clean up first if we do go somewhere."

Rain started falling on our last stretch before the hospital. Not wanting to participate in a wet tshirt contest, I picked up the pace and sprinted for the automatic doors, James right behind me. Just before we slipped inside, James reached out and latched onto the back of my shirt in an effort to slow me down. We speed walked, stumbling and bumping into each other, to the stairwell door, with me giggling behind my hand the whole way. I grabbed his arm to hold him back then shot forward, taking the stairs two at a time.

When my legs started to burn and James was pulling ahead, I switched to every stair and raced past him, arms pumping at my sides. His hand shot out to grab my shirt again, but I twisted out of reach and collapsed, laughing and victorious, against the stairwell wall at the NICU floor. James bent over gasping for breath. I raised both hands above my head and crowed loudly over my win. The noise echoed through the austere stairwell and I crowed again for effect.

James smothered a grin and shook his head at me. "I swear you are trying to kill me," he panted. "Those last three flights never felt so long."

"Oh, quit complaining," I said, still laughing.

He straightened and walked toward me, a glint in his eyes. "You cheated, *Ms.* Sophie…"

My laughter turned to shrieks of protest as he hooked his arm around my neck and rubbed his knuckles across my head. I squirmed out of his hold and put one hand up between us to ward him off as I reached for the door knob with the other.

"Truce," I panted, giggling under my breath. "But maybe you should clean up, too, before we do anything. I was a little too close to your armpit just now."

I opened the door ready to make a break for the NICU when he grabbed my wrist and pulled me back into the stairwell. This caused me to laugh harder, but my laughter faded as he cornered me and with his hands on the wall on either side of my head, looked down into my eyes. His gaze intensified and he lowered his face to mine. I leaned forward, only our mingling breath separating us, when footsteps echoed through the stairwell. James blinked and looked in the direction of the sound, the spell broken. I ducked under his arm and pranced through the door.

Stacy stood from the rocking chair and moved to Dylan's incubator as I walked into the NICU. "You ready?" I asked, watching her get Dylan settled in for the night.

"Yup. Goodnight, little guy," she crooned to her sleeping boy.

"See you later, Stacy," James said stepping into the NICU behind me and heading for his office. "You didn't get out of anything, San Antonio. Just so you know. Paybacks..." he called to me over his shoulder. "I'll check with Andy and call you."

"Sounds good," I giggled. "Oh, and James..."

"Yeah?" he asked turning back slightly, his eyebrow raised in question.

"Zeke's got nothing on you."

Chapter 20

James

"Lookin' good, Doctor," Sophie smiled and gave a small tug on the front of my polo shirt as she walked past me to my car. I reached around her for the handle and she leaned close and sniffed. "Smell good too," she murmured.

I smiled and brought my hand to the small of her back and pressed her to my side for a quick hug. I leaned down and whispered, "You were checking me out." Then I planted a soft kiss on her cheek to let her know I was teasing and released her to get into the car. What was it about this woman that I couldn't get enough of her?

I watched her watch me walk around the front of the car and chuckled. "No I wasn't," she responded with a sniff as I shut my door and started the car. She made a show of wiping at something nonexistent on her capris and then eyed me critically as she said, "I was making sure you cleaned up after our run. I'm starving and don't want to get kicked out of the restaurant for your poor hygiene."

"You were totally checking me out." I grinned at her quickly before returning my eyes to the road and pulling away from her brother's house.

"How could anyone not…"she muttered under her breath and looked out the side window.

"What was that?" I leaned sideways toward her, eyes still on the road.

"I said, you have a bit of snot…" She reached her hand up and brushed her nose.

I laughed out loud and said, "It's okay. I heard you. But then I'm just as guilty because you are looking good too." I reached over and laced my fingers through hers. She squeezed my hand and sighed, settling back in the seat to enjoy the scenery.

Sophie

As hard as I tried, I couldn't keep my gaze from ending up on James again. I could watch him all night. Seriously, how did I get lucky enough to be with him tonight? There are thousands of beautiful girls in the Portland area and he's with me. Every time I say goodbye, I think he can't be as hot the next time as I remember. Then I see him again and he looks even better. Either he gets better looking every time, or my memory is really poor. I'd better get it together.

"You're getting a little shaggy." I reached over and ran my fingers through the hair at the base of his neck that had begun to curl. His hands stilled on the steering wheel and I laughed as he shivered.

"If a haircut from you promises to be anything like last time…" He looked over and waggled his eyebrows at me.

"I'm pretty busy," I hedged. "I was going to suggest you go to Chinatown to get it done this time."

"Uh, uh. I told you there is no going back." I kept my hand at the base of his neck and played with his little curls. What a shame to get rid of them.

James turned the volume up on the radio and I sang along. After a few minutes, I paused my singing by asking, "What would you say if I told you that the buzzing sound a house fly makes is in the key of F?"

"I'd say I absolutely believe it. But only if there are bees present." James grinned at me. "Get it? Honey bees... And B flat is in the F major scale."

"Pretty quick, doctor," I laughed. "How did you know that? Do you play an instrument? Or perhaps you've heard that one before."

James shrugged and reached out to change the radio station. "What about this song? Do you know it?"

"Yup," I smiled and sang along. "Hey," I protested when he switched stations in the middle of my grand finale.

"Let's try this one," he said.

I sang a few lines of the new song before he switched stations again. After the fourth station, I asked, "What gives? I'm beginning to think you are trying to tell me something about my lilting voice."

He reached to turn the volume down. "Is there a song out there you don't know?" he asked. "I've tried 80's, oldies, country, rock, pop…You know everything. I thought a Texas gal like you would be hard core country," he twanged, startling a laugh out of me.

"I try to be well rounded." I sniffed snobbishly with my nose in the air. "You give it a try."

"You don't want to hear me sing," he protested.

"I really do. You can't be that bad."

"I can be and I am."

"No. Come on. Here's a good one." I leaned forward and turned up the volume. "Belt it out. Let me hear you."

He started out soft and hesitant, but then his voice rose in volume as he gained confidence. He was no Clint Black or Tim Mcgraw, but he could carry a tune and had a nice, soothing voice. I could stand to listen to him again, but lest he get a big head…

"Howwwwroooo," I raised my chin and howled. His voice immediately cut out and he blushed. So cute. I grinned and howled again.

He reached back and removed my hand from his hair and held it over my mouth. I howled louder through my fingers. He pushed my hand harder against my mouth. My muffled laughter erupted and I forced my hand away.

"I'm just kidding," I promised. "Not too shabby for a *city* boy. You are pretty good, actually." I leaned over and smacked a kiss on his cheek. "And a really good sport. Thank you." I put my hand back at the nape of his neck and continued playing with his hair.

"I'm glad we are meeting up with Andy and Adri. I can't believe Adri is leaving in two days. It's been so nice to have her here. I didn't realize how much I missed her."

"Speaking of leaving…Dylan is doing so well. What's the plan when he goes home and you aren't needed around the clock like you have been? Is Texas calling your name?" He tried to sound nonchalant, but I sensed an underlying seriousness in his tone.

"Trevor, Stacy, and I have actually talked about that. I'll stay for at least a couple weeks after he comes home so they can all adjust to a new addition. Especially Jeran. We'll play it by ear from there. I can't stay indefinitely. I need to get back and open my clinic."

"Yeah," James agreed softly, eyes trained on the road.

I didn't want him to agree though. I wanted him to latch onto the unspoken idea that had been floating around in my mind lately about setting up a clinic here. I wanted him to tell me he didn't want me to go. I wanted him to tell me he was falling in love with me like I was with him. But if he wasn't feeling that way, he obviously wouldn't say all those things. I suppressed a sigh. What I wanted and what I got were two different things entirely.

We were both quiet the rest of the drive to the restaurant. I took in the slightly run down exterior of the Thai restaurant as James walked around the car to open my door. He took my hand as we walked through the parking lot and into the building, but my mood felt subdued and a little melancholy. James guided us past the hostess desk and lifted our joined hands to point to a table toward the back where Andy and Adri sat, their heads together, studying a menu. They looked very cozy. I looked at James with a raised brow.

"Which one of them is going to be the saddest when she leaves?" James leaned close and whispered as we approached the table.

232

I knew he was talking about Andy and Adri, but I couldn't help thinking it applied to us as well. Apparently, it would be me who was the sadder of the two when I left, but I didn't want to spoil one of the last nights of Adri's visit, so I put on a smile and said brightly, "Hey guys. See anything good?"

"She means besides each other," James teased.

I held up a hand for a high five. That was a good one. We laughed as Andy and Adri exchanged embarrassed grins. James pulled a chair out for me and scooted his closer to mine as he sat down.

"We ordered an appetizer and waters all around," Andy informed us. "The waiter will be back in a few to take our order." Adri handed us some extra menus and went back to the one she and Andy had been studying before we arrived.

"How was the gym?" I asked them.

"Really good," Adri smiled as Andy simultaneously scowled and grunted something unintelligible.

James and I exchanged a glance and I said, "I'm not getting a unanimous 'really good' out of that response."

"Oh, Andy…" Adri waved her hand in an offhand manner and rolled her eyes. "He's mad 'cause he thinks a couple of the guys were hitting on me."

"That's because they were and you encouraged it." Andy interjected, annoyed.

"I didn't encourage it. I was flattered, but I could only see you," she told him and squeezed his muscular arm.

Andy sat back and folded his arms across his strong chest. A satisfied smile stretched across his handsome face. *Oh brother.* I looked at James and smiled when I caught his eye roll. Exactly what I was thinking.

James

"You guys up for a little walk around the town?" I asked as the waiter returned with my card.

"Yeah, James wants to show you where he's getting his hair cut next week," Sophie told Adri and Andy with her mischievous grin.

I raised an eyebrow and shook my finger at her. This made her laugh and I couldn't help but smile. Maybe I'd take her to Tillamook this weekend. She'd need a pick me up after Adri left, right?

"Sure. We could go. I don't really care about your barber, but Adri did want to see what all the hype is," Andy said taking Adri's hand and standing from the table.

I lace my fingers with Sophie's and led her out of the restaurant. We turned right and Andy and Adri followed behind.

"Thanks for the food," Sophie smiled up at me. I ran my thumb across the back of her hand. Man, I could kiss those smiling lips. Instead I asked, "You have plans this weekend?"

"Potty training a disinterested two year old, watching PBS reruns with said two year old, and a few loads of laundry. You have a better offer?"

I glanced back to see Adri pull Andy to a stop in front of a little shop and peer in the window. I leaned in and pressed my lips to the side of her head and whispered, "Come with me to Tillamook?"

She pulled back a little and looked into my eyes. A smile hovered around the corners of her delicious mouth and she shrugged. "I guess I could do that. But it remains to be seen whether or not it's a better offer."

I chuckled and pulled her in for a hug. Just as I felt her arms tighten around my waist, Andy called, "OK, you two, enough PDA. We just ate." I smothered a sigh and took Sophie's hand again.

Sophie

I flopped down on my bed and hugged a pillow to my chest, sitting crossed legged. "So, you and Andy looked pretty cozy tonight."

"He's been a great diversion." A *diversion?* Wait. Did I detect a slight wistfulness in her tone?

"I'll never understand you. You find all these great guys and they all want you, but you won't settle."

"You don't know that Andy wants me. And that's just it. I'd be settling."

"That's not what I meant by settling. You and Andy, though… you are like two peas in a pod."

"Can you say hundreds of mile apart?" she enunciated the last few words. "We haven't even had enough time together to find out real stuff about each other. He's hot, likes to work out, and tolerates Thai food."

"What more do you need to know?" I teased then paused. "It doesn't have to be hundreds of miles. If you want it bad enough, you could compromise."

"Yeah, and what's the compromise you and James have worked out? 'Cause you are totally into him. I've never seen you like this…not even with the 'nearly married him' guy."

"I don't know," I sighed. "We were talking about it on the way to the restaurant tonight and he had the perfect opportunity to ask me to stay, but didn't. Maybe he doesn't feel the same-"

"Whatever," she interrupted. "I saw that look he gave you over the pad beef broccoli. Or was it over the mango rice?"

I rolled my eyes. "What look?"

"That look that said he'd sample you if you had been on the menu."

"Knock it off," I blushed and threw the pillow at her.

She tossed the pillow back and sighed. "There's something there, I'll give you that," she admitted about Andy. "We'll see." When she lifted a shoulder in a shrug, I nearly rolled my eyes again. How could she be so blasé about the whole thing? It drove me crazy. Or maybe it was just my inability to control my own situation that was driving me crazy.

"He asked me to go to Tillamook with him next weekend," I confided, almost keeping the stupid grin hidden.

"Cheese… Now that's romantic," Adri laughed.

"His *parents* live there," I told her dramatically.

Her eyes got big and she smiled. "I told you…" she laughed. "So, you're going, right?"

"Yeah. I'm scared to death, but yeah."

"Keep the trivia under control and you've got it made. He'll be proposing before Christmas."

"I won't even be here that long, crazy girl."

"But if you charm the parents, they'll nag and nag about grand babies and he'll come around."

"Great, so he'd just be marrying me to get his parents off his back."

"No, that would just be a bonus." She laughed as I hit her with the pillow again.

James

The door flew open as I raised my hand to knock. "Hey," Sophie grinned up at me.

"You ready to go?" I asked with an answering grin.

"Need you ask? I've been ready for hours. I didn't even go to sleep last night."

"She hasn't been up for that long," Adri muttered. "But pretty close," she added under her breath as she brushed past us, waving at Andy as she walked to James' car. "Can we go already?" she called over her shoulder. "All this cheeriness is disgusting this early in the morning."

Sophie's grin widened as she watched Adri go, an affectionate look on her face. She closed the door and grabbed my hand, dragging me down the steps to the sidewalk. "She's not much of a morning person, if you couldn't tell." Then, "You can sleep on the way," she called to Adri. "Andy would be happy to lend a shoulder, I'm sure."

"What beach are we going to?" Adri asked a few minutes into the drive.

"Cannon Beach," Sophie eagerly told her. "It's the one I told you about with Haystack Rock."

"Oh, yeah. Is that the one where that nurse, what's his name, wanted to carry you off into the sunset?" Adri giggled and Andy guffawed from the back seat.

I saw Sophie glance quickly at me from the corner of my eye. I schooled my expression and kept my eyes on the road.

"No," Sophie said. "It's the one with the most perfect sand dollars." She leaned over and kissed my cheek. Zeke who? I wondered smugly.

"It is a two hundred thirty-five foot rock in the ocean. There are like five other rocks in Oregon called Haystack Rock also, but this one has other rocks surrounding it called Needles." Sophie was just getting started. "It's the rock that is on the movie The Goonies."

"You sound like a travel brochure. Tell me something I can't read about," Adri told her impatiently.

"I've got something for you that you can't read about." Andy told her. "Well, maybe only in the newspaper or on a police report." I met Andy's eyes in the rear view mirror and laughed. "Back in high school, we wanted to impress the ladies with our unmatched strength and climbing abilities-"

"So not much has changed since then?" Adri asked, biting the inside of her cheek to control a smile.

Andy grinned and flexed his biceps. Adri gave in to the grin and so did I when I saw Sophie's eye roll.

"We decided we'd climb the monolith and repel or jump off. Whichever people wanted. So we skipped school and drove down one afternoon. We didn't really need it to climb, but we had all our climbing gear, our suits were on, and the chicks were plentiful."

Sophie grunted in disgust and I reached over to squeeze her hand. "Just let him go with it. You know you want to hear how we got our juvie record."

I glanced at Andy in the mirror again. "Go on," I told him.

"The girls were all squealing and, 'Oh, we are going to get in so much trouble.' Pssh. We just rolled our eyes at them and told them to prepare to be amazed. I was all strapped in and ready to ascend. They were speechless until one of them pointed to a cop strolling toward us across the beach."

Adri's eyes were huge saucers. "What happened?"

"The cop couldn't get to us without getting his highly polished black boots wet, so he yelled to us about citations and ditching school. He hung around for a while. We knew we shouldn't be trying to climb it anyway, so we packed our stuff and left. Kind of anticlimactic, I know, but we were raised to be law abiding citizens."

I snorted. "Not to mention the fact that your father was running for mayor that year and the police record wouldn't look good for his campaign. They have a group there now that educates the public, answers questions, that sort of thing. People still try to climb it today, but mostly people want to preserve the beauty of it. I guess some chunks fall off it from time to time."

Adri shook her head and mused, "I don't know about you, Sophie. You seem to have a thing for felons."

I turned quick eyes to Sophie while she balked at Adri's statement. "You can't even compare the two," Sophie protested. "Remember we weren't going to resurrect potentially embarrassing situations from our past?" She shot Adri a pointed look.

"The stories she could tell...," Adri continued dramatically. "When it comes to men, she's pretty much seen it all. Remember the guy who took you to his great aunt what's-her-name's open casket viewing/funeral?"

"On a date?" I asked, incredulous. "Were you close friends of the family?"

"Never met her," Sophie said with a shake of her head. "First date."

"And last," Adri shivered.

Andy hooted. "Tell us more."

I nodded mutely in agreement. I admit my curiosity was getting the best of me. Not to mention the fact that I was interested in any past relationships Sophie may have been involved in.

"Adri makes it all sound more interesting than it really is." Sophie assured us, then sighed when we continued to look at her expectantly. "Fine. I almost dated a convicted felon."

Andy crowed from the back seat. "Our good little Sophie dating serial killers."

"Oh, come on," Sophie argued. "It wasn't like that."

"What was it like then?" Andy laughed.

"A friend of my mother's told me she wanted to introduce me to her son. He didn't live in the area, so she said I'd need to write to him. I was thinking email pal's or something. I mean, people meet online all the time, right? I told her I'd be willing to exchange a few emails. But when I got an envelope in the mail with his name and Dominguez State Jail in the return address, I opted out of the correspondence exchange."

"That's cold, Sophie," Andy called to the front seat. "You could have been his inspiration to leave behind a life of crime. Now you will never know." Adri giggled.

"I'll never know," Sophie agreed.

"Hey. What was his name again?" Andy asked, his voice earnest. "I think I saw that name on a wall in the post office the other day."

"He was already locked up, genius, not at large. And they don't put them on the walls anymore," I told him.

"Too bad," Adri said. "I'll bet he'd be there if they did."

"You cannot make me feel bad about turning away a prison inmate," Sophie replied. "My mother was horrified that her good friend would even think of such a thing."

"She wasn't about to turn her lovely *minor* daughter over to the hands of a criminal," Adri laughed.

"I was eighteen," Sophie argued without any conviction. "I just couldn't see myself playing Bonnie and Clyde."

"Never been on your bucket list, huh?" I teased, squeezing her hand.

"No. But now that I know you fall under that category, I'd be willing to rethink it."

I laughed out loud and squeezed her hand again. She was adorable. It took all my willpower to not lean over and kiss her. How could anyone, criminal or not, resist her? I was finding it harder and harder to.

"How long 'til we're there?" Adri asked.

"Just a while more," Sophie promised. She clapped her hands to her chest in excitement. I could tell she was having a hard time sitting still. "Oh, Adri, you are going to love it. It's so cool," she gushed. "And we get to see anemones, crabs, sea stars..." She ticked them off on her fingers as she listed them.

"Would you keep her under control up there, James?" Andy complained. "You two study whatever you want, Adri and I will do our own thing." He bumped Adri with his shoulder and she blushed.

"San Antonio, why don't you dazzle us with some oceanic trivia," I suggested.

Andy and Adri groaned from the back seat. Which made my grin widen. I hadn't felt this happy or content in...well, I couldn't remember when.

"If you insist," she grinned back at me. "Did you know that sea lions are the first non human mammal with the proven ability to keep a beat?"

"Fascinating," Andy remarked dryly.

"And did you also know-"
"No more," Adri interrupted. "Please. We beg you."

"Fine," Sophie sniffed. "Your loss." Then she threw me a surreptitious grin.

Sophie

The miles passed quickly in pleasant scenery and conversation. I grabbed my bag and jumped out of the car as soon as James brought the car to a stop. He pulled a blanket and a basket from the trunk. I skipped down the beach in front of him. Andy and Adri brought up the rear at a more sedate pace.

James set the basket down on the sand and I took one end of the blanket to help him spread it out. I smiled up at him as I kicked off my flip flops and took a seat on the blanket. "You thought of everything." I gestured to the basket.

"I even showered so my cleanliness wouldn't be called into question. I know how ornery you get when you're hungry," he told me. "I have feared for my life the few times we have eaten out."

"Funny," I told him.

"You're such a little girl when you are at the beach," Adri said when she and Andy made it to the blanket.

I shrugged a shoulder. "What can I say? I love it here. It speaks to me like nothing else does," I admitted seriously.

"I know how you feel," James replied, looking out toward the water. In that moment, looking at James as he gazed at the sea, I fell in love with him a little more. As if he felt my eyes on him, he turned to look at me. I turned my face quickly to the ocean. I knew my feelings for him would be plain on my face and I wasn't ready to reveal them to him yet.

James' voice drew my gaze. "I figure we have about thirty minutes or so until the tide traps us at the rock." He spoke directly to me. "If you want to see the tide pools, we'd better save breakfast for later."

I stood and brushed some sand from my jeans. "What are we waiting for?" I asked and walked confidently toward Haystack Rock.

"We are going to stay and eat," Andy called to us before we got too far away." We'll catch up." I waved behind me in acknowledgement without turning from my goal.

Haystack Rock was breathtaking and I leaned my head all the way back to take it all in. Birds who made their nests on its highest points circled overhead, patrolling the seas and searching for their breakfast. The cool morning breeze played with my hair and I sighed contentedly as I brushed it from my face. I shivered and shoved my hands into my hoodie pouch, grateful I had grabbed it before we left.

James stood next to me, our shoulders barely touching. "I like that you are comfortable with silence," I told him.

"There is a lot to be learned and appreciated through observation and contemplation," he responded.

"There aren't many who know that though. I like that you do."

He reached down and took my hand in his. "Why the ocean?" he asked.

"I'm not sure I can describe it. For some people it's the mountains that call to them, speak deeply to their souls. The ocean, in all its powerful fury, has always been a source of calm and peace for me. I just look at it, and my whole body sighs in relief. I feel my breath catch at its beauty and I want to cry with happiness. Does that sound crazy to you?" I looked up at him.

He squeezed my hand and smiled down at me. "No, but this may sound crazy to you. That's how I feel when I look at a perfect heart, working on its own as it should. It's beautiful, miraculous, and indescribable. How can anyone look at the ocean or the human body without seeing the hand of God? There are times during surgery when I feel as though He is guiding my hands to fix those tiny, delicate little people. To give them a chance to see the ocean and experience this majesty and peace that surrounds you when you stand here and speak to me from your soul."

"We understand each other then." I glanced from the Haystack to his face.

A peaceful smile touched his lips as he stared straight ahead at the ocean. "Yes. I believe we do."

"What are you guys looking at?" Andy wanted to know at the same time Adri demanded, "Show me these amazing tide pools." I squeezed James' hand in something of an apology and we both turned at the sound of their voices.

I smiled at Adri. "Right this way." I moved my arm in a sweeping gesture toward the miniature crustacean cities. Adri hooked her arm through mine and James and Andy followed behind.

Adri and Andy stayed by us longer than I thought they would. When the water got a little too high, they slowly wandered away in search of something else to capture their attention for a few minutes more. It just didn't hold the same appeal for them as it did for us. Well, at least for me. And because James knew the depth of my feelings, he stayed by my side until he knew I'd had my fill.

I was captivated and speechless by the underwater world before me. The water was so clear, I would have thought I was staring from behind glass had I not been able to reach down and feel the shock of cold water and spongy softness of the anemones beneath my fingertips. I giggled in delight when the green and pink anemones pulled inside themselves at my touch.

I turned to speak to James just as he leaned forward to see what had captured my attention. We bumped heads and I jerked back quickly. I put my hand down to keep myself from falling over and gasped when it was swallowed up in cold water. Some poor sea creature, disturbed with my inconsiderate hand placement, scuttled about and I pulled back, startled. I lost my balance, falling into James, and sat hard in his lap.

"Whoa. Sorry," I told him, scrambling to get off him.

"It's okay," he assured me as he stood. "Except I'm experiencing deja-vu from the 'peeing my pants' incident."

My eyes got big as understanding dawned and I put my hand over my mouth to stop the giggle that threatened. "James, I am so sorry," I told him between laughs.

"Yes. I can hear how upset you are about the whole thing," he observed. "You are going to have to walk behind me for the rest of the day to block the wind and preserve my ego."

"Wait until Andy hears about this."

"Oh, Andy isn't going to hear about this."

"He's not?" I asked innocently.

"No. He's not." The threatening tone of his voice was downplayed by the humorous glint in his eyes.

He lunged at me, but I side stepped him and took off running. I looked behind me and shrieked when I saw he was almost on top of me. I stepped to the side and put on the brakes. He ran past me a few feet before he managed to stop and turn. I stooped down to pick up some wet sand and held it up between us hoping to use it as a deterrent. He wasn't deterred in the least. He grinned wickedly and kept coming at me.

"Put it down, and you won't get hurt."

"I'm not afraid of you, Doctor," I said, though my voice shook with laughter.

When he was an arms length away, he lunged for me. His clean hand grabbed my gritty one and he pressed his fingers between my own, sandwiching the wet sand between our fingers, forcing it out and onto the beach. He gently tugged me closer, his eyes never leaving mine. The laughter died on my lips when I saw his eyes change from teasing to intense. My breath caught in my throat.

"You're eyes are very green today, San Antonio," he said softly, his gaze penetrating. But the way he said my nickname sounded different this time. More intense. More...something.

"Did you know that reindeer eyeballs turn blue in winter to help them see at lower light levels?" I asked nervously. I rolled my eyes and growled in frustration while James chuckled softly.

"You are just trying to distract me," I breathed.

"No." He tugged on my hand again, pulling me closer, and snagged my waist with his arm. "I think you are trying to distract me."

"Is it working?" I managed to breathe out.

"Maybe a little," he said before he lowered his head and placed his lips on mine. Suddenly the wonders of the ocean and the beach took on new meaning. As James' lips moved slowly over mine, I knew this small spot of heaven on earth would be forever changed for me. I'd never look at another ocean wave, sandy beach, or rising rocky cliff without seeing James.

"We should have done that a long time ago," I murmured breathlessly when we drew apart. "What were we thinking?"

"Well, *I* was thinking that you were a married woman and I was already having trouble steering clear of you without adding kissing into the mix." I laughed at that and leaned in to kiss him again.

James

I was still thinking about our conversation on the way back to Portland later that afternoon. No one, not Andy, Kaley, or even my father understood me deep down like Sophie seemed to. Even though our passions in life were for different things, our feelings about them were similar. We had connected on a deeper level and that scared me. But when it had come right down to it and I was at the edge of the proverbial cliff, I chose to dive right in. I knew what I was doing when I kissed her and I did it willingly. The water was very fine. Now there was no turning back. Attaching the names of all the cities in Texas to her couldn't make her 'just one of the guys'. I could drown in her and never care about coming to the surface.

When we pulled into her brother's driveway, I put the car in park and climbed out. I caught Sophie's hand in mine on the way to the house. "Are your shorts dry so Andy isn't laughing at you while you tell me goodbye?" Sophie wanted to know when we stood on the porch.

"I don't know. Let's test it." I put my hands on Sophie's shoulders and turned us so my back was to the car. With a smile, I lowered my face slowly toward her. She went up on her toes as if she couldn't wait and met me halfway.

I gently kissed her soft lips. She pulled back way too soon, but I couldn't kiss her like I wanted to in front of Andy and Adri anyway, so I said, "So far, so good. I don't hear any laughter." I glanced over my shoulder at the car and then back to Sophie. "I'm glad you forced me from my bed at an unearthly hour today." She smiled up at me again and it was all I could do to not cover her lips with mine.

I lifted my hand and rested it on her cheek. She leaned into my palm and closed her eyes, a small smile still on her lips. "Thanks for today," she murmured. "It was nice."

I leaned down and kissed her once more then took her by the shoulders and turned her toward the door. With a soft shove I told her, "You'd better go while I still let you."

"My, my, doctor…" she drawled as she smiled over her shoulder at me. She waved goodbye to Andy and made a 'come on' motion with her hand to Adri. "See you Monday."

Chapter 21

Sophie

"What a therapeutic day," Adri sighed as she entered the kitchen and plopped an armful of shopping bags on the table.

"We maked cookies again, Adwi," Jeran announced proudly. "Have one."

Adri snatched a cookie off the cooling rack on the counter and sank into a chair. "I think I'd like to marry a really rich man so I can shop all day every day," she said between bites of cookie. "These are really good, Jeran," she commented and smiled at the little flour covered boy standing on the chair that had been pushed up against the counter.

"Me and Aunt Sophie maked them," he told her proudly. "I got to put in the gwedients."

"And you did an excellent job, you little cookie monster," I poked him in his tummy with the spatula.

He shrieked and stumbled down off the chair. Adri opened her arms to him. "I'll save you," she called dramatically and he plowed into her, holding his arms up for rescue. A puff of flour filled the air when his body collided with hers.

"What in those bags?" he asked pointing to the mound.

"Oh, I'll show you," Adri gushed excitedly while wiping flour from her clothes.

I grinned wryly wondering how long clothes and shoes would keep Jeran's attention. Adri opened the first bag and Jeran reached in. He pulled out a shirt and without a second glance, dropped it on the floor. "Whe's the toys?" he wondered peering into the bag again.

I laughed as Adri huffed and snatched her shirt from the dusty floor. "Jeran, I think I hear mommy," I told him when I heard the toilet flush down the hall and the bathroom door open. "Go ask her if she wants a cookie."

"Mommy…" Jeran called as he slid off Adri's lap and barreled out of the kitchen.

I turned off the oven timer and lifted another sheet of cookies out. "Are you still going to the gym with Andy tonight?"

"Yes! Do you want to see my toes?" I glanced over at her as she shrugged off her heels to show me her new pedicure.

"Cute," I responded. "But Andy won't even see your toes. I don't think he'd care overly much even if he did."

"I know. But it's like clean underwear," she informed me as she admired her toes then slipped her feet back into her shoes and stood to collect her bags from the table.

I gave her a questioning look. "How do you figure?"

If something happens, at least I'm not caught with medical people inspecting me and gagging over gross feet with chipped paint."

I laughed and shook my head at her logic. "Do you two want to do something after the gym? I could text James and see if he's not busy."

"You could just text him anyway. You don't need me for an excuse," Adri teased.

"I know. I've heard about this amusement park with rides and roller skating. What do you think?"

"Give him a call. Let me know. I'm going to go change for the gym."

James

Sophie: Plans tonight?

James: With you? Hope so:)

Sophie: Roller skating?

James: Funny

Sophie: Serious

"So, roller skating, huh?" I asked when she answered her phone.

"Adri and I wondered if you and Andy wanted to get together after they go to the gym. I've heard about this amusement park a couple miles from here and thought we could check it out. My treat."

"Do you know how long it's been since I've laced up a pair of roller skates?"

"Too long if you're asking me that."

"Way too long. But since I can't seem to tell you no, come get us when Adri is ready."

"Cool. See you in a few hours."

"I went to Oaks Park once years ago, but I threw up after the Disk'O and Eruption rides and I've never been back," Andy told us.

"You can't expect us to be surprised by that, can you?" Sophie asked.

"Why not?" Adri wanted to know. "Do you have a weak stomach?"

"Baby, there's nothing on me that's weak," Andy responded with a cocky grin. I choked and then grinned at Sophie's scoff of disgust.

Adri looked around the car at us and said, "There's a story here." Andy spent the remainder of the drive filling Adri in on his prom date fiasco.

"They also have roller skating and mini golf if you are feeling queasy. No throwing up in my car." Sophie's warning came out as more of a plea.

"I vote mini golf," Andy said.

"Me too," Adri chimed in. "I can't afford any freak accidents with roller skating when I'm going home soon. And I'd sympathy erupt right along with Andy when he barfed on the Eruption ride."

"Aptly named." Sophie grinned at the irony.

Eighteen holes and two wading expeditions to retrieve balls later, we sat in a dive that Andy suggested and stuffed ourselves with pizza and breadsticks. Talk and laughter circled easily around the table.

After Sophie choked on her breadstick for the third time from laughing at stories she and Adri were reminiscing about, we decided to call it quits.

"Take us home before Sophie dies right here on what's left of the combo pizza," Adri said.

"It is getting pretty late," Sophie agreed, checking the time on her phone. "I'd *hate* to have you miss your flight tomorrow because we slept in." Adri and Sophie grinned at each other.

"I wish I could have been here longer," Adri agreed.

"You've already seen all the important things," Andy reminded her, flexing.

I laughed as Sophie groaned. "Put it away, Andy, or we'll all be revisiting this pizza we just put down."

"She's right, dude," I agreed. "Besides, everyone knows that I have you beat any day of the week."

"Oh, ho," Andy choked out. "Let's take it to the gym and we'll see who beats who."

"Hey, look guys," Sophie interrupted. "It's karaoke night and they're warming up the mics."

Andy's head jerked in Sophie's direction, terror in his eyes. "Since when does this place do karaoke? We're outta here." He scooted out of the booth, pushing Adri with him as he went, and made a beeline for the door.

"I guess that leaves you with the check, Doctor." Sophie grinned over her shoulder in triumph.

"Pretty smooth, San Antonio," I called out to her.

"You ain't seen nothin' yet, cowboy." She winked, causing me to stumble, as she sauntered to the door.

Sophie

"I can't believe you leave tomorrow." I plopped down on my bed and pulled a pillow across my middle. "It's gone by too fast. I'm going to miss you."

Adri took a seat on the bed across from mine, pulling her knees to her chest and wrapping her arms around them. "Have you decided how much longer you are going to stay?"

"I have kind of put off talking to Trevor and Stacy about it," I admitted. "I really want to get back and open my place, but I really don't."

"Does your hesitancy have anything to do with a certain very good looking doctor?" She grinned knowingly. "And what's up with the San Antonio thing?"

I shrugged. "He started calling me that after our first beach trip. We were talking about weather and how I'm always so cold here." I brushed the memory away with a wave of my hand. "Anyway, it's kind of grown on me."

"It's cute. Unique," she said.

"I love him, Ad," I admitted. "I never thought I'd find him, but here he is. I'd be crazy to go back now and not give this thing time. Wouldn't I?"

"I hate to play devil's advocate here, but has he said anything that hints at long term? What if he's the type that will never commit and you are just spinning your wheels?

"No." I shook my head adamantly. "I can't believe he's the type who runs from commitment. Besides, it's way too soon to have that kind of talk." But did I know for sure? He was thirty-two, a doctor, gorgeous, and not married. Why? And what was it he refused to tell me?

"I can't believe how fast the week flew," I told Adri as we rushed into the airport. We were running late and I didn't want her to miss her flight even though I would have loved for her to stay. "Good thing you checked in on-line," I told her when I saw the lines. I hadn't had a chance to ask her about her goodbye to Andy, so I'd go with her as far through the security line as I could.

"How was Andy last night when you left?"

"He was Andy. You know how he is. I couldn't tell if he was just feeding me lines about missing me and will be with someone else the second my plane takes off, or if he really wants to keep in touch." Adri paused for a moment. "You said he and I are a lot alike. Does that mean you think I'm shallow?"

I hesitated. "Only around some people," I replied honestly. "For example, I'd never seen you as crazy about your body and the gym as you

258

were that night we played Trivial Pursuit at their apartment. The days you went to the gym with him, you came back Andy-fied. Don't get me wrong, the gym isn't a bad thing, but you aren't normally that extreme." I watched her closely trying to gauge her reaction to my words.

She sighed, "I know. I could see it in myself and didn't like it. That's why I denied having any feelings for him when we talked the other night. We would have gotten tired of each other, I think. Two selfish, self-centered people together don't last very long."

"You're almost up," I said, pointing to the security guard a few feet away. "I'm sorry that we didn't get to all the places you wanted to go. Someday we will have to do a road trip back here and see it all. Let me know that you got back safely. I love you."

She reached out and pulled me into a hug. "Thanks, Soph. I love you too." She pointed at me as she walked backward. "You better let me know how Tillamook goes." I laughed and waved.

Chapter 22

James

"You sure you are up for this?" I asked Sophie after driving a few minutes in comfortable silence.

She pumped a fist in the air. "Bring it on."

"You're not nervous at all? 'Cause I am, honestly."

"I'm terrified," she confided as she turned toward me in her seat. "You know how I get when I'm nervous. I spout ridiculous stuff. It's so humiliating. They are going to think I'm a freak."

I laughed softly at her dramatics. "It will be okay," I attempted to reassure her. "And anyway, you are just *kind of* a freak." I laughed out loud when she hit my arm with the back of her hand.

"Mean."

I grabbed her hand and gave it a gentle squeeze. "It's really going to be okay. They are as charming and fun to be around as I am." To which she snorted. I tried again. "You like me well enough, right?"

"Don't be too sure about that," she said dryly. I chuckled.

"You like me so you will like them. And if you are a really good girl," I continued as if talking to a small child, "we can go to the beach for a few minutes."

"I better get more than a few minutes of beach time out of this, Doc." She folded her arms. "And a sand dollar. And a sea cucumber. And some seaweed for a wrap…"

I laughed out loud and reached a hand over and pulled her hand from her crossed arms. I threaded my fingers through hers, brought them to my lips and kissed her soft hand, then rested them on the console between us. She was so crazy, so adorable. I wanted to pull her to me and never let go. I had no doubt my parents would love her. If Kaley could be believed, they already did with all she had told them about Sophie.

"…And ice cream at the cheese factory," she added as an afterthought.

"Anything else?" I asked chuckling.

"No, that should do it for this trip. But if they hate me, you're in big trouble."

"Noted."

"So, I brought something." I glanced at her as she leaned forward and dug around in the bag between her feet on the floor. "Ah hah!" she sang and sat back, waving a CD near my face.

"What is it?" I asked.

At her raised eyebrow and "ha, ha", I add, "I mean besides the obvious answer of a CD."

"This, Doctor, is a newly burned beach CD. I could have done something new age like a playlist on my phone or Ipod, but I decided to introduce you to some culture. I made it last night when I couldn't sleep.

261

Take a listen. Tell me what you think." She inserted the CD into the car CD player- I was actually surprised my car had one- and the steady beat of drums and an acoustic guitar filled the car. I smiled when Sophie's alto voice joined the male singer on the CD. I listened as she sang about spending a week at a beach with someone whose heart was still twisting like a beach roller coaster. Minutes later, the music faded and another song took its place. This one about dancing at a seaside pavilion and leaving for Cleveland in the morning. Sophie sang along with each song word for word, harmonizing during some songs and singing in unison with others.

Although I loved listening to her mellow voice, aside from the occasional vague references to sand, water, or summer, I didn't see how this was a beach CD and I told her so.

"How can you say that?" she protested.

"Easy. Just because I swim in the ocean, it doesn't mean I'm a dolphin," I reasoned. "These songs aren't beach songs simply because they reference a few grains of sand or a glass of water."

Sophie laughed. "You know they talk about more water than just a glassful."

"This is your feeble attempt to get me addicted to your country girl jams," I accused. "Admit it."

"I won't admit to anything. What are beach songs, then, if you are such a beach music guru?"

"You know. Something like Surfer Joe, Surfer Girl, Surfin' Safari," I listed off a few in a hurry.

"So, they have to have the word 'surf' in them to be considered beach music?" she questioned, making quote marks with her fingers.

"No. They just need to have more surf than spurs."

"Although I do not agree, I have anticipated you," she informed me. She leaned forward in her seat to push the skip button and skipped ahead a few songs. "Number six." She sat back with a satisfied smile. The first strains of Surfin' USA by the Beach Boys filled the car.

I cranked up the volume. "That's what I'm talking about," I hooted over the music, tapping the steering wheel to the beat of the music with my right hand. I glanced over at her scrunched up nose and laughed. "How many more of these do you have on here?" I yelled over the chorus.

"This is the only one," she yelled back and rolled down her window. The wind caught her hair and whipped it into my face. I spluttered and pushed it away. She laughed and gathered it in her hand and secured it in a ponytail.

I reached forward and lowered the volume, throwing her a questioning look. "This is the only beach song on this CD?"

"By your definition, yes," she sniffed.

I shook my head and laughed. "A *beach* CD."

"Fine. Laugh all you want. I'll have you know that forty percent of Americans, more or less, listen to country music. I was trying to help you acquire a bit of culture, diversity," she sniffed.

I grinned at her. "Or you were trying to up the percentage to a less embarrassing number." She scoffed, not believing I'd accuse her of such a thing. In my most humble voice I said, "Thank you for attempting to make me a Renaissance man."

"I can see some people are more prone to acquisitions than others. I am willing to compromise, however."

"Yeah?" I asked, intrigued.

"To show you I harbor no hard feelings about your insulting remarks, assumptions, and backward thinking-"

"Backward thinking," I objected.

"- I…" she held up a hand and continued over me. "I am willing to change the title of the CD from beach tunes to summer tunes if you are willing to admit that country music could grow on you."

"That is very magnanimous of you, pretty girl." I grinned at her blush. "And in an attempt to right any wrongs, I accept your suggestion of a title change, agreeing that summer tunes is a better title, and make a counter offer."

"I'm listening," she said.

"Take a moment to listen to my talk radio. See what that does for you."

"You won't agree that listening to my music has changed your opinion of country music?"

"Not even to up the percentage a little bit."

She pushed another button. Gone was the country twang and the monotone voice of a radio announcer informed us we could buy previously owned cars for a great price.

"Never mind," she said in disgust.

I tsked and reached out and turned the radio off.

Sophie

After a few minutes of comfortable silence, I asked, "Do you want to play a form of twenty questions since you balked at my beach music and we have over an hour to kill?"

"Now, now. I believe we called a truce," James reminded me. "But sure. I'm game. And I get to ask the first question."

"Okay. Just know that if you ask a good question, I can ask you the same question back without it counting as one of my questions."

"How is that fair?" he complained. "That way you get like forty questions to my twenty."

"I said it was a *form* of twenty questions. I came up with the game, so I get to make the rules."

"Fine, I guess. Okay, first question. Indoors or out?" he asked.

"Depends. If it's bathroom usage, definitely indoors. But if it's skinning rodents, I'd go without." I had to grab the wheel when he started to laugh or we would have crashed.

"Please tell me you have never actually skinned a rodent." He glanced at me and then back at the road.

"Skinned it, cooked it up, and ate it." At his horrified look, I said, "Kidding. Rodents give me the heebie jeebies. Seriously, though, I'd rather be outside doing something than sitting and watching television, but I love sitting down with a good book. I love kayaking, but swimming isn't my strong point. I love walks and riding my bike. Now you, same question."

"Outdoors for everything except surgery. That gets pretty tricky outside. I guess the bathroom too."

"You've had to perform surgery outside?" I couldn't believe it.

"Well, not a major surgery. When I was in South America on a medical humanitarian trip, our guide tripped and fell on his own machete. I had to sew him up right there in the middle of the jungle."

Sophie gasped. "Holy cow. I couldn't have done that in a hospital let alone a jungle."

"We came upon a guy that had been bitten by a snake. We were too far in the middle of nowhere to get him to a hospital in time. I had to slice him open and suck the venom out, then sew him back up."

"No way!"

"You're right," I admitted with a mischievous smile. "I had some anti-venom."

"Man, I totally fell for that," she laughed. "Did he live?"

"Yeah. We got him taken care of. There were other medical procedures we had to perform, but they were in a tent in the center of a village. So not technically outside."

"Wow. That's all I can say. Wow." I looked at James, admiration in my eyes. "My turn. Car or truck?"

"Well, you can probably tell I like cars given that I drive one. I've wondered how it would be to race cars on a track." His eyes lit up. "That would be awesome. Haven't ever really had a need for a truck. Now you, same question."

"Truck all the way. Cars are so limited in where they can take you. But I've recently acquired a taste for Lexus. This is one sweet ride, Doctor." He smiled and reached for my hand. I looked down at our intertwined hands. Mine was tanner than his because I spent more time in the Texas sun, but his was big and strong, gentle- the hands of a surgeon. Could hands be sexy? Well, his were.

I looked up and saw him glance over at me with a question in his eyes. I cleared my throat in an attempt to stop the blush filling my cheeks. Thank heaven he couldn't read my mind.

I cleared my throat again. "I love a little off-roading, mud on the tires, that kind of stuff. Adri and I went out with a couple guys once who had these diesel trucks with lifts. We told them the pond was too deep, but they were real hicks. I think they had probably already thrown back a few.

Anyway, they gunned it and took off into the pond. We got about halfway through when the engines stalled. They were cussin' and water started seeping in through the doors. Adri and I bailed and swam back to shore, but not before we had a scary little run in with an alligator. They aren't common that far north, but they aren't unheard of either."

"Hence the no swimming thing."

"Yes. Adri and I can laugh about it now, but we weren't laughing then."

"Did you ever go out with them again?" James wanted to know.

"Are you kidding? I'd have to be as drunk as they were before I'd go out with them again."

James laughed. "I wonder what you'd be like drunk. That would be funny."

"Yeah, well, you'll never know. The closest I've come is when I got my wisdom teeth out and was on pain meds. My parents still laugh about that day. Lots of blackmail material came from a couple pulled teeth."

"What should I look up on YouTube?" He pretended to search the console and his pocket blindly for his phone.

"I'll never tell," I laughed.

"Ok. My turn. What were you thinking when you looked at our hands a few minutes ago?"

I blushed and asked, "Do I really have to answer that question?"

"With that blush? Absolutely." He grinned.

"I was thinking that if I ever had to have surgery," I improvised, "your hands are the hands I'd want performing it. You have nice hands." I had told the truth. Mostly.

"Now you are making me blush," he said.

"Well, you'd blush even more if I hadn't paraphrased what I was thinking and had repeated it verbatim."

"Now you have to tell me," he insisted.

"It's better this way. Trust me. Just know that I think everything about you looks good, including your hands." Mercy, did I ever. "My turn. Best and worst date ever?"

"Do you mean that one date had to be both good and bad in the same date? Or do you mean which date was the best and then which separate date was the worst? And do I have to vote one of our dates as the best or you'll get all bent out of shape and not talk to me the whole weekend? Or do I…Oh, would you look at that. We're here," James announced.

My heart rate kicked into high gear as we pulled up in front of the Anderson's home. Then my eyes narrowed. "You cheater. You stalled on purpose with those meaningless find out questions so you didn't have to answer the question."

James chuckled. "You can't know that for sure."

He reached for the door handle but paused a moment before opening his door and looked at me. My face must have registered my panic because he grinned. "Did you know..." I began almost against my will.

James quickly leaned in and planted a soft kiss on my slightly parted lips. "Soph, it's going to be fine. You'll see." I exhaled a deep breath I didn't know I was holding and touched my fingers to my tingling lips. Shock from that kiss left me speechless. Perhaps that was his intention. I sucked in a breath and wondered what a real kiss from him would feel like. I opened the door and took James' outstretched hand.

"Mom, Dad? We're here," James called as we stepped into the tiled entry. I glanced around. Pictures adorned the walls and a baby grand piano sat sleek and silent in the immaculate great room.

"Dad's probably out in his shop," James speculated, heading for the kitchen.

I paused in the hall and touched the frame holding a picture of a younger James hanging on the wall. The once skinny teen had been replaced by a more physically defined, more mature man. He had been cute even as a teen, but that's not what held my interest. The eyes staring back at me from the photo were happy, carefree, and filled with excitement and determination for an unknown, but anticipated future.

The eyes I had looked into everyday this past week and multiple days for weeks before that, the eyes of James Anderson- the man- held pain. Sure he had the beginnings of soft laugh lines that crinkled at the corners of his eyes and mouth when he smiled. They held that same determination and excitement when we ran together or he talked about his career as a devoted doctor to sick babies. I saw a maturity and wisdom in his eyes born of years of hard work, sleepless night shifts, and life experiences, but until I saw this high school picture, I'd never recognized the pain.

I had sensed hesitation mixed with a little fear just before he kissed me or right after Zeke or Andy teased him about our relationship. But up until this point, I hadn't known what hovered on the edges of his eyes and soul. Now that I knew, what did I do with that knowledge? I had a sinking feeling that whatever was behind the pain was linked directly to our disagreement a few weeks ago and he wasn't open to discussing that.

I was okay with that for now, but whatever was holding him back from fully opening his heart to me and our relationship, could hold his heart captive in chains so thick and unyielding that he'd never be free to entrust it to me. I suddenly felt sick to my stomach and swallowed down the lump rising in my throat.

James

"Dad?" I called as I approached his open shop door. The sound of power tools met my ears and I knew he wouldn't be able to hear me even with his hearing aids in. I paused in the doorway and watched him working at his jigsaw. Other than a little more grey up top, he looked the same as the last time I visited.

I stepped farther into the room and my movement caught his attention. He lifted a hand in greeting and turned his saw off. "Son, you made it," his voice boomed across the shop to me. He made a show of looking around the shop. "Weren't you supposed to be bringing someone to meet us?"

"I think she got lost in the house. I'll go find her in a minute. I wanted to come say hello first. How have you been?"

"I'm great," he said, watching me closely. His eyes narrowed marginally and he asked, "How are *you*?"

"I'm good, Dad." I smiled and slapped him on the back.

"Well, you look good. Different, but good." His eyes narrowed further and he asked, "What's different?"

"What are you talking about? I could use a haircut..." I shrugged. "Hey," I protested and waved him off when he cuffed me on the back of my head.

"I'm not talking about a haircut, James. Give me a little credit."

"I don't know what you want me to say," I chuckled. "I'm still me." I patted myself all over my upper body as proof.

"Whatever it is, it looks good on you." He swatted at his pants in an effort to get the sawdust off. "How's the hospital?"

"Great," I replied enthusiastically. "A couple babies are on target to head home in the next few weeks. I'm really pleased with their progress. Sophie, the girl I brought with me," I gestured toward the house, "her nephew is one of the little guys slated for a discharge. The hospital is good."

Dad nodded. "Good to hear. How's rooming with that crazy cousin of yours going?"

I laughed and shook my head. "Andy is still Andy. But it hasn't been too bad. Gives me someone to come home to instead of an empty apartment."

I tried not to laugh as Dad's eyebrow rose at that statement. "I'm not sure he's the one I'd want to be coming home to every night, but that's just me. Personally, I love snuggling up with your mother at the end of the day. Be kind of hard to stomach getting that close to Andy." His eyes glazed over for a moment then he shook his head as if to clear the disturbing image from his mind. I laughed again.

"What are you working on this time?" I moved over to the saw he had been using before I interrupted.

He held up a partially cut piece of wood. "One more thing to cross off that list I mentioned during your last visit. Some of those craft projects your mother likes to paint and girly up with ribbons and such. It will say FAMILY when it is finished. After this one, I'll get started on an autumnal decoration- a sunflower, I think. It's all nonsense to me, but it keeps your mother happy. And if she's happy, I'm happy." He winked. "I think because it keeps us out of each other's hair. But if it means the difference between cuddling or sleeping alone on the couch, I'll do it.

"Ah, there's a method to the madness," I chuckled, but I knew that all the slave driver talk was just that. He loved his power tools almost as much as he loved his children. *Maybe more*, I thought with a rueful shake of my head, remembering our conversation in this same shop a few months ago. "Speaking of the conversation we had a few months ago, can I ask you a question?"

Dad picked up a sheet of sandpaper and began sanding his project. "Sure." He shrugged.

"How did you know? I mean *I* didn't even know what was bugging me on a conscious level."

He paused in his sanding and glanced up at me. "You said yourself that your sister was doing well. You are happier at work than any man has a right to be. What else was there?" He continued sanding.

"What else, indeed?" I chuckled and held my hand out to him. He grasped it firmly and pulled me into a one-armed hug.

When he stepped back, he appraised me. I could see when a light turned on and something clicked. "That's what is different about you." His eyebrows pulled together. "You fixed things." I kicked at a pile of sawdust on the floor. "Feels good, doesn't it?" He grinned when I refused to look at him.

"Well, your mother keeps pestering me to make her a frame that spells out GRANDKIDS with spots to put pictures, but I told her I wasn't going to make that until we had more grandchildren to fill the slots." He looked at me pointedly.

"Whoa. Don't look at me." I put up my hands to ward off any more discussion.

"Who else am I going to look at? Do you see any other children around here?

"You're getting a little ahead of yourself. Anyway, that ship has sailed. If you are looking for more grandchildren, you need to take it up with Kaley."

"Speaking of Kaley, she said you are dating a pretty thing. She the one you dragged here with you and then left alone in my house to steal all the valuables?"

I snorted. "Yes, Dad. I picked her up from the prison on my way here. She was let out for good behavior, though, so you have nothing to worry about. Your *valuables* are safe for now." I shook my head. "Good grief."

"It's the pretty ones you have to watch out for. They'll rob you blind while you sleep. I should know. Look at your mother."

"I'm telling mom you called her a petty thief."

"Now don't go putting words in my mouth and getting me into trouble," he warned.

"Speaking of pretty little thieves, do you remember that song Grandpa used to sing about marrying an ugly woman? Andy and I were talking about that a few weeks ago."

"Of course I remember." He paused then a look of concern crossed his face. "What does this girl look like? Should I be planning for something?" He chuckled at the look of terror that crossed my face.

"Let's just say that if I was following the advice from the song, I couldn't marry Sophie. She and ugly are on opposite ends of the spectrum. But again, nothing to worry about."

"You can't help your taste in women. You inherited that from me." He slapped me on the back. "Go on and find that girl before she robs me blind. And tell your mother that I will be in in a while." I turned toward the house and smiled when I heard him whistling a familiar song as the saw started up again.

Sophie

"Oh." The surprised voice behind me made me jump and I swiped quickly at my eyes before turning around. "I didn't know you had arrived yet. You must be Sophie. I'm Caroline Anderson, James' mom." A sophisticated woman in her late fifties approached me with a smile. Her trim body and dark hair belied her age, but I would have known her anywhere the minute I looked into her eyes. When I did, I saw James staring back at me. I held out my hand to her, but grinned when she pulled me into a hug. Her arms were warm and inviting like a mother's should be. I liked her instantly.

"Nice to meet you, Mrs. Anderson." I released her and stepped back. "James is around here somewhere. I think he mentioned something about his dad and a shop out back. I got distracted by these photos."

"Please call me Caroline. I just finished up some work in the office and was going to start on some lunch. Have you two eaten?" She talked over her shoulder as she moved into the kitchen.

I touched the picture frame one last time and turned to follow James' mom into the kitchen. "No, but he and I can grab something later. You don't need to go to any trouble."

I wasn't vomiting at the mouth yet, but if we stayed for lunch, gathered around an intimate table setting, I may not be able to control myself. Especially if the attention should happen to focus on me for any length of time. Best to avoid that situation. As much as I immediately liked and felt comfortable with James' mom, I couldn't' trust myself to not stick my foot in my mouth.

"Please stay. We'd love to have you. I want to catch up with James. You can help me make it if it will help you feel better."

How could I keep her son from her? "Sounds good. Tell me where you want me." I leaned against the granite topped island as she opened the refrigerator and began pulling out chicken and vegetables.

"You can cut up and cook this chicken while I work my magic on the croissants and secret sauce." I laughed lightly. It was nice to be around a mother again. I couldn't wait for my own mother's return.

"Sophie?" Mrs. Anderson and I both turned at the sound of James coming in the back door. "Thought I lost you." He smiled and walked to stand beside me at the counter. "She put you to work already, huh?"

"Oh, get over here and give me a hug." I watched as Caroline wiped her hands and met James halfway, pulling him into a big hug. "It's been too long," she scolded even though it had only been a couple of weeks. "How are you?" She pulled back and looked at him. I mean really looked. What was she looking for? What did she see? It must have pleased her, whatever it was, because she glanced over at me and then back at James, a speculative look crossing her face. "You look good, happy," she told him and he glanced my way. "That makes me happy." She reached up and placed her hand on his cheek for a moment and smiled.

Uncomfortable with her scrutiny, he shrugged out from under her hand and put his hands in his back pockets, turning toward me again. "What do we have here?" he asked, his chin resting lightly on my shoulder as he leaned over to look into the pan in the silence that followed.

"Chicken salad sandwiches," his mother answered and continued to cut vegetables. "Go tell your father that lunch will be ready in twenty minutes."

James turned his face slightly to whisper, "You okay if I leave again for a minute?" His warm breath made me shiver and I felt him smile against my ear. I pulled back to look into his eyes and returned his smile.

"I'm perfect," I said softly.

His gaze slowly wandered down to my lips and back up to my eyes. His expression intensified and I read desire there. I felt his mother's gaze and glanced at her out of the corner of my eye. James suddenly straightened as if just remembering she stood five feet away, gave me a side hug, and strolled over to the back door. I watched him go, admiring his swagger, and turned back to the stove to stir the chicken.

"Kaley told me you have a nanny position in Portland," Caroline said conversationally.

"Well, that's partly correct. My brother and sister-in-law just had a baby born with a congenital heart defect. I came for a few months to help them out with my other nephew, Jeran. That's how I met James. He's Dylan's doctor."

"Well, he's in good hands then. How is the baby doing?"

"He's doing so much better," I answered with a smile. "James says if all goes well, Dylan will be able to go home soon."

"Does that mean you will be heading for home soon, too?" Was that merely curiosity in her voice? "Where is home?"

"I'm from San Antonio. I'm opening a sports therapy clinic there when I get back, so the sooner I can get back, the better."

Caroline's eyebrow rose at that information and a disappointed "Oh" came from her mouth. "How long have you and James been dating?"

"We've known each other for about eight weeks, but we've only been dating for about half that time. It's a pretty funny story, actually-"

"And one she isn't going to hear because you aren't going to tell it." James cut me off as he came in the back door.

I laughed and turned to find a warning look on his face. Clasping my hands together in front of me, I begged, "Oh, please? It's such a good story."

"A good story for who? It's humiliating."

"If it's going to humiliate my son, it's a story we've got to hear. Right, dear?" A big bear of a man followed behind James and slung an arm around his shoulder. James' father. I studied him only to find an older version of James looking back at me.

"Thanks, Dad," James said wryly.

"It's okay. If he won't let you tell us, I can always get it out of Kaley," Caroline threatened. "She'd be more than happy-"

James' loud protests cut her off. "Kaley will butcher it. Fine." He looked at me. "Tell your story. I'll go cry softly in the corner." But he took a stack of plates into the dining room and set them on the table instead.

"I'm Max, by the way." James' dad came forward and shook my hand. "It's good to meet you. Real good." I watched with furrowed brows as Max walked into the dining room. If I didn't know better, I'd think his eyes had gotten misty. When Caroline sniffed, I turned to look at her. She read the question in my eyes and came closer.

"It's good to have James back," she said quietly, patting me on the shoulder. Weird.

"How long has it been since he visited?" I wondered aloud. The way he talked on our drive here, it hadn't been but a few weeks since they'd seen each other.

"No, not physically, but emotionally. He's different. The only change in his life recently has been you, so we have to think that you are the reason for the change. Thank you." She patted my shoulder again and followed her husband into the dining room with the chicken salad and croissants. I followed at a slower pace with the pitcher of lemonade, not exactly sure what just happened. I was happy that they were happy, but they gave me too much credit.

We sat around the table talking and laughing long after the food was gone. I felt as comfortable here as I did at my parents' house with my own family. Max and Caroline laughed so hard when they heard that James thought I was married to my brother that tears rolled down their cheeks. James was a good sport.

After lunch was cleared, James gave his mom a kiss on the cheek and grabbed his keys off the counter. "I promised Sophie I would take her to the cheese factory and the beach. I'm not sure when we'll be back, so don't wait up."

"Thank you for the delicious lunch. I've really enjoyed myself." I gave Caroline and Max a hug.

"Yeah, at my expense," James muttered under his breath.

I put my arm through his and looked up at him with mock hero worship. "Don't think of it that way. Think of it as being the life of the party. You made your parents so happy. You are such a good son," I cooed like I was talking to a child and reached up to pinch one of his cheeks.

"No seaweed wrap for you." He untangled his arm from mine and slung it around my shoulders. I laughed and wrapped both of my arms around his waist as we walked to his car.

"I don't know why you were worried," James said as we drove in the direction of the Tillamook Cheese Factory. "They love you, I think, more than they love me."

"What's not to love," I boasted. When James didn't respond, I looked over at him. "I was kidding," I told him.

"I know. I also agree."

I sucked in a breath. Was he saying what I think he was saying? Before I could question him about it, he asked, "What is your favorite type of cheese?"

What? Cheese? "Uh, I don't know. I thought they were all pretty much the same."

He glanced at me incredulously. "Must we have this discussion again, O Queen of Trivia? You honestly can't tell the difference between pepperjack and cheddar?"

"I've never given it much thought." I shrugged. "When I eat food with cheese, I only worry about whether or not it tastes good. I do know that parmesan tastes different than cheddar if that makes you feel better."

"Only slightly. What a sheltered life you have lived." He shook his head in exaggerated disappointment.

"It's a good thing we are going to a cheese factory so I can educate myself. I will stay up the whole night tonight studying different types of cheese." I solemnly crossed my heart with a finger.

We took the factory tour that ended with samples of a variety of cheeses. I was proud to be able to tell James that the smoked cheddars and bleu cheese weren't my favorite, but the pepper jack and gouda were high on the likes list.

After hitting the gift shop for a stuffed Tillamook cow for Jeran, James purchased five or six different types of cheese. When I questioned his need for that much cheese, he grinned mischievously and said it was for a quiz later. We got a passerby to snap a picture of us in the orange bus just inside the factory entrance and headed for the beach.

I watched out my window as the scenery changed from houses to fields to green coast. Excitement bubbled up inside in anticipation of that first glimpse of the ocean surrounded by dark rock formations, evergreens, and ferns.

I turned in my seat to study James' profile. Even all the breath-taking beauty out my window couldn't compete with the mind numbing creation in the seat next to me. "If you could live anywhere, where would you live?"

James turned a lazy gaze on me. "Well...I went on a humanitarian mission to South Africa with a youth group from my church. I've told you about the medical missions in South America. And then my residency, of course, in Boston. I am spoiled and love the comforts of the States, so definitely in the US. I really like coastal climates. There's a charming, historical feel to the towns back east. The town we are going to, Oceanside, is like that, but with an unbeatable view of the Pacific. I don't know..." James shrugged.

"I didn't know about South Africa. That's fascinating. I can't imagine all you've seen. I toured Europe with some friends right after high school, but other than a few trips to Houston and the Gulf, I've stayed right around San Antonio and now Oregon. Tell me about the humanitarian mission in Africa." I turned sideways in my seat and pulled my legs up and settled in for a good story.

James grinned and reached a hand out to touch my cheek. "I love that you get so excited about life. Whether it's running by the river, sampling cheese, or listening to my boring stories, you have this infectious childlike enthusiasm about you." He took my hand and kissed the back of it. "It's cute."

"Okay, great." I blushed. "We don't have much time. Story please."

He laughed and began weaving a tale of poverty and neglect, of hope and true joy. I sat mesmerized by the stories themselves, but also of his ability to capture moments so vividly in his mind that I felt as though I was experiencing them first hand with the retelling.

Suddenly I put up my hand. "Stop," I commanded loudly, cutting him off in the middle of his sentence. He signaled to pull over while looking wildly around and quickly came to a stop on the side of the road.

"What?" he asked, his eyes moving.

"Do you smell that?"

He paused and cocked his head. "Do I smell what?" he asked, looking at me strangely.

"Do you have a strawberry air freshener or strawberry candy or something? Don't you smell strawberries?

James started to laugh. He reached over and took my head in both hands, tilted my head down, and kissed the top of my head soundly. "*That's* why you scared me to death? Strawberries?"

"Well yeah. Don't you smell them?" My cheeks flamed red.

"Look out your window." He gestured around us with his hand. "We are surrounded by strawberry fields. That's where the strawberry scent is coming from." He shook his head and chuckled. "I can't believe I almost got us killed over strawberries. There is never a dull moment with you in it."

I gazed out my window in wonder at the green fields stretching and covering the ground as far as the eye could see. If I looked closely and squinted a little, I could see bright red fruit scattered amidst the dark green leaves.

"Sorry," I said sheepishly and sank down in my seat. "But that's so cool. I've never experienced anything like this." I paused to look at the plants out the window once more then I said, "We can go. Geez, what are we still doing here at the side of the road like there's some emergency?" I peeked up at him through my lashes.

He gave me an exasperated look then signaled and checked over his shoulder. As he pulled back onto the road, he asked, "Where was I before I was so rudely interrupted?" He picked up his narrative where he left off and I was quickly caught up in the tales again.

I was so enthralled that I blinked and looked around, disoriented, when he stopped the car and announced we were at the beach. That nine or so miles went by lightning fast. I was loathe to leave my peaceful cocoon. I told James as much and he looked at me in disbelief.

"You love the beach. There are some amazing things to see. Way better than any of my riveting tales. When you see what I'm about to show you, you'll never want to leave," he promised.

"Okay, but I reserve the right to pick the topic of conversation on the way back. And I pick you and your captivating stories." I sighed and shoved my door open ready to hit the beach. I paused and took in a deep breath of salty sea air while James grabbed his ball cap and a blanket from the back seat. Excitement for the picturesque scenery took hold and I grabbed his hand and pulled him down the rocky stairs to the beach.

"So this is Oceanside, huh?" I asked in awe, turning in a complete circle. The mountainous rocks jutting up in the middle of the ocean were breathtaking.

"If you think this is cool, wait until we walk a little ways down. There's a tunnel under one of the cliffs that leads to another beach," he told me. "Three Arch Rocks is only a half mile away. We can go watch the sea lions. Or if you are into lighthouses, Cape Meares is only a couple miles north."

I stealthily took my phone from my back pocket and whipped it up to snap a picture of him in his ball cap with the cliffs and ocean behind him. "What the..." he made a grab for my phone.

I swatted his hand away and smiled smugly. "Just taking in the local scenery. I didn't even get you in it." *Well, at least not from the waist down.* He snorted, clearly not believing my explanation. "Come stand by me and I'll get one of us together. We need to capture this moment to fix it in our brains forever." I watched him saunter closer and breathed in his scent as he leaned in, placing his cheek against mine. I fumbled my camera and he put a hand over mine to steady it. I don't know which of us snapped the picture. All I knew in that moment was the slight stubble on his cheek tickling mine and his erratic minty breathing keeping pace with the beat of my flustered heart. He turned his lips to caress my cheek, dropping his hand from my phone to my face. I closed my eyes and felt him shift and stand in front of me. I sucked in a breath, fearing my heart would burst from my chest, as he leaned in and placed a kiss on the corner of my mouth.

Tease. "Uh, uh." I grabbed for his shirt to hold him in place when I felt him start to pull away. He smiled against my lips, pulled me tight against him, and covered my lips with his. I don't know how long we stood there wrapped up in each other, the sound of the waves crashing against the rocks behind us and the cry of gulls in the brilliant blue sky, but I felt like all the pieces finally slid into place and I could see clearly for the first time in my life. If he asked, I'd stay. I'd make my life here with him because there was no life without him.

James

As I stood there getting lost in everything Sophie, I felt something shift. In me, in her, I didn't know. It wasn't anything tangible that I could put my finger on, but it terrified me anyway. I pulled back so abruptly that she would have fallen had I not kept my hands at her waist to hold her steady. We were both breathing hard, but she looked up at me in confusion. I felt that same confusion roiling inside me. I needed a minute, but didn't want to hurt her feelings. How could I not get close enough one second and then not far enough away to leave the fear behind in the next? I dropped my hands from her waist and bent to pick up the blanket that had fallen to the ground when I needed both hands to pull her ever closer. I reached up and turned my hat forward and looked around.

"I forgot the water." Even I wanted to hit my forehead. Who breaks off the greatest kiss of all time for water? Nothing to do now but go with it. I shoved the blanket at her. "I'm going to go grab a couple water bottles from the car. Don't stray too far," With that, I turned and hurried away. I quickly made my way to the car, my mind going a million miles a minute. I popped the trunk and rested my hands on either side, dropping my chin to my chest. With my eyes closed, I took a couple deep breaths to calm my racing heart and mind. I thought I could do this. Hoped I could.

All the things that drew me to Sophie were the same things that forced me to push her away-- out of fear. But I was tired of being alone. I teased my dad about going home to Andy, but going home to just anyone wasn't actually *coming* home. I didn't need someone there just to fill space. I wanted the kind of home I'd caught a glimpse of when Sophie was in my arms. The home where she ran her fingers through my hair as we drove in the car somewhere or nowhere. The home where I constantly laughed at her zaniness. The home where everything in life seemed brighter and more manageable because I knew I'd be seeing her in a couple hours. The same home I'd tried but failed to achieve with Nicole.

And that right there was the problem.

Nicole showed me that it's not possible for my heart to find a home. It's better to keep it boarded up than to let someone take up occupancy only to tear through it with a sledge hammer, destroying every room. The pain would bulldoze over the top of me and leave me demolished.

And Sophie wasn't staying.

This wasn't her home.

I couldn't do it again.

"Hey."

I jumped at her soft touch on my shoulder and the sound of her voice. I straightened quickly and barely missed hitting my head on the inside of the trunk.

"Are you okay?" She peered closely at me, the blanket dangling from her hand at her side.

"What? Oh, yeah. I'm good. But I'm actually not feeling the greatest. Do you care if we head back to my parents?" Her eyebrows rose in surprise and then furrowed in concern.

"No. Sure. Let's go. I'm sorry. I didn't know you weren't feeling well. You should have said something sooner." She quickly folded the blanket and set it in the trunk. I grabbed two water bottles and shut the trunk. "Are you okay to drive," she asked over the top of the car as we walked around to our separate doors.

"Yeah. It was probably too much cheese. Apparently, it doesn't just plug you up when you eat too much."

She made an attempt to laugh at my lameness, but it fell flat. We both knew it wasn't the cheese. She sat silently with her hands folded in her lap the twenty minutes to my parents' house. I wanted to say something to rid the car of the awkwardness that smothered us like a thick fog blanketing the ocean before an early morning sun rise, but I didn't know what I could say that wouldn't hurt her or reveal too much of the fear that had nearly paralyzed me back there.

She was out of the car with a 'Thanks, James' thrown over her shoulder the second we pulled to a stop in the driveway. A humorless laugh escaped me, but she wasn't around to hear it.

"Sure. Anytime I can rip myself from your lips with no explanation and follow it up with a bunch of lies to get as far away from you as possible, you just let me know." *Water.* Hah.

I bypassed the house for my dad's shop in the back. I didn't care one way or the other if he was in the shop. I wasn't in the mood to talk to anyone either way.

Chapter 23

James

The utter silence that met me at the shop door filled me with relief. I guess I did care if he was in there. I flipped on the light and breathed in the soothing scent of sawdust that covered every surface like a thin blanket. I made my way over to one of the many work benches against the far wall and pulled down a box, whose original job was to hold Christmas oranges, from a shelf above the bench. The orange box now housed years of discarded potential masked as pieces of wood. *It had to be in here somewhere.* Near the bottom of the box, my fingers touched on its smooth surface and I pulled it from the box. I lifted it to the light and blew off remnants of the other wood it slept with over the years.

I was ten years old again standing in this very spot holding a large rectangular block of wood. "Make a boat out of this?" I questioned my father in disbelief. "I told you I want to build a *real* boat." I slapped the block of wood down roughly on the workbench.

"And I told you that if you finished a boat out of this block of wood, I will help you build your real boat." My dad turned back to his scroll saw and turned it on, high-pitched metal noise filling the small shop.

I sat and stared at that block for what seemed like hours that cold winter day. I could picture the finished product, but had no idea the hours it would take to get to that point. For weeks, I sanded and shaped that block of wood. Slowly, it began to take shape and I was thrilled one day when I went out to work on it again how much it had actually started resembling the boat I had pictured in my mind all those long weeks before. But as weeks turned into months and winter turned to spring and then summer, baseball and basketball, skateboards and trips to the ocean took me away from the boat and it moved from the bench to the orange box on the shelf. Oh, I'd come out to the shop every so often and dig the nearly completed boat from among the useless pieces of wood when a friend was out of town or I had ticked mom off and was looking for a place to lay low for a while, but I never went back and finished that boat. My father knew something my ten, eleven, and twelve year old mind didn't. Shaping and crafting things in life takes time, effort, and dedication. The real things that matter don't just happen overnight. My father had gained wisdom from life's experiences that told him to start me out with the small block of wood before I took on a life-sized boat. He knew I would be biting off more than I could chew at any age, but especially at the age of ten.

Now as I held that boat up and studied it, a new meaning flowed into the crevices of my brain and anger swelled deep in my chest. Besides med school, had there ever been anything I had seen through to completion in my life? Was this unfinished boat a metaphor for my incomplete, unraveling life?

"Agggh," I cried out and cocked my arm back to throw that piece of wood at the shop wall as hard as I could.

"Son," my father's voice reached me through the angry haze.

I dropped my arm to my side, the boat falling to the floor, and fell to my knees, sobbing over what never was and what never would be. I was broken inside and didn't see how I could be made whole now. Too much time had passed. Too much fear had been allowed to fester and had taken control of my heart.

I felt my father's strong arms around me as we knelt in a broken pile on the shop floor. "It will be okay, son. We'll work through this."

For a list of cities and states where sleeping in Walmart parking lots is frowned upon visit:

http://www.allstays.com/c/walmart-locations-noparking.htm

Works cited

Book of Mormon-Another Testament of Jesus Christ, 1989, 422-429 & 440-441

Where did all that trivia come from?

http://health.usnews.com/best-hospitals/area/or/oregon-health-and-science-university-6920570http://circ.ahajournals.org/content/96/2/550.full

http://www.heart.org/HEARTORG/Conditions/CongenitalHeartDefects/SymptomsDiagnosisofCongenitalHeartDefects/Detection-of-a-Heart-Defect-in-the-Fetus_UCM_315673_Article.jsp

http://www.heart.org/HEARTORG/Conditions/CongenitalHeartDefects/AboutCongenitalHeartDefects/Ventricular-Septal-Defect-VSD_UCM_307041_Article.jsp#.ViB8wf2FOP8

http://www.nursingschools.net/blog/2010/12/20-incredible-facts-about-breast-milk/

http://www.mnn.com/earth-matters/animals/blogs/36-random-animal-facts-that-may-surprise-you

http://www.thefactsite.com/2010/09/300-random-animal-facts.html

http://www.whowhatwear.com/fun-facts-shoes/slide13

http://www.movoto.com/guide/or/oregon-facts/

Songs mentioned, but not cited in the story:

Real Men Love Jesus-Michael Ray, 2015

If You Wanna Be Happy-Jimmy Soul, 1963

Anything But Mine-Kenny Chesney, 2004

Roller Coaster-Luke Bryan, 2013

Surfer Joe-The Surfaris, 1963

Surfin' Safari-The Beach Boys, 1962

Surfer Girl-The Beach Boys, 1963

Surfin' USA-The Beach Boys, 1963

Soundtrack for the book:

You Can-David Archuleta, 2008

In Case You Didn't Know-Brett Young, 2017

Making Memories Of Us-Keith Urban, 2004

Nobody In His Right Mind-George Strait, 1986

Give Your Heart A Break-Demi Lovato, 2011

Falling Stars-David Archuleta, 2010

Demons-Imagine Dragons, 2012

Nobody Knows-Tony Rich, 1996

Life After You-Daughtry, 2009

Ask Me How I Know-Garth Brooks, 2017

A sneak peak into <u>The Heart of the Matter</u>

James

"Where are we going?" Sophie asked and looked at me in confusion when I pointed the car

west toward the coast instead of to Portland.

"I promised you a trip to the beach if you behaved. You lived up to your end of the bargain, so I'm living up to mine." *It's the least I can do,* I admitted to myself.

"We don't have to do this, James," she told me tiredly. "Let's just get home."

"No, Sophie. A promise is a promise."

"We went there yesterday." Had it only been a day ago? "It didn't go so well," Sophie reminded me. I cringed at the pain in her voice.

"Well, today is going to be different. We can't leave the beach on a sour note. It's against the rules."

"Really," she drawled. "Whose rules?"

"Probably yours, for starters," I said. "We didn't get to see Three Arch Rocks and that's something you can't miss."

"I can see it some other time," she tried again.

"You have somewhere you need to be, San Antonio? Some hot date or something?" I glanced over at her.

"Yes." She rolled her eyes. "No. I just-"

"You just need to enjoy this ride," I interrupted. "And prepare to be awed by what you are about to see." I needed to remove the hurt from her voice and see her beautiful smile. "I'll even turn on this new beach CD I dug up somewhere. I think you'll like it." I reached for the stereo.

Sophie laughed and pushed my hand away. "You lost your CD listening privileges."

"But how will I ever educate myself on the fine art of country music?" Despair laced my voice, but I grinned in triumph at her laugh.

"You should have thought about that before you made fun of my music."

"You are absolutely right, little lady," I drawled. "Can y'all ever forgive a backward city boy?"

"Only if you promise to give my music another try. And only if you promise to never talk like that a..." her voice trailed off. "James," she breathed, staring out the window at the ocean.

"May I present the Three Arch Rocks." I gestured out to sea like a tour guide. I laughed when she bounced lightly in her seat in excitement. "Don't jump out," I told her. "I'll park right here."

As soon as the car stopped, Sophie jumped out and headed for the trail that led to the beach. She raised a hand to shield her eyes from the sun and turned back to me with a childlike grin on her face. She waved for me to hurry and continued to the sand where she slipped her sandals off and practically skipped to the water.

My heart twisted in my chest at her happiness. It was contagious. I felt a smile grow on my face in direct proportion to the feeling welling inside. I had thought a lot about what my father said earlier this morning about the life I was choosing. I hadn't realized how lonely and incomplete I was until Sophie came along and completed me. I wanted to be the one to bring the smile to her beautiful face and put that sparkle in her eyes. I wanted to introduce her to all the wonders she had never experienced before. I wanted to have her look at me with the same longing she looked at the beach. I wanted her to love me as desperately as I was coming to love her. I rubbed my chest above my heart where an aching need started. I would put it all out there. I would tell her what she wanted to know about my past. I would let go and free myself from the memories and heartache and fill up the empty space with her.

I spread a blanket on the sand and sat down to watch her comb the beach and glance at the occasional bird that passed overhead. I grinned when her head jerked up and her eyes squinted and roved the rocks a half mile out at a sea lion's call. I laughed at her startled squeal when a wave lapped up and over her feet. I knew I was grinning like a fool, but I couldn't help it.

I hopped up from the blanket and walked toward her. When I was a couple feet away, I held out my hand to her. "Walk with me?" She smiled up at me and placed her hand in mine.

"The Meares Lighthouse is up ahead," I pointed out to her as we walked.

She sighed. "I love lighthouses. It's hard to describe. Just like the way I feel about the ocean. Maybe it's that they lead boats away from danger. Maybe it's that they are a beacon on a stormy sea. Maybe it's that darkness can't exist where there is even a little light. Or maybe it's that where there is a lighthouse, there is an ocean. And I've already told you how I feel about the ocean."

I squeezed her hand. "I love how passionate you are about life. Whether it's the ocean or physical therapy or your family." My voice sounded strained and my heart was threatening to burst from my chest. And not in a good way. It was time. I knew I needed to tell her, but terror gripped my heart.

After a few minutes of walking in silence, Sophie asked, "What's wrong, James?"

Might as well get it over with. "For years, I've locked my heart up. First with Nicole and then with my career." She glanced at me questioningly. "You remember a couple months back when you asked about my biggest regret from my past?" I gave a rueful laugh. "How could you forget, right?" I stopped and turned to face her. "Have I apologized enough for that?" I rubbed my thumb across the back of her hand.

"Who is Nicole?" she asked, curiosity and confusion warring with each other in her eyes. Or maybe it was wariness.

I took a deep breath. "I was married once," I began.

Coming Soon...

About the Author

Heather graduated with a Bachelor's degree in Elementary Education with a Special Education emphasis from Weber State University. She writes whenever she can squeeze time in between taxiing five children around and carving wooden key chains for souvenir shops. She lives in Ogden, UT with her husband and children, two dogs, one goldfish, one bird, and a snake. This is her debut novel.

Made in the USA
Monee, IL
20 June 2023

35979267R00177